A Mallick Brothers Novel
--

Jessica Gadziala

Copyright © 2017   Jessica Gadziala
All rights reserved. In accordance with the U.S Copyright Act of 1976, the scanning, uploading, and electronic sharing of any part of this book without permission of the publisher is unlawful piracy and theft of the author's intellectual property. This book or any portion thereof may not be reproduced or used in any manner whatsoever without the express written permission of the author except for brief quotations used in a book review.

"This book is a work of fiction. The names, characters, places and incidents are products of the writer's imagination or have been used fictitiously and are not to be construed as real. Any resemblance to persons, living or dead, actual events, locales or organizations is entirely coincidental."

Cover image credit: Shutterstock .com/gpointstudio

DEDICATION

To Autumn Schmidt.
For the name.
For your instantaneous and unrelenting love of Eli.
And for being an awesome human being <3

PROLOGUE

Autumn

No one buys dildos at eight o'clock in the morning.

I learned that my first year of business while I fought with spreadsheets, cried over the light bill, and stocked bright pink butt plugs onto shelves.

It was also why I was sitting outside a coffeeshop in Hollydell right outside of Navesink Bank because, apparently, in a town full of twenty different fast food restaurants, having an actual coffeeshop was too much to ask.

The season was proving temperamental. I had woken up to forty degrees, but it was steadily on its way to the sixties, so I had grabbed my double shot mocha frappe to sit at one of the wrought iron tables-for-two right out front, flipping through the pages of a glossy magazine like I had all the time in the world.

I did.

I opened my store around ten-thirty on weekdays which gave the moms plenty of time to drop the kiddos off at school before

ELI

dropping in for a new Rabbit, or tongue vibe, or - if there was an anniversary coming up - a mutually enjoyable cock ring or set of edible panties.

In case it wasn't infinitely clear here - I own a sex store.

They call it, officially, a "novelty" store or an "adult toy store." But let's be real - it's a sex store. I deal in making sex even better than it usually was. I was a smut-slinging, vibrator-advising, proud owner of Navesink Bank's only sex store: Phallus-opy. Because naming it "X-anything" or "toy-something" was cheesy and unimaginative. Plus, when you went the "toy" route, there was the off-chance of someone getting the wrong idea and coming in with a kid. With "phallus" in the name, there was almost no chance of that kind of awkward screw-up.

Don't want to scar the kids for life with the sight of a twelve-inch monster cock in rainbow leopard print or a unicorn-horn-shaped, glitter-infused butt plug.

Heaven forbid.

I shook my drink, watching the full-fat whipped cream melt down into the skim concoction. Call it balance. Like how I was going to have a salad for dinner. Followed by a huge slice of the chocolate cake I had picked up at the bakery over the weekend. And don't try to tell me that the fat and sugar in the oversized slice of cake actually made the choice of a light salad null and void because, well, no one wants that negativity in their life. Just let me live with my delusions.

"You've got to be fucking kidding me!" a woman's shrill voice had my head popping up. Shrill was not a good sign at eight in the morning. Someone was going to get his balls handed to him. "You won't even stop to talk to me? Seriously?"

Oh, boy.

Crazy chick then.

This would be good.

I sat back in my chair, taking a sip out of my straw, watching as the duo came into view from the side of the building where the lot was situated.

And, yeah, damn.

Maybe it was my underused libido talking, but he might have been the best-looking man I had ever seen.

He was tall with a lean, strong body. A swimmer's build, it might be called. Even though the morning was running toward chilly,

ELI

he had on a white tee, showing off some ink on his arms that I had a sudden urge to inspect closer.

Naked.

After we'd toured my bedsheets.

Okay there Autumn, get a grip of your hormones.

The body was nice, sure. He definitely wouldn't get kicked out of any woman's bed. But it was the face that made you feel like you were gut-punched.

Gorgeous.

That was the only word even close to good enough to describe him.

He had those good, old-fashioned chiseled, masculine features - a cut jaw, strong brows, a straight nose, lips that were pressed in a firm line but you knew would feel good kissing and sucking you all over. His hair was black, a little long, falling down his forehead. But the eyes, damn. Those eyes. They were the lightest kind of blue, almost transparent. With that dark hair and that perfect face? Oh, yeah, I could see why this woman was willing to go full-on crazy-ex-girlfriend at eight in the morning for a man like that.

She was pretty too. Gorgeous really, but in a cold kind of way. She was tall, lean, with long ice-blonde hair, blue eyes, and just a tad too much makeup considering she was naturally attractive.

"Eli, come the hell on," she said, grabbing the man's arm, making him stop, exhaling his breath slowly, like he was trying to prepare himself for something wholly unpleasant. "I know you couldn't have been serious about it being the dog or me."

Oh, yeah, he had a dog too.

Somehow, I had been so wrapped up in his face that I hadn't noticed the bright orange leash in his hand that led to, well, the ugliest dog in the world.

His hair was sticking up in patches, a mix of colors like that of a border collie, but with a flatter snout, straight-up ears, giant feet, one bright blue eye, and one gray one.

U-G-L-Y.

But, let's face it, he was a puppy. So no matter what, he was adorable with his flopping pink tongue, twitching ears, and wagging tail.

My eyes went back up, shamelessly eavesdropping. I felt a smile tugging at my lips.

ELI

He chose his dog over her?

Now that was a good man, wasn't it?

"We've been through this," the man, Eli, told her in a patient, but barely holding onto it, tone.

"Yeah, and it's ridiculous!" she hissed, jutting out a hip, her hand waving down her body. "You'd trade all this - and let's not forget the wild sex - for a stupid, hideous dog that destroys your apartment. And, I might add, my very expensive shoes."

"For which I bought you new ones," Eli shot back in a calm tone. "In fact, I bought you three pairs because you threw such a fit."

This was better than TV.

"I was with you before you found that hellbeast."

Oh, boy. She was jealous of the dog. Bad enough that she felt that, but she was expressing it? Yeah, jealousy was never a good look to wear on your sleeve. It was even worse when it was jealousy for a hideous, troublesome, but obviously loved puppy.

"And it wasn't working then either, babe," he said, shaking his head at her, eyes almost a little sympathetic.

"It was working just fine. What? Just because I didn't fit in with those freaking chicks..."

"My sisters-in-law," he corrected.

"Yeah, whatever. Just because we didn't get along, you were going to dump me?"

"Honestly, yes," he said, shrugging.

"Choosing your family over your girlfriend, Eli. What the fuck kind of man are you? Oh, wait, I know. One I won't be wasting this good pussy on anymore." With that, she stormed off, adding a bit too much hitch in her giddy-up as she did, thinking she was showing him what he would be missing.

Oh, shit.

I actually had to press my lips together to keep from laughing out loud at that.

Because, quite frankly, it was sad.

Not for him.

But because that whole display was a bit, ah, needy on her part. First, the begging for attention. Then, when it was clear she wasn't going to get it, trying to have the last word.

Pride, that woman had a lot of it.

ELI

What was with people not being mature enough to just... accept that things weren't working out, and move on? Scenes at coffeeshops before a decent hour in the morning were, well, kinda pathetic.

"Don't listen, Coop," the man said, drawing my attention again because, yeah, what a voice. I always had a thing for voices. I drooled over accents, over those gravel-and-glass ones that some men had. This guy, though, his voice was smooth. I swear it slid over the skin like silk, bringing shivers. He was kneeling down at the post out front that had clips to tie up your dogs so you could run inside, threading the orange handle in through one of the holders. "You're not ugly. You're... alright, you're fucking ugly. Sorry, there's no way around that fact. But those shoes you ate were hideous to begin with," he told him, rubbing his head as the dog's tail wagged obsessively. "I'll bring you a treat," he declared, moving off inside.

He didn't even look at me.

This maybe should have offended me.

Most women wanted to be noticed by hot guys.

Hell, I even was apparently his type with my height and blonde hair, though I was just a sight more curvy than his ex.

That being said, I was pretty secure in who I was.

And, you know, sometimes you just weren't in the mood to interact with the opposite sex. We've all been there, in the grocery store running late, feeling sweaty and annoyed at life in general, and some dude's eyes catch yours, and you just know they are going to engage you, so you hurry off in the other direction.

After a run-in with a, ah, spirited ex, the dude likely just wanted a double shot of coffee, and to get on with his day.

I looked over at the dog whose different colored eyes were watching the door where his owner disappeared with clear devotion. A dog that ugly, he had to be a rescue, a street pup, some accidental one-night-stand between two dogs who likely looked decent on their own, but never should have procreated. His devotion to his owner likely ran deeper because he had known the mean pang of hunger, of cold, of being alone in the world.

Gotta love a man who rescued dogs.

And loved his family.

And dumped chicks who got along with neither.

ELI

As if my thoughts had summoned him back, the door chimed as it opened, bringing a gust of sweet air from all the varied sugar syrups inside. He walked out with an extra large hot coffee, one I figured he took black because men like him usually did, and a doggy bag for, well, his actual dog.

It must have been a tradition too, because the dog was jumping and whining as soon as he saw it.

"Alright, how about we try that sit thing again?" he suggested, putting down his coffee, reaching into the bag to produce one of the beige, somewhat lumpy-looking dog cookies the shop offered for this very reason. Hollydell was a shopping town, all the stores close together, and most people walked their dogs around when the weather permitted. It was smart business. "Coop, sit," he ordered, trying for a demanding tone that the dog took to mean: jump around like a lunatic. "Coop, sit down."

I was smiling at the show when it happened.

It came out of nowhere, making my stomach plummet, and my heart fly upward, a fluttering, foreign thing somehow lodged up in my throat.

One second, the man was trying to train his unruly dog.

The next, sirens were screaming, and tires were screeching as two police cruisers came to an abrupt stop right beside the man and his dog.

The doors flew open, producing a cop from each car in their typical blues.

"Eli Mallick!" the first cop, someone on the young side and a bit too - ah - out of shape to be able to chase down any perp, called, his voice full of the cocky authority a badge gave some weaker men. "Stop right there!" he added, hand touching his holster on his belt, despite the fact that the man hadn't moved an inch.

No, in fact, he almost seemed to let out a held breath, like he had been hoarding it for a week, and gave a small nod.

I reached for my hand instinctively, bringing up the camera on my phone and switching to video, having seen far too many instances of abuse of power from cops not only on the news, but with my own two eyes in Navesink Bank. And these *were* NBPD cops, not Hollydell. I knew better than to try to interfere, but it was smart to record it. You know, just in case.

ELI

"We have a warrant for your arrest," the second cop added, tone much more reasonable, body relaxed, hand holding out a sheet of paper.

My stomach twisted at the scene, realizing that this hot guy, this dude with the crazy ex-girlfriend who his family didn't like, with the ugly and untrainable dog, was about to be locked up.

I had seen more than a few guys in Navesink Bank get picked up. When you lived within a hotbed of criminal activity as I did, it wasn't even an unusual sight.

But somehow, this one was making me uncomfortable. Maybe it was as simple as the fact that the man didn't seem like a criminal. I mean, not that anyone actually did look like a criminal, but still. He just seemed like an average dude.

Possibly he just had a lot of unpaid parking tickets, right?

"For aggravated assault."

Oh.

Okay.

Well then.

Not parking tickets.

"Put your hands behind your back, asshole," the jackass cop demanded, reaching for cuffs. Eli moved to comply, but for some reason, the jackass cop grabbed his wrists and the back of his neck, turning him, and slamming him down onto the hood of the cruiser.

The impact made my stomach twist as an objection worked its way up my throat.

But then Eli's eyes were on mine from his position bent over the hood. Seeing my lips part to say something, he shook his head at me. My shoulders slumped as the metal click of cuffs - a sound I was maybe familiar with for *other* reasons - filled the air, and the man was yanked back upward.

"Finally got one of you motherfuckers," the cop added, shoving him down into the back of the cruiser.

I ended the video as the cars moved off, my heart a frantic beating, my hands oddly shaky even though I hadn't been involved at all.

Then I heard it.

Whining.

I looked over to find Coop jumping hard, lunging toward the street. Each attempt had his body flying back as the leash pulled

ELI

against the post. But there was no stopping him. He whined, whimpered, barked as he tried desperately to get free, to get to his owner.

"Okay," I said, standing, trying to keep a soothing voice. "Okay, buddy. It's okay," I crooned as I got closer, making a reach for his collar. "Calm down. You're going to strangle yourself," I went on, untying the leash as I reached for the body of the dog, trying to hold him still from the midsection, so he didn't keep pulling on his neck.

Feeling my touch, he looked over at me. And I swear, his little mismatched puppy eyes were frantic. Don't try to tell me dogs didn't have emotions like that, because they totally did. Coop did. He was worried about his owner.

An owner who he likely wouldn't see for a good, long time.

What was I supposed to do here?

I couldn't just leave the dog there, tied to a post, losing his ever-loving mind. The owners of the coffeeshop would likely call animal control or something. Then, what? He would end up at the pound? Ugly and untrainable as he was, he wasn't going to get adopted. And our local shelter was open-admission. They put the dogs down when they had been around too long.

I wasn't going to let some dog be killed because his owner beat someone and went to jail.

So, ah, I guess I just got a dog?

I liked dogs.

In fact, I loved dogs.

Growing up, I had always had one.

They always slept at my feet, followed me around.

Dogs, as far as I was concerned, were the only things on the planet that would love you more than they loved themselves.

That was, well, something any sane person would want.

The problem being, I lived in an apartment that didn't allow pets. So I had just sacrificed that lifelong love because the rent was fair, the place was huge, and I worked quite a bit.

That being said, I did *own* my business. If I could maybe try to train the crazy thing, I could take him to work with me so he wasn't alone.

The no-dog rule, well, I would find a way around that.

ELI

"Coop," I said, making the dog's head twist, looking up at me with curiosity. "Want a cookie?" I asked, reaching to the table where his owner had put his coffee and the bag down. I reached in, producing the thing that smelled heavily of peanut butter.

And, I kid you freaking not, the dog sat without being told to.

"Good boy!" I cheered, giving him the whole damn cookie as I reached down to ruffle his hair that stuck up all over his head in patches. "Good, good boy. I'm sorry about your owner," I said as he ate his cookie. "I know I'm not him. But I am kinda rescuing you right now too. You can learn to love me, right?" I asked as he finished the cookie, then planted his feet on my bent knees, and gave me a huge, peanut butter kiss.

So, yeah, I had a dog.

--

"Um, 1A," the super called as I stepped up the walk from the main lot toward the building.

The super was somewhere in his fifties, thin to the point of gaunt, with stringy brown hair, a godawful porn stash, and these leering black eyes that made you feel slimy whenever his gaze slid in your direction.

He was also a dick who never learned tenants names, no matter how long you lived there, and called you by your apartment number instead.

"Yeah, Randy?" I asked innocently as I led my illegal dog up the path, holding half a dozen bags from the pet store in the other, full of wet and dry food samples so I could figure out what he liked, toys, and bowls. The bed was in the trunk. I'd have to make a dreaded second trip for it.

"That's a dog."

ELI

"Really?" I asked, brows drawn low. "I thought he was just a supremely ugly child. Huh."

"Dogs are against the rules, 1A."

He said this while eye-fucking me and scratching his balls. Yeah, he was a real peach, let me tell you.

"Hey, you know what?" I asked, ducking my head to the side. "I'm pretty sure leering in the window while my sister takes a bath isn't just against the *rules* but the *law*."

That, well, it made his whole body stiffen.

See, my sister was a bit of an - ah - exhibitionist. She didn't mind having a Peeping Tom. In fact, the crazy chick would put on a show when she knew she was being watched.

I know, so what, she had said when I told her about seeing Randy 'walking by' the windows to 'do his rounds' whenever she was bathing. *They're just tits. I flashed them at that holier-than-thou dude who told me my tattoos were satanic and that I was going to hell last week. He didn't seem to grasp the concept that all my favorite people will be down in hell. Fornicating and sodomizing each other while listening to death metal and drinking vodka straight from the bottle. Sounds like a killer party to me.*

When I had tried to press it, she had shrugged. *Autumn, I'd close the curtains if it bothered me.*

And since he seemed only to spy on her, I never felt the need to report him before.

But I wasn't above using it as leverage.

"I never..."

"I have pictures," I added. And I did. Just in case I ever needed them.

His face fell at that.

"If I let you have a dog, then everyone else will want to have one."

"That sounds a whole lot like *your problem*," I said with a shrug. "Sounds better than being charged with a misdemeanor though, doesn't it?" I asked, turning, not even bothering to hide my smile as I made my way to the door.

I dealt in sex.

I knew the ins and outs of every kink that existed.

I knew that voyeurism and exhibitionism were valid fetishes that were engaged in by many people. That being said, it was only

ELI

fun when both parties were fully aware of the situation. It was a *crime* when someone watched you when you didn't want to be watched. I understood that, in this case, it was different. My sister didn't care. Hell, I had heard her flick on a vibrator when she knew he had been watching her once. But Randy still rubbed me the wrong way. Because his behavior was criminal, even if my sister was permitting it.

So it felt good to hand him his balls about it, to remind him that it wasn't right.

He probably got the wrong idea about me because I owned a sex store. Most people did. Guys, when they figured it out, thought I was a slut who engaged in all kinds of kinks from BDSM to threesomes.

Now, I loved sex.

Sex was amazing.

It was something that made life just better than it was.

And I *did* enjoy toys and games and such in the bedroom.

That being said, I was a serial monogamist. I had never been able to enjoy casual sex. It just felt empty and unfulfilling to me. I had tried a time or two when I was younger before I decided it simply wasn't for me. A part of me - especially when stuck in a long dry spell - really envied women who enjoyed hookups. But, hey, we all had different things that got us off. Mine simply wasn't that.

I hadn't been in a relationship in about eight months.

So I hadn't had sex in eight months.

I bought liberally from my own store.

You know, vibrator *research*.

So people could go ahead and think what they wanted.

I wasn't a slut.

And I personally took offense to the term.

And to sexual deviants like Randy thinking he had any right to think them.

"Alright, buddy," I said, unlocking my door. "I am praying you are house trained. And I guess I should lock up my closet. My shoes aren't all that great, but y'know, I need stuff on my feet." I went to close the doors to the bedrooms, figuring any mess would best be contained in the main living space. I walked back out to take the toys out of the bag, smiling as he hopped up on his back legs and barked for each one, never losing enthusiasm even after the sixth toy. Then I

ELI

put out some water and dry food. "I gotta get to work now," I told him as though he could understand. "Can you try not to eat the furniture? It's nothing fancy, but it would be nice for it to not have bite marks. I'll be back at dinner time to walk you."

That was a perk to owning your own place.

Have a doctor's appointment, or meeting with your finance guy, or a dog that needed walking? Hang a sign on the door saying when you'll be back. Maybe people wouldn't be happy about having to wait to get their sour apple lube or Fleshlight, but they would survive. Besides, it was either wait the hour or wait two days to get it on Prime or seven days to get it from a discreet online supply store.

You had to love being the only game in town.

"And, ah, yeah. See you later, buddy. Try not to be too depressed about him, okay? We are going to have a good life, you and me."

That was the plan.

Then we went right ahead and started living it.

ONE

Eli - 1 year later

You'd have heard it all by now.
Don't drop the soap.
Hang a 'do not disturb' sign on your ass.
If you're someone's bitch, they'll protect you.
If you do chores, you can curry favor to keep a dick out of your ass.

And, to be fair, those were actually pretty sound pieces of advice. Prison rape was daily and brutal. If you were new, and especially if you were new and young and small, your ass was open game. One of the guys I got bussed in with was immediately taken in by the Neo-Nazis and became a bitch to the big guy. By the time I noticed him again six weeks later, he was thin, bruised, and a shell of the man he had been when we arrived.

You could avoid all that drama if you came in connected to one of the organizations within all prison systems. If you had a history of being a white supremacist, a wise guy, a Blood, a Crip, or

ELI

one of the dozens of Latino prison gangs, you were likely to be protected.

If you weren't, well, you had to get crafty.

"What you think you're all big and bad because you beat the shit out of that politician's son?" I had been pushed up against the wall my third day there by some low-level Irish mob jackass. "You're in *prison* now, pretty boy. We know how to fight back. You want to start with me? Huh? Come on, throw a fucking punch, pussy."

See, I didn't want to start.

I had made the decision to keep my head down, do my time, and then move the fuck on with my life.

But when his hand landed on my shoulder, shoving me back into the wall, well, let's just say *it happened.*

You know what I mean.

The rage.

That thing that moved through my veins, that burned them like battery acid, that made rational thought impossible, that turned me into a monster I wasn't at any other time.

By the time the alarms went off, and the C.O. came running, the Irish dude's face was all blood and broken bones.

Me, well, I went to the SHU.

And had time added onto my sentence.

Not much since I was new, he was a bully, and the warden knew how it went, but time. They jacked me up to seven years, but I was told I would only serve six, then have a year of parole on the outside. Not a lot of time in the grand scheme of things. But time.

Extra time.

Because of the exact same thing that got me shipped off to prison in the first place.

Naked. In a cement floor and walled room with no window, no nothing except for a hard bed with no mattress and a stainless steel sink and toilet combo. For months.

Yeah.

It set a man to thinking.

It was the only way not to go crazy.

And, being I am who I am, my thoughts went first to my family. They'd been there. At my trial. Of course. I wouldn't have expected anything less. Hell, I had them tattooed on my arm.

Vis necia vinci.

ELI

A power ignorant of defeat.

It was right there on my skin, though anyone who knew the Mallicks knew that shit - that mentality, that loyalty, that love - that went right down into the marrow.

I hadn't engaged them. I hadn't even looked their way. Just like I hadn't given them what they needed from me at the police station the night of my arrest. They needed to hear it was okay, that I would be okay.

They needed that from me.

The problem was, I couldn't give it to them.

I didn't have it.

At the time, shame was something not unknown to me. I had felt it time and time again when I came back out of my spiral, when I realized what I had done. It had never been a lasting thing, though. I guess that was the difference. Because there had never been any kind of repercussions from my actions - mostly due to the fact that I only ever beat people who were in the underbelly and had it coming - I could accept it and move on.

This time, I couldn't do that.

Every single day I was paying for what I had done.

There was no accepting it and moving on when it was the very reason I was eating slop, showering with other men, and having lights out at nine at night like a fucking eleven-year-old.

It wasn't that the bastard didn't have it coming.

I'd never forget the sound of that woman's screams, her pleas for it to stop, for someone to help her. I could still see her face when I closed my eyes at night - all bloodied and broken open.

He deserved every last punch the motherfucker got for putting his hands on a woman.

But he wasn't in the underbelly.

He was connected.

And daddy-o wanted my nuts in a noose.

So he got that.

I would have gotten off if it was anyone else. No jury would have convicted me when they saw the pictures of that woman from the hospital. You know, the ones the nurses took before her husband's lawyer showed up and ushered her out for 'home treatment.'

It was a case of right time, right act, wrong family.

ELI

The shame didn't start until I was trying to get Coop to sit down for his treat, and the cops came out of nowhere with a warrant.

If there was one word to describe how I felt when they pulled up, sirens going, attitudes getting thrown around, my face getting slammed onto a hood as bracelets went around my wrists, that word was *humiliation*.

It was embarrassment I had never known before.

And it didn't stop there as I had been paraded through the station, interrogated, gotten called a lowlife piece of shit.

I heard it enough, I started to agree with it.

Off to jail to wait for trial. Strip search. Blue overalls.

Fucking animals, the guards would say.

To trial.

Like any other lowlife piece of shit.

Sentence handed down.

Bus to prison. Strip search. Orange pants and white tee. Trapped in a cage.

Fucking animals.

Given a toothbrush, travel paste, a bar of soap, and a roll of toilet paper.

Like every other lowlife piece of shit.

It wasn't until three weeks in the SHU that I realized it.

There would be no end to it.

The rage outs.

My own personal battle between Bruce Banner and Hulk.

The monster I had been groomed to become when violence hadn't come as easily to me as it had to Ryan, Mark, and especially Shane.

It was something that had become a part of me, something I used to help keep control over the family business, something that was an asset more than a flaw.

So as long as I was that man, the Eli Mallick I had been raised to be, so long as I was him, yeah, I could never hope to see an end to the rage-outs.

I would live the rest of my life worried I might flip again, get sent back to jail. Maybe kill someone and never get out.

That could very well be my fate.

So, alone in that cell, starved for fresh air, light, or any human contact, knowing this was no life for me, I made the decision.

ELI

I couldn't be that man anymore.

I couldn't live that life.

I couldn't - fucking forgive me - be a part of my family.

For my own good.

But for theirs as well.

See, I might not have been acknowledging them at the police station or my trial, but that didn't mean I wasn't aware. When my mother broke down. Hardass, take-no-shit, balls-to-the-wall Helen goddamn Mallick *broke down*. Fee and Lea had lost it too. My brothers, though they weren't exactly criers, you could feel the devastation even from across a crowded room.

And while they weren't there because it was no place for them, my fucking nieces...

I just took something from them. I took a person they loved from them, someone they trusted and depended on. I ripped that away from them. I took a little piece of the blissful oblivion of childhood from their perfect little hands.

By the time I was out, they wouldn't even remember me.

They wouldn't know me.

I would be some strange guy, not Uncle Eli.

I had done that. I had made my mother and sisters-in-law cry. I had crushed my brothers. I had let down my nieces.

I could never be that person again.

By the time I got out of SHU, the decisions had been made.

I would be cutting off contact.

It would make it easier on all involved. They could move the fuck on. Not have my memory hanging like a ghost in corners for six years, not having to be a spirit kept alive. They didn't deserve that. They deserved to be happy. They deserved to have Thanksgiving and Christmas without thinking *Poor Eli, all alone at Christmas in prison.*

I was giving them back their freedom.

They wouldn't see it as that at first. They would think I was punishing myself, I was adjusting, I was in a bad headspace. But, eventually, after a year or two, they could move on. They would have to. That was how life went.

It. Moved. On.

As for me, I was giving myself a chance.

ELI

If I never wanted the rage to win again, I needed to stay away from anything that triggered it.

Like the family business.

Like anyone at all who might mean them harm.

Like every single other inmate in prison.

The assault stunt that got me into SHU and got some extra time on my sentence, it had been enough to keep people from fucking with me. Even when I got out fifteen pounds thinner, pale, with sleep deprivation bruises, and shoulders that had the weight of the world on them.

No one fucked with me again.

Eventually, I just became invisible.

"Damn, man, your family fills your commissary every fucking week, huh?"

I used it for essentials at first, figuring it was a necessary evil, knowing the money came from one of my legit businesses. I stocked up on some extra toothpaste, deodorant, fucking toilet paper.

But then my focus switched as I passed an old man - a lifer, in for killing the man who had fucked his wife... with an electric meat slicer - painting in his cell.

I hadn't been aware that items like that could be gotten through commissary. When I went to check, sure enough, right there under domino or chess sets, there was a list of art supplies that could be gotten. Sketch books, canvas, watercolor paint, colored pencils, crayons, markers, and graphite.

So I stopped buying shit like shaving cream and detergent.

And I bought as many art supplies as I could with my money each week.

Spend your time well, an old man had told me when I got out of the SHU. I figured he meant that I should take college courses, get a prison job, and stay out of trouble. Maybe that was what he meant. But I didn't have any interest in the college courses offered. My job only kept me busy in the laundry a few hours a day. And thanks to becoming invisible and having some affable enough ex-junkie and ex-heroin dealer as a cellmate, I didn't have to worry about the third thing.

But if I was going to spend my time, he was right, I should do it right. I should do it being useful. I should do it engaged in something that had always made me happy.

ELI

Outside, in my old life, I had time to scribble here and there, to design shit for the menu at Chaz's or the flyers for Fee's business or shit like that.

But I never got to immerse myself.

So that was what I did.

That was how I chose to spend my time.

And when you work at something twelve hours a day for a year, yeah, you got good. The kind of good that got noticed. The kind of good that even guards were saying I should make a career out of it when I got out. The kind of good where some fucking old school wise guy gives you the name of a gallery and tells you to tell them to say that Anthony Galleo sent you and that he wants your art on the walls.

As much as I wanted to cut ties with the criminal underbelly, I kept that name scribbled on the back of one of the canvases. Just in case I wanted to use the contact.

Things were going par for the course.

Except I had underestimated my family.

One year down the line, they still hadn't given up. They still tried to call, tried to visit, tried to write.

I dreaded mail day.

Because it was like a motherfucking knife to the gut every time I had to return shit to sender.

It didn't matter that I had made my mind up. They were still there, in the marrow, buried too deep ever to be extracted. And a huge part of me wanted that contact, wanted to read what was going on. Shane and Lea had to have been starting their own hoard by then. Had Scotti and Mark gotten married? Were Mom and Pops well?

Fee had found a way around my rule.

Because, no matter how hard I tried to hand them back, I couldn't force my fingers to let go of the letters from the girls. I had walls plastered with their adorably terrible artwork. Even though it was painful to look at them, knowing I would never be a part of their lives again.

It was dirty on Fee's part.

But she liked to play that way.

"Yeah yeah yeah," the C.O. said, shaking his head as he flipped through the letters. "I know the drill by now. Oh, wait. This

ELI

one isn't a Mallick." He held out the envelope with a shrug, showing me the name.

Autumn Reid.

Weird.

"I'll take that one," I agreed, reaching for it.

"Oh, and here, kid writing," he added, handing me a fat envelope.

So far, they hadn't been letters. The girls weren't great at writing yet, let alone getting their thoughts together enough to formulate an actual letter.

Just artwork.

It was hard enough.

Letters would fucking ruin me.

I took them back to my cell, opening the one from Becca first, finding a surprisingly improved picture of Coop.

Another knife in the heart.

I loved that fucking dog.

And I didn't have the damnedest idea what had happened to him. Had my family found him? If so, why was Becca still drawing him as a puppy? He would have been full-grown by now. If not them, then who? The pound. Ugh. I sure as fuck hoped not. Maybe Mark and Scotti took him on since Scotti wasn't like Lea who had a shoe collection that rivaled a department store.

I could hope at least.

I put that down to be hung later, climbing up into my bunk to rip open the letter from the Autumn woman, careful to leave the return address intact in case, for some unknown reason, I might actually need to write her back.

Eli,

You don't know me. Well, actually, you saw me once. On, um, the day you were arrested. Outside the coffeeshop. I was the girl filming the cop getting a little police-brutality-ish with you. Blonde hair. Blue eyes? Yeah, anyway. It took me this long to figure out who you *are and, well,* where *you are.*

Sorry for the delay.

ELI

I'm sure you've been worried.

After you were taken away, your dog started flipping out. No offense, but he was one ugly little sucker, and I didn't want him ending up in the pound. So I took him home with me.

He has a happy, active, shoe-chewing life.

He got enormous.

And he still likes those peanut butter treats from the coffeeshop.

You seemed pretty attached to him, so I wanted you to know he had a safe and happy home where he has learned a few manners - and disregarded all others.

I enclosed a picture. As you can see, he still won't be winning any beauty contests, but I think he is officially so ugly that he is cute. So he has that going for him.

- Autumn

My heart seized in my chest as I read the words, not realizing just how badly I had needed to hear them. It was a bit crazy, maybe, to have become so attached to a dog so quickly. Especially one as poorly behaved as he was. But, what can I say, I had never had a dog growing up and had always wanted one, but just never got around to it. Finding him had been fucking fate.

The worst part of getting arrested was sitting in a cell that night wondering what happened to Coop.

All for naught, it would seem, since he had been with this Autumn woman all along.

I remembered her too.

Kind of hard not to.

She was a knockout with her tall, lean but womanly body, long blonde hair, blue eyes, and a certain kind of laid-back confidence she wore around her like a perfume.

Hell, she had been shamelessly watching the whole scene with my ex, not even trying to hide how much she was enjoying the show.

She was gorgeous.

ELI

Then when shit went down and got a little uglier than it needed to, she had been quick to try to get it on tape, to make sure there would be evidence to back-up a claim if something ever happened to me.

So beautiful, with her head on straight, and a dog lover?

Sounded a lot like the perfect woman.

Sounded a lot like somewhere I wanted Coop to be raised.

I reached into the envelope to find a picture of the dog that had still been a bit of a puppy in my mind - small-bodied but big-footed. He still had big feet, sure, but the rest of him had caught up with them. She was right too; he hadn't gotten even the smallest bit better looking with age. He was now just a giant ugly dog.

He seemed happy too with his big bright blue collar that matched his eyes, sitting on a sidewalk with a cookie half-hanging out of his mouth. You'd swear he was smiling.

Curious, I looked past him at the store he was situated in front of, squinting at the picture that was taken from a distance.

But then my lips curled up when I made out the sign.

Phallus-opy.

She took a picture of my dog outside a sex store? What's more, she *sent me* a picture of my dog taken out front of a sex store?

Either it was a mistake, or this Autumn woman was one interesting character.

I'd say time would tell, but, well, let's face it, it wouldn't.

I had five more years behind bars.

I would never meet this woman.

It shouldn't have, but that knowledge gave me a small pang to the left side of my chest, deep in the black hole I didn't even recognize as a heart anymore.

I figured time inside would do that to a man.

It was harder for those who had a wife or girl on the outside, knowing they were away for a while and unable to fill her needs, worrying that she might step out on him, or get rid of him completely while he spends every night with his dick in his hand thinking about her.

I was in the lucky minority in that I didn't have that worry. I didn't have a girl, and I sure as fuck would never have demanded she wait for me even if I did.

ELI

So I wasn't plagued with that insecurity. And, well, I had a sex drive like anyone else, but suppressing it wasn't exactly hard in a place full of men, that smelled constantly of a bathroom and sweat and shitty food.

"Jesus, the fuck happened to his hair?" my cellmate, Tank, though his actual name was Bobby, asked as he came in, leaning up into my bunk because the idea of 'personal boundaries' was wholly lost on the man.

"Dunno. I found him like that when he was a puppy."

"Thought you said you have no close family," Bobby observed. "You know, aside from the kids."

"I don't," I agreed. *Knife, meet gut.* I still hadn't gotten used to the sensation. I wondered if I ever would.

"Who has the dog then?"

"Some chick at the coffeeshop where I got arrested. Took him home with her."

Bobby's lips tipped up, giving his already good-looking face a little charm. "She hot?"

"Incredibly," I agreed.

"Well," he went on with a shrug. "I guess when you get out, you're gonna have to go take him back from her," he said with a twinkle in his eyes before he dropped down into his own bunk to read the half a dozen letters he got each week from various family members who never gave up on him, even though this was his fourth trip to prison since he was sixteen.

Honestly, the idea never even occurred to me.

Six years was probably more than half of Coop's lifetime. He wouldn't even fucking remember me. He had a good life with the Autumn chick.

I had no right to go back and reclaim him when I got out.

But, somehow, once the idea got planted thanks to Bobby, there was no stopping it from starting to sprout and grow.

3 years

ELI

"I wish my hustle was half as good as yours," Bobby said, shaking his head over my shoulder as I counted the cash that Big Tony had handed me for the huge canvas I had just painted for him. It was a massively detailed piece of him, his wife, their kids, and their grandkids that I had needed to put together from a dozen photographs he had handed to me and, well, my pure imagination since there wasn't a single picture of more than two of them together and it needed to look like it was made from a real family photo session.

It had taken me three weeks to finish it, just under the line for him to be able to get it to his wife in time for their fortieth wedding anniversary.

How he was going to get it out to her, what palms he would need to grease to get that kind of shit done, yeah that was none of my business, but he apparently had it all worked out.

The piece had set him back six-hundred, a number he hadn't even raised a brow at. You had to love the wise guys. They always had cash to throw around.

"You need a hustle that won't add any more time to your fucking sentence, Bobby."

A hustle was a prison term for some kind of job that you did that the prison didn't know about - or pretended not to know about - that made you some extra cash to spend at commissary or use to barter for other shit within the prison.

My hustle was portraits or artwork. One guy had me do an album cover for him, even though he had another eight years left on his bid.

Bobby's hustle was selling pot.

How he got pot into the facility, quite frankly, I didn't want to know. All I did know was that he had almost been caught dealing it three times, and was looking at another couple of years if he did.

"Easy for you to say. Not all of us are talented, man."

"It took work," I told him truthfully, knowing the shit I had been putting out when I first arrived paled in comparison to what I could do now. "And there are plenty of guys in here with a clean

ELI

hustle. Fucking Rick proofreads letters to families, lawyers, and nonprofits, so the guys don't sound like idiots."

"Barely finished eleventh grade here, boss," Bobby reminded me, shaking his head as he dropped down across from me at one of the chess tables.

"Poet writes poems for anniversaries and birthdays. Marty cleans cells for commissary money. Andy fixes all the busted electronics. Thomas fixes shoes and clothes. Fucking Al makes candy in his cell. Plenty of hustles if you're actually willing to do a little work."

That was perhaps a little bit pointed.

See, Bobby was getting out in six months. He got time shaved off for good behavior since no one ever caught him handing out the pot. And I had a sick feeling that the bastard would be right back in again in less than a year if someone didn't try to push him toward a life that didn't involve ending up on the wrong side of the law.

"That's your privilege talking, man."

I snorted at that, shaking my head.

Privilege.

I grew up in a crime family. I was raised in a town that was nothing but criminal enterprises. Financial security didn't come until I was in my teens. Until then, we had to scrimp and save and barely get by just like anyone else. I didn't go to college; it wasn't even an option.

Both of our stories were similar.

We had good families in somewhat shady areas. We were both male, white, around the same age, and had the same chances in life.

The fact that he continued to choose easy money whereas I planned on going straight, well, that wasn't privilege. That was a choice. A bad one. But a *choice*.

It wasn't like when he got out, he was going to have no place to go, no one to help him get back on his feet. He didn't have to go live in a slum where the only money to be made was in illegal jobs.

That was the reality for more than half of the prison population. But it wasn't for Bobby.

He was just fucking lazy.

"You got the same chance as me of getting out and keeping your nose clean."

ELI

"Yeah, sure. You ain't never been in here before and gone back out there. When you do, then you can talk to me about readjusting. You don't know shit about it."

Bobby blew hot too easily.

Another reason he couldn't keep a straight job.

The fact of the matter was, the time, it wasn't hard. For me anyway.

It wasn't the hours locked in the cell, the fact that other people told you when to eat, shower, go outside, sleep. It wasn't the random shakedowns. It wasn't the shitty healthcare. It wasn't being stuck.

All that, I dunno, I had adjusted well enough. It becomes rote after a while. If you weren't the type to bemoan your fate, the time wasn't awful.

What was hard was the man I had needed to become to ensure my life could never go down this road again. What was hard was denying thirty-some-odd years of traditions, of loyalty, of love. What was hard was hollowing out a heart that used to be full of my parents, brothers, sisters-in-law, and nieces, and making it *stay* empty. What was hard was knowing that three years in, they still weren't accepting that the Eli they knew and loved ceased to exist when he walked into these walls. What was hard was knowing that while I was a hollowed-out shell, they were still holding onto hope that I would come around.

After three years, that wasn't even possible anymore.

There was none of that man left.

All that was left was the cold, the detached, the depersonalized psyche that the shrinks had wanted to medicate, thinking it was due to some prison horror that I wouldn't discuss.

They refused to accept that it was self-inflicted.

And, well, once you carved enough away inside, there weren't even any edges that could grow back together. You were just pieces.

Disconnected was a state I lived in.

I got up, I made my bed, I did checks, I brushed my teeth, I ate breakfast, I went to work, I showered on days it was allowed, I had my hour or two in the yard, I worked on my art, I slept.

Rinse.

Repeat.

Feel fucking nothing.

ELI

The only time there was even a hint of anything other than absolute and complete disconnection was when a letter would show up from one of the girls.

Yeah, letters.

Because they were big enough to write them now.

Three years of Fee keeping that candle lit for them, not knowing she was only hurting them, not accepting that just banking it out would be the kindest course of action.

Once I got the first letter, in all caps and full of information about her new cousins - you know, babies I would never get to see - I had felt a pain akin to something being ripped out inside. From then on, I accepted them, but couldn't bring myself to open anymore. Not even when they started not only coming from Becca, but Izzy and even Mayla. Then, soon after them, artwork started from Jason who couldn't have been more than a toddler by the looks of things, and whose parents, yeah, I didn't even fucking know which of my brothers had him.

That realization was the last, most lethal, painful pang of my dying fucking heart.

I kept all of them unopened now, locking them away in a box under the bunks. I tried not to even look at the names on the address labels.

Better not to pry open that can of worms.

Better to treat it like junk mail you keep forgetting to throw away.

Better to not have a family at all.

Better to shut it all the fuck down.

"Yo, Mallick," the guard called, stopping outside my cell. "Missed mail call," he said, holding up a small white envelope.

Normally, you missed mail call, you were fucked. But I had made this guy a portrait of his baby that died of SIDS to keep on his mantle, so he was a little more forgiving of any of my small indiscretions.

"You know the deal," I said, exhaling hard. Mail days sucked.

"Nah. Not your family, less you got some distant relative with the last name Reid."

I turned fast, too fast, showing just a hint of a weak spot that I didn't want anyone - not even a guard - to see.

"Girlfriend?"

ELI

"Chick that stole my dog," I corrected, going for a calm tone as I took the envelope.

"Stealing a man's dog then writing him. What a shit move," he said, shaking his head as he ambled off.

My hands went almost a little frantically for the tab, sliding my finger under to rip it open.

Why was she writing again? After two years of nothing?

Did Coop get sick? Die?

Why put that on some dude already in prison if that was the case?

It was a pretty dick move.

I couldn't tell you why I was so desperate to read it, aside from genuinely hoping my dog was okay. Maybe it was a genuine need for human connection, for a contact on the outside, to be reminded of normal life.

It was easy to adjust to prison.

When there weren't reminders that there was another way to live.

I had successfully stayed clear of them.

Except for now.

Eli,

Coop wanted to show you his Halloween costume.
I hope prison is better than it looked on Oz.

- Autumn

What the fuck was that?

Even as I reached for the picture still in the envelope, I couldn't for the life of me figure out why the fuck she was sending me a letter.

ELI

She was a good-looking woman. She didn't need to write some shithead in prison so she could get some male attention.

What was her motivation?

I pulled out the picture, unable to hold back a laugh/snort hybrid that escaped me at what was staring back at me.

Autumn, whoever the fuck she was, was either really creative herself, or shelled out a shitload of money to have a three-headed dog costume made. With two extra of Coop's heads. One was missing an ear as if the real Coop had maybe gotten to it. Which, well, was very much like him.

Unfortunately, looking down at it, my first thought was how much Becca, Izzy, and Mayla would have liked seeing him like that.

This Autumn chick was making it hard to forget about my old life the way I wanted, to seclude myself away from it, to avoid any thoughts that could conjure up images of my family.

Why then did I reach for a pencil and paper?

Why did I write back?

Why the ever-loving hell did I actually mail it when I did?

5 years -

It was wrong to think.

I knew that.

I knew that there were men in here, men with women and children they desperately wanted to get back to, but likely wouldn't until the kids were grown, if ever at all.

They would kill for it.

To be on their last leg.

To be one foot out the door.

ELI

And here I was, half not wanting to leave.

What can I say, after over five years, even a place like prison can start to feel like home. You get used to the rhythms, find a certain comfort in the sameness. Nothing changed. Faces did, power dynamics as well, but every single day was almost identical to the last.

It wasn't the routine, though, that had a fist of trepidation settled in my stomach. I liked my old life, being able to come and go as I pleased, eat what I wanted, go to bed if or when I wanted, go for a drive, see movies, buy shit without a strict budget set in place by someone other than me.

It was what I knew would be waiting for me when I left.

Hell, I would bet my left nut that someone - if not a group of them - would be sitting outside the jail on release day.

The letters still came.

Even the ones from the adults.

And now it wasn't just Becca, Izzy, Mayla, and Jason.

Now there were new names too.

Jake. Joey. Danny. Ford.

And, to top the cake. Eli. Little Eli.

If I had any heart left, that would have fucking sank it down in acid.

One of them, and I had no idea which, had named a child after me. Even after not seeing me, hearing from me for five years. Even after having letters and gifts sent back. Even after I turned my back on all of them, they still had hope.

Only fools had hope.

I didn't have hope anymore.

I had plans.

I had goals.

I had a system of things to set in place to make a new life.

A life I couldn't allow them into.

A life they wouldn't want to be in if they knew the man I had become.

Or, knowing them, they would still want in, but only because they thought they could fix me, they could undo the five years, the shame, the humiliation, the regret, the disappointment in myself.

There was no fixing that.

ELI

But they were good people, and they loved me, so if they found me, they would work their asses off to get me back.

Unfortunately, I was getting paroled to Navesink Bank, so I had no choice but to set up shop there.

According to my lawyer who was the only connection to my old life I allowed, my family had kept up my apartment for me to go back to. I thanked him, not telling him that that wasn't my intention. I would deal with it eventually, but I wasn't going back to it, right where they would look for me.

Instead, I had had Bobby, who was surprisingly *not* back in a cell yet, work out a duplex for me in a crummy area of town. They were somewhat secluded, and I could come and go without being seen. He was in one of the duplexes across the street with his girl and, if he was being honest, working a straight job. I figured he wasn't being honest, but I needed someone on the outside who wasn't connected with my family to help me arrange shit for release day.

Once I was out, I had my accounts to get me going.

Then I had my plans to work selling my art to keep me going.

Would I be living as large as I used to? No. But it would keep me from that world, keep me from becoming that man who could transform into some rage-monster without warning.

And it would keep from hurting my family when they realized what I had to become to get rid of the person they once knew.

I knew it would happen eventually, a run-in.

It was inevitable.

The town wasn't exactly small, but it wasn't a big city either.

I would see one of them.

And then I would have to rip their hearts out like I had needed to my own.

The difference was, theirs would mend. They would sew one another back together. They would be mostly whole again.

That simply wasn't in the cards for me.

TWO

Autumn

"Is it another letter from Prison Blue Hottie?" my sister asked as I came through the front door with a small stack of bills in my hand.

Okay, so... I couldn't tell you why the hell I wrote him at all.

I really had no idea.

I mean, the first time was because I knew he loved his dog, and would want to know that he was okay. That was just the right thing to do.

I would have sent it sooner had I realized who he was. I had heard his name when he got arrested, but among rushing to get dog supplies, dealing with Randy, texting my sister to tell her we had a new pet, going to work, coming home to clean up the mess that Coop made, yeah, I had totally forgotten his name.

It wasn't until I was out with friends one night at Chaz's, celebrating the big three-two (every single year after thirty, in my humble opinion, called for adding 'big' before the actual number), I

ELI

had seen a man walking around who looked a suspiciously lot like Coop's former owner. He had the same tall build, the dark hair, the light eyes.

Then someone had yelled out *Hey, Mallick!*

And the name flew right back into my head.

Eli Mallick.

That was his name.

And if you had a name, you could do a computer search that would tell you about his crime, his trial, and where he was going to prison.

It was maybe only a matter of days between getting the name and his letter being in circulation.

That letter I understood completely.

The second one? The Halloween one? Yeah, man. I had absolutely no idea where that came from.

Okay, fine.

It was maybe, just maybe born out of the fact that once I had his name back, and, ah, did a social media search, yeah... that gorgeous face and those amazing eyes - let's not even discuss the body because there was a poolside picture of water dripping down his abs that had nearly made my ovaries freaking explode - had been haunting me. They crept in in quiet moments. You know, between weighing the pros and cons of various floggers to a newbie to BDSM and having to explain to a set of obnoxious barely-eighteen-year-olds that, no, the Ben Wa balls were not for some weird BDSM beating, that they, in fact, got inserted into the vagina to strengthen the muscles of the pelvic floor, a fact that shut them up and had them promptly leaving the store.

In the moments when the store was quiet save for the music overhead, constantly set to an ever-growing sexy playlist because it would be weird to walk into a sex store to hear, I don't know, Taylor Swift playing.

Don't get me wrong, I love me some Swift, but yeah, it wasn't exactly the kind of music you wanted to hear while picking out your first Wand.

You had to keep it sexy.

Even if you heard the song about 'riding' for the four-hundred-and-thirty-thousandth time.

ELI

But yeah, when the store was still as it often was in the afternoon and early evening, he crept into my mind.

Blame sexual frustration while around a room full of toys meant to ease it.

I could have been fantasizing about the hot UPS guy and his little short shorts and muscular ass. I could have thought about the guy in the leather cut who said 'baby, fucking gorgeous' in a very matter-of-fact way as he passed me on the way out of She's Bean Around. I could have even gone back to my favorite go-to, the silver fox who once stopped - in his expensive *suit!* - and fixed my busted tire. I never even got the poor man's name. Boy, would he be surprised how many times I slipped on a finger vibe with his image in my head.

But they weren't where my mind went.

No.

It was all about those ocean eyes, that dark hair, that amazing bone structure, that smooth voice. And, well, the damn dripping abs too. They couldn't be left out.

Maybe it was because we, sort of, shared a dog.

Maybe it was because he was in prison for doing what, in my opinion, was the right thing.

Whatever it was, he was there. In my head. A lot of the time.

When I looked at Coop, sometimes his image would flash up of him trying to make the dog sit. He totally did sit. And lay down. And come. Other than that, he was a wild freaking animal still.

When I saw that asshole cop cruising around, yeah, then too.

And, well, when I started watching reruns of *Oz* when I really, really hated watching violence, and the show was full of it, so I could only blame the fact that I knew of a real-life prisoner, and was a bit curious about life behind bars.

In fact, I had just gone off a pretty serious prison documentary show binge the week before Halloween.

Maybe that was it.

Maybe it was all the stories of all the men who had been abandoned in the penal system. Who had no one to write them. Who had no updates on the outside world.

What can I say, I was always a sucker for that type of thing.

ELI

So I sent him a picture of the costume my sister had made for Coop - because she was quirky like that - and sent it off, not expecting anything.

One could say I was a bit, well, floored when three days later, I got a letter back.

Autumn,

Thus far, no one has been crucified to the gym floor. We got that going for us.

- Eli

He wrote me back.

He even referenced the show I mentioned.

Granted, it was only two sentences, but it was a response. And, I felt, maybe a bit of a cry for help. If he was responding to me, a complete and utter stranger, then maybe his family had disowned him, or just slowly lost touch.

He was trying to reach out.

I just figured... what harm could it do to keep in touch, right?

I mean, maybe I had laughed at the people who kept prison pen pals before, thinking it was a little strange to keep up a relationship with someone you never met who was in for a violent crime.

I guess I never fully understood it.

Until I was faced with it too.

If someone who was locked up for five years needed some lifeline on the outside, and you were the one holding it, could you really hold back from tossing it out there?

I knew I couldn't.

At first, I always started mine with comments about Coop and the occasional talk about some prison TV show or even the weather. But before long, once he seemed to loosen up a little - and once I did as well - they were just letters.

ELI

I learned the names of the prisoners he talked about and what their respective 'hustles' were, noting that all the ones he mentioned seemed to have legit businesses, not selling drugs or prostituting themselves. I jokingly asked what his hustle was, if maybe he was the in-house Hallmark Card writer.

In response, he sent me back a folded-up piece of sketch paper.

With me on it.

I was sitting outside the coffeeshop, leaned back in my chair casually, frappe in front by my chest, straw in front of my lips like I had just taken a sip, my mouth curved up in a small smirk, eyes dancing, hair kicked up slightly in the wind.

Like I had been when I had been watching him and his crazy ex.

And, God, it was *good* too.

It was better than the art I had on my walls that I paid an arm and a leg for at a gallery featuring local artists. It was leaps and bounds better than the portraits my family had had commissioned of my sister and I growing up, shelling out thousands of dollars for work this man could do inside concrete and barbed wire from memory.

That was insane.

I wondered how he used it to make money, and even told him about wondering. He'd informed me that prisoners would pay a pretty penny for family portraits to have in their cells, or to send home to family members. He even told me that he had designed a piece of artwork or two for tattoos, but that wasn't something he liked to do, saying that that was 'a job for another brother,' and I got the distinct impression he meant his own. He was careful to never speak of them - his family. I didn't know - and didn't feel it was my place to ask - why.

So, instead, we stuck to more neutral topics like prison life, like TV, movies, and music. Like the weather. Like what businesses were popping up in and around Navesink Bank since his departure. When I had once mentioned She's Bean Around, his response had been almost immediate, though we usually went weeks or months between letters.

ELI

Autumn,

    No shit? They actually did it? The coffee truck girls opened the shop? How is it?

    - Eli

    It was maybe the first letter I had ever received from him that hadn't had a sort of disconnect, a coolness, that showed actual excitement about something.
    But there was no way to describe how amazing She's Bean Around was. It was the kind of place - and coffee! - one had to see to truly appreciate. With my caffeine addiction, I had been to many a coffeeshop in my day, all to varying degrees of corporate or indie. None had even come close to the flair Jazzy and Gala gave their shop.
    So, aside from describing the decor that I warned was often changing, that was what I told him - that it needed to be one of his first stops when he got out. That the salted caramel hot coffee was the stuff caffeine addicts wet dreams were made of.
    His response had been more of a typical one for him, telling me simply that he would keep that in mind.
    After that, there was nothing for almost six months, until I had a Coop Christmas card to send.
    I had actually even looked into sending him a package, believing that everyone should get a little something for Christmas, but the rules had been vague, but strict at the same time, leaving me too confused to make a decision. So I just stuck with the card.

Autumn,

ELI

How the fuck'd you keep reindeer horns on him for long enough to take a picture?

Also, who the hell are you sending an entire box of finger vibes to for Christmas?

- Eli

My eyes went huge as I scrambled to my fridge to get the Christmas card, you know, the Christmas card I sent out to literally everyone I knew. And, yep, sure enough, I had a supply box of multi-colored finger vibrators sitting off in a corner. They actually were a Christmas promotion for the store. I had a loyalty card for frequent customers. And the top twenty of them got a free gift at Christmas and Valentine's Day. I had brought them home to package up so I didn't have to stay late at the store.

And there they were.

In my Christmas card picture.

Granted, they were off to the back and barely in focus, but there nonetheless.

Oh well.

Anyone who knew me knew - whether they liked it or not - that I owned a sex toy store. They would just chalk it up to me being quirky like that. Or as proof of my descent into the fires of hell. You know, whichever.

I looked back down at the note, at his somewhat slanted, but small and neat writing.

And there wasn't, there absolutely was *not* a fluttering sensation in my sex at seeing the words *finger vibes* from him.

Nope.

Because that would be nuts.

No matter how long a dry spell I had been in.

I had written back something witty, brushing the subject away, knowing if I said anything suggestive, that it would get tossed out and he would never receive it. I mean, not that I was thinking of saying anything suggestive.

Fine.

I thought about it.

ELI

I thought of about fifteen suggestive things to say.

Then needed a goddamn session with my own finger vibe after.

But then... that had been it.

Suddenly, I didn't get another letter.

And I had no reason to write him, so I didn't, not wanting to seem like I was being pushy or whatever.

That was December.

This was April.

And, apparently, I still looked at my mail hopefully every day if my sister's response was anything to go by.

"Just bills," I said as I moved into the kitchen, dropping them on the small island with the special, shiny, white quartz countertop I had finally saved enough money for over the winter.

The apartment had been a special project over the past year. I guess I had always seen it as a transition for me when I moved in, figuring it was a stepping stone to a townhouse or just a house someday, something that I owned with a yard and some equity. As such, I hadn't been overly concerned with fixing up the apartment. But, it seemed, I was likely in it for the long haul, and I had even started to be completely okay with that.

But if I was staying, it needed work.

So I set to it.

I had the carpets ripped up, and laid wood flooring. I skimmed the walls, then painted them a soothing light sage color. I ripped out all the old kitchen cabinets that were straight out of the seventies, and replaced them with nice, clean white ones. The apartment didn't get a lot of natural light, so I tried to keep everything inside it as bright as possible.

The couch my sister was sitting on was a light cream color and still on a payment plan as were the two accent chairs, end tables, coffee table, and the cream and green carpet beneath them.

Slowly, but surely, it was all coming together.

My room was my current project, but I had hit a snag with, well, money for the new furniture. I would get there eventually. Then I would do the renovation of the bathroom.

"Don't try to act like you're not disappointed. You can put on a good show, but these here walls are thin," she said, waving her book around in the air. "I hear those good vibrations when you get a

ELI

letter. You want that bad boy D. And, well, who wouldn't? Just think of the solid dicking you would get after six years of abstinence in prison. You wouldn't walk right for two weeks. Man, maybe I should get me a Prison Blues Hottie of my very own."

My sister was, well, a character.

We had been raised in a very, ah, what's the nice word here, *conservative* household where we were taught abstinence-only education, had purity pledges (ha!), weren't allowed to wear any shorts shorter than our knees or any tank tops at all. We had eight o'clock curfews all through high school where we weren't allowed to wear makeup, listen to inappropriate music, or, of course, date.

To say we had rebelled would be the understatement of the century.

My cherry got popped at barely sixteen; my sister followed suit.

We bought makeup that we hoarded under floorboards like contraband in a fascist dictatorship.

At eighteen, my ass had high-tailed it out of there into a shitty apartment with a shitty boyfriend.

A few years later, as I was just about ready to open my store, my sister moved out and joined me.

She promptly pierced her ears and nose, tatted her arms and chest, and colored her hair like a mermaid.

Peyton was, well, the best roommate you could ask for.

And the best sister there was on the planet.

It had never really even occurred to either of us to live apart. It simply worked. Men came and went, all of us either fitting comfortably, or us spending more time at their apartments. I worked mostly days; Peyton worked mostly nights. Someone was always around for Coop.

It was the best arrangement.

But, ah, yeah, Peyton was not the kind of sister or friend to have all kinds of limits. No topic of discussion was off the table, from dick size to period products, we discussed it all. As far as I was concerned, nothing in the whole damn world would ever be half as funny as Peyton discussing her misadventures with a Diva Cup after having half a bottle of Citron vodka in her system. There were props involved. Including ketchup. And she had made a 'Flo' chart, the name of which made her laugh until she almost peed her pants.

ELI

She had been right there beside me on the couch watching *Oz*, cheering on the eye-gouging and stabbing and hangings. See, where I cringed at violence, Peyton loved it. She watched all the shows my stomach couldn't handle that everyone else in the world adored. From *Sons of Anarchy* to *Game of Thrones*, she was my own little story teller. She would watch the episodes, then tell them to me, going light on the murder and rape stuff she knew I couldn't handle. Her love of gore and horror extended most extensively to her book collection. *You wouldn't believe the stuff these twisted psychos come up with*, she once gushed, talking about why she chose to read indie over traditional. *No way would any publishing house touch this content.*

If there was a single person in the world who I could hide absolutely nothing from, it was Peyton.

So there was no use even trying to deny that I was disappointed about the sudden lack of contact.

"I hope he didn't get killed or something."

"He's probably in the hole," she tried to comfort, in her very Peyton-way - meaning a bit matter-of-fact and aloof even on a heavy subject. "That should get the vibe going don't you think?"

"Ah, how so?"

"You know," she said, climbing off the couch, lips twitching. "In a cell. Naked. Nothing to do but jerk-off. Likely to the memory of you. That's some hot shit right there."

Okay, maybe it was mildly hot.

Maybe the image of him naked with his hard cock in his hand was, well, scorching. But, for me, the whole punishment in a cold, dark, damp cell somewhere kind of ruined the image for me.

Not for my sister, mind you, because that was just her kind of twisted.

But for me.

I would definitely rather he be in a cell jerking off than dead, though, so I had to hold onto that, erm, *hope*.

It shouldn't have mattered.

He was just some dude who got arrested, who occasionally wrote me letters in his detached way, who had a really pain in the ass, but wholly lovable, dog that I happened to adopt.

What we had was a whole lot of little nothings.

ELI

But even a lot of little nothings could add up to something, right?

A whole lot of tiny grains of sand made up the entire shoreline.

Oh, good God.

What was wrong with me?

"What?" Peyton asked, over her shoulder from where she was bent looking in the fridge, brow raised, making me realize that the growling noise I thought I had made internally, actually came out of my mouth.

"Nothing."

"Don't you be going 'nothing-ing' me, young lady!" she snapped in the absolute perfect imitation of our father.

We hadn't exactly cut ties with our parents, but one could say things were rather, ah, strained. They couldn't have us at their Thanksgiving table. I mean, what would they tell their other ultra conservative friends?

My eldest daughter slings smut for a living and, as you can see, our youngest is intent on becoming a human canvas.

Since we both moved out, there had always been this unspoken rule that we didn't show our faces at their events, but we must call on Christmas, Mother's Day, Father's Day, and their anniversary.

It was a system that worked out well for all involved since we were all such different people. That being said, Peyton liked to imitate the way they continued to speak to us on occasion. You know, to remind us what we weren't missing by not being too in touch.

"Were you having impure thoughts about a boy?" she went on, this time making her voice high and just slightly nasal - a spot-on mother impersonation. "Because you know what you're supposed to do when you have impure thoughts, dear," she went on, but then came back with a big cucumber and wiggled her eyebrows at me.

I laughed, snatching it away from her, deciding a salad was in order for dinner. Mainly because I planned to hit the local bakery and bring home half a dozen donuts just for myself.

"It's not that," I said, then rolled my eyes at her raised brow. "Okay, there is a little bit of that. But it's more that... I shouldn't care.

ELI

Right? I mean, it's crazy. I don't even know the man. I haven't even officially met him."

"And yet you share a dog with him."

"I don't *share* Coop with anyone. Except you. I mean, I've had him for almost six years now. He's mine."

"You send him pictures. And updates. Let's face it, your doggy-daddy is serving time in the penn, and you are making sure he gets to watch him grow up."

"Be serious."

"I mean, this will be new for me, but I can sure try," she agreed, pressing her lips into firm lines, but her eyes were dancing. "This is my serious face." It took two seconds for her face to break out into a grin. "Come on, Autumn!" she said, shoving her shoulder into mine. "What does it matter if you maybe get the downstairs tinglies about some guy you saw once?"

"It's not the 'downstairs tinglies' as you so maturely put it," I countered. "It's more that, I dunno."

"You give a shit about him?" she suggested, her shoulder moving up to her ear as her nose scrunched up, like the idea was completely foreign to her. "And you think you shouldn't because he's a prisoner."

"It's less the prison thing--" though maybe that should have been more of a factor, "and more that I don't even know him! But I think about him way too much."

"You know what it is?"

"No, what?" I asked, turning toward her.

"You desperately need to play sink the sausage." At my snort/laugh hybrid, her smile curled further upward. "When was the last time you rocked the Casbah? Or kneeled at the altar? Given someone your lunchbox? Oh, wait, I know. It's been almost two *years*. Years, Autumn. Years."

"I can't do..."

"Sex without a commitment. I know, I know," Peyton finished for me, shaking her head. "I'm just saying. If you're wondering why you can't get Hottie Mc Death Row--"

"He's not on death row!"

"Off your mind," she went on. "It's because you haven't done the four-legged foxtrot in far too long."

"Nice alliteration."

ELI

"Just saying," she said, raising the cucumber again, giving me a serious nod.

"I own a sex store! I can more than keep my sexual appetites appeased."

"Oh, please. You and I both know that that is not the same. You need to feel a man's weight on you, have his hands sink into your ass, have his mouth over your tits, hear his grunts and growls while he fucks you... it's different. You know it is."

I did.

That was maybe the worst part.

I loved sex.

I mean I *loved* it.

I almost felt bad for the men I did end up dating because they needed to mainline Gatorade and protein shakes to be able to keep up with me.

And I loved all the amazing, brilliant nuances of the act. The feels, the tastes, the smells, the sounds. It was the best creation in the universe - the way two bodies entwined.

I missed it.

But I couldn't foxtrot with a partner who was going to tap someone else's shoulder for the next song.

"Yeah, I know," I agreed, wondering how many sessions with a vibrator it would take to even get the edge off my frustration.

I had a feeling there weren't enough batteries in the world.

But it would have to do.

And no matter how much I told myself to think of the UPS guy, the biker, or the silver fox, oh yeah, I thought of *him*.

THREE

Eli

There was some kind of ingrained, internal barrier as I took my belongings from the officer at the desk and moved toward the door.
The door that would lead me outside.
To freedom.
I actually stopped in my tracks and had to force my legs to keep moving forward.
The early fall air met me as I walked out the door wearing a beanie I had bought at commissary and clothes that I had traded with someone else inside, clothes that were baggy and nothing like I would normally wear - a dark blue button-up mechanic shirt with a white name tag belonging to the owner, Mitch, and a pair of huge wide-leg jeans that were eerily reminiscent of the JNCO phase I had luckily been slightly too old to indulge in when they were around. I left the shirt open, sporting a white wifebeater I'd never have been caught dead wearing as an outer garment before.

ELI

When I had looked at myself, I gave my reflection a nod.

They wouldn't recognize me, not from a distance, and they wouldn't be allowed to park right out front.

As I walked down the chain and barbed wire path that led to the road, there was an odd churning inside. I had been preparing for months, but it still felt surreal. I understood why so many people had a hard time staying out when it felt so strange to be free.

I spotted a black SUV with dark windows parked almost near the corner. I didn't have to see in to know it was them. Not my brothers, though. No. They would be waiting back at my parents' home. It was Mom and Pops.

I had expected - no matter how much I had prepared myself, steeled myself, cooled myself toward them - to feel a pang.

I was surprised to feel nothing but that hollow space in my chest where my heart should have been as I turned my back on them and made my way up to the waiting beat-up, rusted blue sedan that Bobby was driving.

He didn't bother to get out; he knew the deal.

I needed to get the fuck out of Dodge.

I dropped down into the white fake leather seat. Before I could even reach for my belt, he was peeling away.

"You need a decent fucking burger and a drink," he declared.

And, in a rush though I was to get to my new place, to get into clothes that didn't smell like someone else, to start rebuilding my life, well, I had to admit, I needed a fucking burger and a drink.

Thirty minutes later, my stomach almost bursting for the first time in six fucking years, Bobby and I were pulling into the cul-de-sac where the duplexes were located, all varying degrees of worn out. A couple six-packs of beer were sweating in the backseat.

"Home sweet home," he said, parking, and waving at the hunter green duplex with matching half-rotted front porches, chipped paint windows, and a shared crumbling path.

Work.

It needed some serious work.

I didn't need to live in a fancy place, but I wasn't going to sit in a house that was falling down around my feet either.

"I scoped it out for you. Two bedroom, one full bath. Kitchen is straight out of the seventies. The floors are shit. And the radiator likes it rough, but works after you go at it for a while. It's not bad.

ELI

I've stayed in a lot worse. And that's me and Nat," he went on, getting out, and waving across the street at a slightly better-looking brown duplex. "I'll help you bring your shit in."

And he did.

Right inside the door.

Before handing me a burner I had requested, and the keys to my place. "Been in your place a few too many times. Know you need to settle back in alone. My number is in the phone. I'm across the street. Don't forget to call your parole officer." He moved to walk away, then turned back, whacking me on the shoulder. "Glad to see you out, man."

"You too," I agreed, giving him a nod.

With that, he was gone.

And I was truly alone for the first time in six years.

There was no such thing as alone in prison. Not even when I was between cellmates after Bobby left. Even then, I was in a fishbowl.

It was almost foreign after so long.

I turned, looking around the main area of the house. It was narrow, as all duplexes are, with a staircase leading up right inside the door. The small living room with windows that peeped out onto the porch ran beside the stairs and back toward the kitchen that, yep, was straight out of the seventies. And the *ugly* seventies with yellow cabinets, floral backsplashes, and faux wood linoleum on the floor.

With a head shake, I moved back out toward the living room, grabbing one of my bags to take up the stairs that creaked loudly enough for the neighbors to hear me each time I went up or down. Which, in turn, meant I would hear them as well. But, whatever, it was the price that came with freedom and detachment from the life that would make a shitty duplex a laughable concept.

I would fix it up.

I would make it home.

The upstairs was cursed with thick brown shag carpeting in every room except the bathroom that had small black and white tile, a shower stall that needed a serious bleaching, and a cracked mirror over the pedestal sink.

The spare bedroom was maybe eight by nine with a window looking right into the window to the next set of duplexes. But it was

ELI

plenty big for the studio I had planned for it. It was certainly more than I was used to.

The master bedroom was maybe ten by ten with a decent set of windows overlooking a courtyard that it seemed all the duplexes on this side of the street shared, littered with bikes, plastic slides, skate boards, a plastic kiddie pool full of sand, and a push mower wrapped in tarp.

I made a mental note to hit the local home improvement store for flooring, cabinet solutions, and window treatment options when I went to buy a cot to hold me over until I could order furniture.

I'd never truly started over again.

Not completely.

Anytime I had moved, from my parents' to my first apartment, from my first to my second, second to third, I had always had shit with me, the little stuff you compile over time that you need. Cleaning supplies, towels, sheets. Life stuff.

I shot Bobby a text asking to borrow his car until I got around to getting one for myself. I couldn't even fucking shower and wash off the penn because I didn't even have any goddamned soap.

Three hours later, my apartment had more bags and supplies than actual floorspace.

Once I got my bearings, things like withdrawing money from my bank as I waited for up-to-date cards to get sent to me, like shopping, like unpacking, like cleaning with actual supplies, yeah, it all came back as easily as you might expect, no matter how much time had passed.

By the time mid-afternoon passed, I had a clean enough place, a spot to sleep on, some food in the fridge, three beers in me, and a sense of self-satisfaction I hadn't experienced in far too long.

I dragged myself into the bathroom, tossing the clothes I would never wear again, showering, and changing into the new digs I picked up at the store.

Then I paced.

Like I did in prison.

Like a caged animal.

It took an almost embarrassingly long time to realize I didn't *have* to pace, that I could just... go for a walk. I could get back whenever I wanted.

ELI

So I called my parole officer, grabbed my keys and wallet, and headed out, waving a hand to Bobby who I was pretending not to notice was handing out pot to a couple of kids who were likely still in high school.

Not my business.

I learned that motto in prison.

It was something you had to roll around your head a dozen times a day, no matter what crazy shit was going on around you.

Not my business.

I had no real plan in mind, maybe just a walk up the street and back, just clearing my head, just trying to keep focused.

But then I saw it.

She's Bean Around.

I swear to shit, I literally stopped dead in my tracks, making the guy who was walking behind me ram into my shoulder with a muttered curse.

See, I tried.

To stop writing her when she wrote me. To put an end to that connection.

Not because I didn't want it.

I wanted it too much.

That was the problem.

When I found myself going out into the common room when it was time for mail, finding myself disappointed each time there was nothing, even though that was generally the pattern - a few months between each letter, though there were times when it was more frequent.

When I found myself reading and re-reading her sometimes several page-long letters about the prison shows she was watching, or the new places popping up in Navesink Bank, or whatever new trouble Coop was getting himself into that week, and fucking smiling at myself all alone in my bunk, yeah, I knew I needed to get it together.

I couldn't be creating connections with some chick who didn't understand what a monster I could be.

I couldn't drag a seemingly good woman down with me.

That wasn't in my cards.

Why she was even contacting me was beyond me. She was beautiful, smart, funny, and warm. She should have been out there

ELI

getting worshipped by some normal man, not sitting and penning letters to a fucking criminal.

Maybe it was just Coop.

Maybe it was a way for her to get her kicks, learning about the ins and outs of prison without actually having to experience it herself.

Maybe she felt a weird connection because she watched me get arrested.

Who knew.

Whatever it was, it probably wasn't healthy for her.

And it definitely wasn't good for me.

It was making me think things, giving me hopes for a life I knew I couldn't have anymore.

And on Christmas, after I sent off the letter, and got into my bunk, and thought about those fucking finger vibes, my cock got a mind of its own for the first time in a long goddamn time.

That, well, yeah, was that.

She wrote me back, but I had decided by then to cut ties.

It was better for the both of us.

Even if I had to steel myself and plant my feet every single fucking mail day.

But slowly, over time, like I had needed to do with the roots that planted much, much deeper - my family - I had been able to phase it out, to put it on a shelf, to refuse to think about it.

Until I saw that fucking sign, man.

It all came rushing back.

And I knew I had to.

I fucking had to.

I hadn't even consciously made the decision to go in before my legs were already carrying me in that direction.

Hot salted caramel coffee.

She had called it a 'food... you-know-what' because, obviously, the woman had done some research about the content allowed in letters, and was worried the word 'foodgasm' might raise a red flag. She was careful about that. If the word she was using was a curse, she put stars in it. She never used staples or paperclips. She never sent any images that were suggestive in any way.

ELI

She had sat down and brought up her computer, and went to Google and fucking looked up how she was allowed to correspond with someone in prison.

It made no sense.

But she did it.

And, even though I had been determined to do my time in my detached, cold way for the good of myself and everyone around me, I had looked forward to it; I had taken a small bit of comfort in the contact.

Which was why I cut it off.

I shut it down.

I pretended to forget.

Until I saw that sign.

I hadn't had a decent cup of coffee in six fucking years. And given my old addiction to it, there was no way I was passing up a foodgasm even if flavored coffee wasn't usually my thing.

I walked up to the door, not sure what I was expecting despite getting a detailed letter about it. Autumn had claimed that the inside changed as often as one of the women who owned it changed her hair.

Before I even moved inside, I could hear the music, loud and thrashing, some kind of post-hardcore slash NU metal band I wasn't familiar with. And, apparently, it was about dismembering corpses.

No one sitting at one of the dozen or so tables scattered inside seemed the least bit phased by the choice of song or the ear-splitting volume. And as I walked up near the counter, I saw a sign claiming that they would not change the music or turn it down because it was the only thing keeping them from slapping rude customers.

My lips curved up as I stepped in front of a woman with a mass of wavy and curly red hair around her pale face complete with a light smattering of freckles and almost see-through light blue eyes. Tall and thin, she still managed to make her simple jeans and She's Bean Around black tank look like the sexiest outfit a woman could wear. There was just something in the air about her.

There's this redhead named Gala (yes, like the apple) who kind of has this sweet, innocent face, but is a complete shameless flirt who every man goes completely gaga for.

That was Autumn's description. And it was accurate.

ELI

"Rough day, huh?" I asked, motioning toward the speakers in the ceiling.

"Some out of town suit came up to the counter on his cell phone then had the nerve to tell *me* - not the person on the phone - to wait a minute. The call went on for five minutes, then without apologizing, he called me 'toots,' and demanded I just give him a shot."

"Did you throw it at him?" I asked, smiling a little at her level of anger. But, having worked in the service industry when I bartended at Chaz's when I was younger, I knew that it was never just one rude customer. It was a slew of them in varying degrees of awful that led to a mood such as hers.

"Oh, I gave him his stupid shot, but didn't inform him like I normally would that there is more caffeine in a medium coffee than there is in a shot of espresso and that if he wanted the biggest bang for his buck, getting a medium with a shot or two is what was going to get you going and keep you going all day. You know two-hundred-eighty grams of caffeine versus just the eighty in an espresso. But whatever, dude, peter out at noon and need another shot. Not my problem you suck at life. So what do you want?"

I laughed at that, charmed by her somewhat prickly greeting, and how she managed to talk to me like I was a regular she bitched with every day and not a complete stranger.

"I need two medium hot salted caramels. With a shot each," I added, giving her a smirk.

Yeah, two.

Because I was out of my fucking mind, that's why.

It was the only possible explanation.

"Salted caramel, huh?" another woman asked, coming out from a door that led into the back.

She was every bit the complete opposite of her business partner, aside from them both being tall. Where Gala was thin, this woman had more curves than any one woman had a right to. Gala's skin was pale; this woman was maybe Puerto Rican or Dominican with her medium skin-tone. She had full lips, sleepily sexy dark eyes, and dyed gray hair with light purple ends.

Jazzy, she was called.

"I didn't have you pegged for a flavor guy. Usually, those are the suits."

ELI

"Or the indie kids," Gala chimed in.

"Usually it's just black. But a... friend suggested the salted caramel, so I am giving it a try."

"Oh, a *friend,* huh?" Gala asked as Jazzy went to pour the coffees. "I'm going to take a wild guess that this friend is a girl. I mean, look at you."

It had been so fucking long since I had seen a woman at all - save for the one or two working as corrections officers at the prison - that I almost didn't even grasp at first what she was doing. She was flirting with me.

You'd think after six years inside, that fucking would have been the first thing on my mind, but somehow, it fell back in importance behind a slew of other pressing matters.

"At least tell me she's not just a pretty face," Gala implored.

She was that, a pretty face.

Gorgeous.

Fucking beautiful.

But she was much, much more than that.

"She's not just a pretty face."

"Then I will contain my heartbreak," Gala offered as she handed me my coffee.

"That's six," Jazzy said as I reached for my wallet.

I handed her a ten, nodding toward the two separate tip jars. "Put me in for Freeman," I said, choosing him over Christopher Walken to narrate my life.

"What, no cow bells?" Gala asked as she threw the extra money in the jar. "Enjoy your coffee," she offered, going over to the music, lowering it a few decibels, and changing it to something more classic rock.

I guess I helped wash away the memory of the under-caffeinated suit.

And the reality of what I was doing didn't actually hit me until I turned away from the counter.

What the fuck was I thinking, ordering an extra coffee?

I had no right to seek her out on the outside.

Hell, I had been the one to stop communication in the first place, to think it was best to create a disconnect.

ELI

Why then, was I turning out of the coffeeshop and moving down the street that would lead to a side street that would lead to Navesink Bank's only sex store?

I mean, chances were, she had just taken the picture of Coop there by happenstance. It was pointless to go there.

But I refused to be the kind of freak who would show up at her house. That was a whole other level of creepy.

As I made my turn down the street toward the storefront, I figured there was no harm, right?

If I went there and it was just a sex store, fine.

That was a sign.

It was done.

But if I went there and saw her there by chance...

That was its own sign as well, wasn't it?

A sign of what, I wasn't sure.

But I guess I was going to find out.

FOUR

Autumn

If I had to deal with *one* more comment from a male customer about how he doesn't need one of those penis enlargement devices - nudge nudge, wink wink - I was going to scream.

It was just one of those days.

The ones from hell.

When the POS system was down for a few hours, then my shipment ran late, and then I had to sit with a maid-of-honor for *two and a half hours* to help her decide on what toys and supplies she wanted at the bachelorette party. When I offered to make it a Phallusopy event - meaning I could be hired to come in and give sex tips, hand out the best erotica, explain the different types of sex toys and how they were used, you know, since she didn't know diddly squat about any of it - she refused, insisting it had to be her giving all the information out. Which meant that I had to, essentially, give her a free class that I would normally charge for if I wanted her to buy

ELI

supplies from me and not, as she so charmingly put it, buy online where it was cheaper.

So I guess that "shop small" bag you carry around is for show, huh?

It took everything I had to keep my mouth shut about that.

Add on top of that the aforementioned creepy dudes giving me the eye-fucking of a lifetime, yeah, I was having a crummy day.

Normally, I would look forward to grabbing some Chinese, and heading home to pick out a movie, waiting for Peyton to get off her shift at the library so we could veg out and I could put a decent spin on a blah day.

But Peyton had a date with some dude she met at a Tractor Supply & Co, or, as she called it, Men R Us.

Why she was even *at* a Tractor Supply & Co was completely beyond me, but she better not have given in and bought one of the damn ducks she always eyed up when she was there.

Coop would probably try to play with it. But Coop's play would mean an untimely - and likely bloody - end to the poor dude's life.

I had to rescue a baby bunny once.

Thankfully, before the little fluff ball got hurt.

I was still planning on Chinese *and* maybe some gelato because it was one of those days when you just had to say 'fuck it' to balance, and indulge yourself.

It just wouldn't be quite as uplifting without Peyton there to say something smartass or off-the-wall, something that never failed to turn around a bad mood.

I heard the bell over the door ring and actually felt my eyes rolling before I reminded myself to get my head out of my ass and be a professional. Even if this person was another stubborn maid-of-honor, I needed to keep it together.

By the time the footsteps came closer, I was sure I was ready for anything.

Apparently, I was very, very wrong about that.

But, really, how could I have ever prepared for this?

For him?

Walking into my store like it was the most normal thing in the world?

It was weird seeing him there.

ELI

It didn't matter that, when I first saw him, he was a free man.

I swear it was like seeing a bear outside on a vacation, then for the next half a decade, only seeing them in zoos. Then walking into work to see one sitting at a desk.

It was weird.

Unexpected.

God, he looked *good* too.

He was a bit different, sure, than the pictures that had been on his Instagram before he went away. He seemed a bit thinner. His hair was much shorter. He had grown some stubble on his face. But age had - as it only ever seemed to do with men - only served to make him even more attractive.

And maybe the attraction factor was also amplified by the fact that this man, his dark hair, his light eyes, his impeccable body, had been invading my dreams and waking fantasies for years. As awful as this is to admit, I had been dating a man for six months, and the relationship was in the toilet, and the sex was just mandatory and uninspiring, then I had caught myself fantasizing about my prison pen pal while in the act.

I had never come so hard in my life.

I had felt so guilty about it that I had actually broken it off the next day. You didn't stay with a man when you caught yourself fantasizing about another.

There was nothing awe-inspiring about his wardrobe - perfectly fitting dark wash blue jeans and a white tee - but somehow, it was the sexiest thing a man could ever wear.

My eyes trailed down his arms, seeing some kind of tattoo peeking out from his sleeve, a tattoo I had seen in pictures that looked a bit like a family crest, but I wasn't sure. They grazed over his strong forearms, his neat nails, then finally, his wide palms that were wrapped around...

She's Bean Around coffee mugs.

Holy shit.

No.

That required more emphasis.

Holy shit!

He was here. In my sex store. With *two* cups of, what I could only imagine, was salted caramel coffee.

What universe was I living in?

ELI

Whose life was this?

Because it certainly wasn't my own.

He was closing in on me, only maybe three feet away from the counter, those hypnotic light eyes trained on me, not seeming to pay any mind to the very explicit display of a flesh-like pussy to the side of him - something that seemed to catch everyone's eye.

No.

He was looking at me, walking toward me, like a wild cat stalking prey.

Maybe I wanted to be eaten.

Oh, good God.

Okay.

Focus.

I needed to focus.

And force my lips to move and form words.

Only I couldn't.

And he was right in front of me.

His head tilted to the side a little, a smile toying with the ends of his lips as he watched me.

"Someone once told me that the salted caramel coffee from She's Bean Around will give me a food-you-know-what," he said, that smooth voice of his shivering through my insides, making my sex clench hard with an unexpectedly intense surge of desire. "And by 'you-know-what,' I'm pretty sure she meant food*gasm*."

Could a person come just from hearing that word?

I mean, I taught tantra for a living; I knew people could come just from breathing properly. But, ah, yeah, this was a new experience for me. I felt right on the verge. I could tip over at any moment.

I was pretty sure it was my turn to talk, but words proved impossible still.

"You gonna make me drink it alone, sweetheart?"

Oh, my poor poor lady parts.

That was just cruel and unusual punishment using an endearment like that.

My hand reached out as he pushed the cup across the counter, making sure my fingers didn't brush his, or else I was sure that would be the last push I needed.

"So, you work here."

ELI

"I own here," I heard myself say automatically, my pride in my hustle a bit stronger than my almost overpowering sexual frustration right then.

My life wasn't big or glamourous. I didn't go out and party all the time. I wasn't a world traveler. But I had my business. I busted my ass to get it, to keep it. And I was extremely proud of what I had accomplished on that front.

His brow raised as he looked around. "Explains the finger vibes, huh?" he asked, raising the to-go cup to his lips, and taking a sip.

I didn't watch his Adam's apple, I swear!

"Fuck, yeah, okay. This is pretty good."

I forgot mine was even in my hand.

I shook my head, raising it to take a sip, hoping it would help my dry-mouth situation.

"So, you're here," I said, hearing the wonder in my own voice.

"I'm here," he agreed, head still ducked to the side slightly, and I couldn't figure out why that was so endearing to me.

"How are you here?" I asked when he didn't explain further.

"I got out earlier today."

"And you came... here?"

"I took a walk and came across She's Bean Around. Didn't even think about it when I ordered two."

"But... how did you know to come here?"

"That's the thing..." he started, only to be cut off by the sound of the chime of the door.

"No, you heel! Heel, you hellbeast, you!" That was Peyton. And she almost never called Coop by his name, choosing instead her own spin on the concept of endearments. I once caught her telling him in a sweet-talking tone 'Who's a ugly little rabbit shit eater? Who is? You are! That's right. You know it was you, you oaf.'

I looked up at the clock, realizing the best part of the day had somehow gotten away from me. If she was taking the time to drop off Coop on her way to work, he must have gotten into something at home. Again.

"Autumn, I swear he wants..."

ELI

She lost the rest of her sentence because when she came into view, Coop got an eyeful of Eli and freaking *lunged* forward, pulling the leash right out of her hand as he ran for his old owner.

I didn't think he would remember him.

I mean, not that I actually ever thought this day would come, but yeah, even if it did... six years was such a long time. And he was only a couple months old when he had been with Eli last.

But he remembered.

And at the last possible second, the crazy animal leaped upward and into the *arms* of the man who had originally rescued him.

"Oh Doggy-Daddy," Peyton greeted, taken aback long enough to give me a *what the fuck* look before turning back to him. "So, what? You just show up after six years, no child support, no nothing, and expect visitation?" she asked, going for serious, but her lips were twitching. "You owe us some Milk Bones up in this bitch. And about ten pairs of shoes for Autumn and a very, very precious signed paperback of *Die Muthafucka* that he ate last year."

"*Die Muthafucka?*" Eli asked as he dodged his head to the side to avoid the searching tongue of Coop.

"Limited paperback edition of an indie genius named Neil Jenkens. He ate the cover. And about half of the pages."

"Alright, buddy. Relax," Eli said, but he was smiling as he tried to untangle from the dog and put him back on his own feet. "Hi, yes, hi," he cooed at him as he squatted down to give the belly rubs Coop shamelessly flopped down, rolled over, and begged for. He said it so lowly that I couldn't say for absolute sure, but I was pretty certain I heard him murmur, "I know. I missed you too."

And damn if I didn't have to look away and fast-blink the little shimmer that crept into my eyes.

I caught Peyton's gaze from several feet away.

She said nothing, but I somehow knew exactly what she was thinking.

Hottie Mc Death Row is in your sex store. You know, the guy you've been polishing the pearl to for years. He's here. In your sex store. *Where there are plenty of devices for you two to consummate your weird prison love affair with. Why are your clothes still on?*

Uncomfortable, I shifted my feet. "What did he do? Why did you bring him here?"

ELI

"He kept body slamming the door when I tried to leave. Like full force. Then he would fall, whine, and charge at it again. But he's here now, all safe and sound with Mommy and Daddy," she added a bit pointedly, letting her lips twitch. "And I have a job to get to. Doggy-Daddy, nice to put a face to the abs," she said, making my cheeks heat. "And sis, I'm just saying... foxtrot lessons are *never* a waste of time. Usually mutually rewarding too," she added, waving a hand as she turned and went to the door. "Cock God," she said, steepling her hands in front of her nose, and bowing her head to the six-foot-tall penis statue that sat beside the front door. "May your blessings rain... actually, ew, no. *Goodnight!*"

Then she was gone.

We were alone again.

And I was praying to hell that he had no idea what 'foxtrot lessons' actually meant.

"That's your sister?" he asked, moving to stand, still reaching downward to pet Coop's head as he whacked it against his leg.

"That's my sister," I agreed.

"She's a character."

"You have no idea," I agreed, smiling a little because, no matter how much she might try to embarrass me at times, she was still my favorite person.

"Where does she work?"

"The library."

"You've got to be shitting me," he said, smile wry.

"Nope. She enjoys scaring all the old people with her colored hair and tattooed body."

"And piercings."

"Those too."

There was a long, uncomfortable silence following that, neither of us seeming to have any idea what to say. What could you say in a situation like this?

So, I never expected to meet my prison pen pal. Oh, and by the way, I think about you when I masturbate?

That wasn't going to work.

You're so beautiful it makes me forget that you were a felon locked up for aggravated assault.

I was pretty sure that wouldn't be appropriate either.

ELI

"Autumn," Eli said, voice a mix of soft, but also heavy at the same time. "Thank you."

Startled, I felt myself jerking back, brows drawing together. "For what?"

"Take your pick," he said, shrugging. "For taping the arrest when you thought it was getting too rough. For taking Coop in because he was too fucking ugly for the pound. For dealing with his crazy ass all these years. I know he is a chore. For writing me to tell me you had him so I didn't worry. For fucking writing me at all. Thank you."

There was almost a weighted feeling in my chest, somehow reacting to the depth in his tone. "You're welcome. For all of that. But, I mean, I think any decent person would have done the same thing."

"Take the compliment, sweetheart," he said, smiling.

I gave him a small one back. "Fine. I take it. I'm an awesome human being."

"There you go," he agreed, giving me a smile that suddenly didn't reach his eyes. "I don't want to keep you from work," he said after a minute, looking torn. Between what, I wasn't sure.

"Yes, because there seems to be an absolute rush on floggers right now," I laughed, waving a hand at my empty store.

"I know this is weird," he went on, looking apologetic.

"It was... unexpected," I countered. "I hadn't heard from you for so long. Peyton was convinced you got shanked in the shower," I added, lips twitching.

He chuckled at that, the low, rumbling noise moving around my belly deliciously. "Nah, I got out this morning," he admitted.

He got out this morning and one of his first stops was to share She's Bean Around coffee with me?

That was crazy.

And like super sweet.

But mostly crazy, right?

Unless, maybe it wasn't.

What man didn't get out of prison and think of a woman first? Right? And, clearly, he and his ex weren't going to happen again. Sure, he could hit a bar and find a woman. He was gorgeous and charming. But why not go right to the chick who was writing you prison letters for years like some freak, right?

ELI

Ugh.

Great.

I made myself seem like some chick with a prison fetish or something. The kind of girl who always wanted to fuck a bad boy.

That, well, it absolutely wasn't me.

Writing him had been completely out of the norm. And having sexual fantasies about a man who did criminal things was just insane for me.

It was, what was the term, an *isolated incident*.

I mean, of course, I was incredibly attracted to him. Anyone with eyes would be.

But that didn't mean that, now that he was free, I was going to drop to my knees at the, as Peyton put it, altar.

That wasn't my style.

No matter how hot he was.

"What's that look for?" he asked, making me shock back, not having realized I had swum out into an ocean of not-great thoughts.

"What look?" I asked, reaching under the counter for one of the specialty biscuits we kept just about everywhere for Coop. Milk Bones comment aside, Peyton refused to let Coop eat the 'mass produced crap' you would get at a local pet store. She actually spent one of her days off every week *baking homemade dog treats,* dehydrating meat for his bedtime snacks, and making a special dog stew that she read about in some veterinarian's book.

I might have brought him home, but Coop was every bit hers as he was mine.

"Is that in the shape of brass knuckles?" Eli asked as Coop jumped clear off the floor to take it from me.

"Peyton has an interesting cookie cutter collection."

"I believe it," he agreed, watching Coop devour his food.

"He's a bottomless pit. I swear he has thirty treats a day on top of his food. But he never sits still, so he burns it all off. The vet said his weight was perfect."

"He got huge," he agreed, giving the dog a bit of a sad smile.

And, hell, every ounce of me wanted to find a way to take that look off his face.

Even if that meant stripping naked and demanding he do as he pleases.

ELI

Okay, so maybe that was just my libido talking, not my common sense.

But yeah.

I didn't like seeing him sad.

He spent six years inside; he should have been over-the-moon to be out.

"Do you want to come with me to take Coop on a walk? If I don't tire him out now, he'll be pacing my apartment all night, chasing shadows, and waking everyone up."

There was a second of hesitation, something inside him seeming to have a battle before he nodded and reached for the leash. "What about the store?"

"Closing early is a perk of ownership," I told him, reaching for my purse under the counter.

"But what if there is a flogger emergency?" he asked, deadpan, making me let out a mildly embarrassing snort/laugh hybrid as I made my way through the main aisle of the store, letting him lead Coop out onto the sidewalk.

I turned to flip the sign on the door and lock up. "Then I guess they will have to experiment with bare-handed spanking for one night. It's not the same, but it will do in a pinch."

When I turned, I realized I needed to pay more attention to the things I said around this man. My life revolved so much around throwing out sexual comments all willy-nilly. It hardly ever occurred to me to temper what I said, around adults at least. If you couldn't handle some dildo talk, then we probably had no business being around one another.

But, yeah.

Sex talk around this particular adult was, ah, problematic.

Because those hypnotic eyes of his got just a bit deeper, went heavy-lidded.

Noticing it did this dropping sensation in my belly followed by a pressure on my lower stomach that everyone who had ever been turned on before would know for a deep desire.

"So, what direction?" I asked when he said nothing, as I tried to remind my body that we didn't do casual sex. Not even if the guy was as hot as this one.

ELI

Eli jerked his head to the side, surprising me when he didn't want to go toward the center of town where there might be storefronts to look in.

Maybe, at this point, I should have been wary, I should have been hyper-aware of the fact that this man was a violent criminal fresh out of jail, and that the streets toward the side of town he was indicating were somewhat dead thanks to many abandoned storefronts.

That being said, I had researched his case.

He hadn't hurt the woman. He had been *defending* the woman against her abusive husband. Normally, he would be hailed a hero for something like that. It was just his bad luck that the husband was the son to a prominent politician who had way too many connections, and who was able to force the battered wife to testify against him at trial. To, ugh, as the disgusting phrase went - *stand by her man*. As if any woman should be made to feel like she didn't have any other choice but to lie on the stand and convict the man who had tried to save her.

But anyway, yeah, I didn't figure this man was any threat to me.

That being said, I owned a sex store that I often was in alone a lot of the time, and left late at night.

So my bag was like a mini self-defense store.

Mace? Check.

Mini expandable baton? Check.

Taser? The best one on the market. I wasn't even sure it was legal in Jersey, but I didn't care.

And, for about six months, I took self-defense classes at the local gym.

So, yeah, even if his intentions weren't honorable - though I very much doubted that - I was prepared to take him down.

"So, ah, are you staying in Navesink Bank?" I asked.

"At least for the next year. I don't have much choice in the matter."

"You don't want to be here?" Why was that information making my heart sink a little?

"It's the only place I've ever called home," he hedged, pulling back on the leash when Coop looked like he was about to lunge at a shadow.

ELI

"But you feel done here?" I asked, understanding.

"Been there?"

"I grew up in the sticks in Pennsylvania," I offered. "Very rural. Very conservative community."

He looked over at me, smirk devilish. "You sure showed them, huh?"

I laughed at that. "It wasn't that I set out to raise eyebrows. Once I was an adult and realized how far we, as a community, still had to go in being open about sex, and giving comprehensive sexual education, I kinda figured this was a niche I would do well in."

"So you do more than sell sex toys?"

"I won't lie; that is the majority of my income. But I teach classes too."

"What kind of classes?"

Okay, so I know I said that the sex store thing wasn't a good idea for topics of conversation. But Eli, unlike most men I tried to have this kind of conversation with, wasn't making double-entendres or leering at me. He was genuinely curious. In a casual way.

"I offer a class for parents and kids about 'the talk' for when the parents are too embarrassed to do it themselves, but want their kids to get accurate information not based on shame and taboo. Then there are couples classes like tantra. I have classes - and these are usually done at bridal showers or bachelorette parties - just about sex toy education."

"Rabbits verses eggs?" he suggested, managing to simultaneously pique my interest - because, let's face it, any man up-to-date on his vibrators was intriguing - and send another surge of desire through my system. There was simply no way to keep my brain from imagining being in bed with him. With a rabbit. Or an egg. Or, hell, *just* him.

"Exactly," I agreed, hoping my voice wasn't as airy as I was worried it might be.

There was another tense silence as Coop - as he usually did - led us his way, which was down a dead-end side street where there were only two stores, both of which were closed, likely following the scent of a mouse or stray cat. Or both.

Eli turned suddenly, light eyes so intense under those thick black lashes.

"Autumn, why the fuck did you write me?"

ELI

Oh, so we were doing this.

And me, well, I didn't have any good, satisfactory answers for him.

"The first time, just so you knew your dog wasn't at the pound on death row. After that," I said, shrugging my shoulders. "I honestly don't know."

"You knew what I did?"

"I looked into you once I remembered your name."

"Remembered my name?"

"Yeah, you know. Between the arrest, then trying to take care of Coop, and work, and life... I kinda forgot what the cop called you. It wasn't until right before I wrote you the first time that I was at a bar, and someone called another man with the last name Mallick. Then it clicked."

"Did you talk to them?"

"To whom?"

"My brother or father."

There was a noticeable tension in his body right then. His shoulders squared; his spine went fully straight; his jaw looked like it was clenched painfully.

So family.

That was a sore, sore topic for him.

The nosy part of me wanted to know why, wanted to ask for the details, wanted to understand. But I also understood that wasn't my place, that wounds like that hurt when they got uncovered, ripped open again.

"Ah, no. No. I was at Chaz's for my birthday, and someone just called out the name Mallick. It clicked, so I turned, and I saw someone who looked a lot like you. But in a fancy suit."

"Ryan."

"I'm sorry?"

"That was Ryan."

Ugh.

There was pain in his voice.

Whatever story that was there, it could not have been a good one.

Had they disowned him when he got arrested?

Was there a disconnect even before then?

ELI

It was clear that, at some point, his family must have meant something to him. That was the only way to describe the depth of tortured emotion in his tone.

Something about hearing that in a man's voice, maybe just in *this* man's voice, it gave my insides a tug, something I couldn't place at first, but was ultimately just a bone-deep desire to ease it slightly.

Without thought, truly without realizing it was going to happen until I felt the contact myself, my hand moved out to close around the outside of his hand.

At the contact, his body jerked, like he wasn't expecting it, like he was unfamiliar with touch. And, I guess, that made sense.

His eyes sought mine, full of questions.

I had no answers.

But I had a small bit of comfort.

"You don't have to talk about them," I offered, shrugging.

Like my touch, I wasn't sure that his was exactly intentional either. Because he seemed almost as taken aback as I was when his thumb moved to slide between my thumb and forefinger, allowing it to move gently over the top of my hand.

Shivers, I tell you.

There were actual, real-life shivers.

I couldn't claim to have experienced everything there was to experience with a man, but I had known enough to know that the shivers you read about, hear songs about, see in movies, they didn't happen often. In fact, I had gone all my years without having felt them at all.

Feeling them now, in this quiet, badly lit street, with a man I had only officially just met, whose past was a mystery, whose previous six years had been spent in a prison cell, it couldn't have been any more unexpected.

"Don't," he said, his voice barely above a rough whisper, but somehow still pleading.

"Don't what?" I asked, hearing the neediness in my voice, but finding myself suddenly completely unconcerned by it.

His hand slid from mine, leaving an odd tingling in its wake as his arm lifted, and his fingertips brushed near my eye. "Don't give me this look," he finished, fingers moving back toward my temple, brushing my hair behind my ear.

"What look?"

ELI

As if I didn't know exactly what look it was.

It was the shameless slut inside all of us screaming out *take me, take me now!*

"The one that looks a hell of a lot like permission."

Because it was.

It so, so was.

To hell with rational thought, with consequences, with the knowledge that this was likely a horrible idea.

All I could focus on was the way his touch was making my belly go liquid, making the pressure on my lower stomach all but impossible to bear, was making my heart race and skip.

And I just wanted more.

"It is permission."

That was apparently that.

Whatever thread of control he had been holding onto, snapped.

His fingers slid back into my hair, grabbing my head at the base, and yanking me forward.

I collided with his body hard enough to make my body jerk.

But I couldn't even focus on that for a second.

Because as soon as my body hit his, his lips crashed down on mine.

And the world ceased to exist.

I'd been kissed wildly before, without restraint, without anything but primal need.

But, apparently, that was nothing like getting kissed by a man who hadn't known the touch of a woman in six years.

His lips bruised into mine as his fingers curled into my skull, holding me flush to his body as his teeth bit my lower lip, as his tongue took the opportunity when I moaned to slip inside and claim mine.

A shudder racked through my body, making a low, guttural, almost pained groan rumble from deep in his chest as he turned us suddenly, slamming me back against the brick wall to a building, his hand taking the impact as his thigh slid between mine, pressing them open slightly so he could move in closer.

My hands went up, one clawing at the skin on the back of his neck, the other low on his hip, dangerously close to grabbing his ass.

ELI

His lips took mine again just as his body shifted, and his hard cock pressed against my sex, pressing right where I needed contact most.

There wasn't a force on Earth strong enough to contain the pained whimper that escaped me as my hand forgot all about things like how to act in a civilized society when you were in, for all intents and purposes, a public place. My hand sank into the firm cheek of his ass, dragging him against me, begging for more.

On a growl, as his teeth snagged my lower lip and pulled hard, he gave me more, grinding his cock against my pussy as my leg rose to the side of his hip, opening up to him more.

His lips moved from mine, going down the column of my neck as he kept grinding against me, as I kept moving my hips against him, already almost to the brink of oblivion.

His lips sucked in the sensitive skin of my neck as his cock hit my clit.

And it was close.

So so close.

His hips pulled back to thrust again, sure to make me completely explode into an orgasm the intensity of which I wasn't sure I had felt before.

It was that precise moment Coop not only became a shoe-eater, book-destroyer, attention-demander, but also a cock-block.

He jumped up with a bark, one foot landing on my side, one on Eli's, making us both spring apart unexpectedly.

Coop hopped back down, oddly silent as the sound of our heavy breathing seemed to fill the air around us.

Eli's eyes looked as heavy as mine felt.

His cock was as hard as my pussy was wet.

"Fuck," he said, the sound a mix of angry, turned on, and resigned. "Fuck," he repeated, dropping Coop's leash into my hand, turning, and walking away.

I sank my ass back against the wall, not sure my legs would be able to hold me any longer.

My heart was thudding alarmingly in my chest as my sex clenched painfully with the need for release.

Beside me, Coop wagged his tail as I turned to watch Eli disappear into the night.

Fuck.

ELI
That had been his parting word.
And, well, that just about covered it.
Fuck.

FIVE

Shane

They had all been out looking for him for fucking hours. It was starting to seem hopeless. Hell, even Scotti's four brothers were scouring the town along with them.
Nothing.
Everyone was pretty much ready to start heading home to help out with the kids, to see their women.
And that was where Shane was heading, coming back from Third Street territory where no one would claim to having seen Eli.
He had slowed down for a stop sign when something big and multi-colored and oddly familiar caught his peripheral.
There was no stopping the laugh that burst out of him at the sight of that hideous, oversized mutt that the entire family had been looking for for years. Right there. Down a side street. On a leash. Looking well taken care of.
At that thought, his eyes drifted over and up.

ELI

And fuck if he didn't hit two birds with one motherfucking stone.

Because there was Eli.

Mouth and hands all over some woman.

If he figured right, it was likely the woman who had been taking care of Coop all these years.

And that was right where Eli went when he got out.

Maybe he should have stopped, charged down there, demanded an explanation for the years of disconnect. But, well, the poor fuck had been on the inside for six years. He didn't blame him for wanting to get some action first thing.

What mattered was, he was in town.

He was okay.

The rest would fall into place.

Wait until he told the rest of the fucks this shit...

SIX

Eli

I had no right to put my hands on her.
Not even if I had fucking permission.
She didn't need to be near a man like me.
I had no right to even show up at her store, to exploit some weakness she obviously had toward me, for whatever reason she had it.
Then I went and kissed her?
And it wasn't just any kiss either.
It was the holy fucking grail of them.
It was like a dying man after a meal.
She should have pushed me away, scolded me for pushing too hard too fast. Instead, she was rubbing her hips against my cock, practically begging for fulfillment.
As for me, I was too fucking far gone even to realize the lines I was crossing with her.
Until Coop reminded me.

ELI

Was it a dick move to turn and walk away from her right then? Ah, yeah. But it would have been an even bigger dick move to keep going, to take advantage, to fuck her right against the wall in that alley, no matter how much every cell in my body was begging for me to do just that.

I walked back to my place more sexually frustrated than I had ever been in my life.

And I didn't relieve myself of it either.

Apparently, after six years of punishment, I still wasn't done getting down on myself.

Maybe I never would be.

On a growl, I grabbed a bunch of the bags left in the living room and hauled ass upstairs to my studio, planning to lose myself in some project until my brain cleared up, until I got the thoughts of her out.

I realized, just shy of sunrise, how impossible that would be.

Because, brain focused for the first time in hours, I realized what I had been so focused on.

A goddamn portrait of her.

Standing in her store.

Seeing me for the first time.

On her gorgeous face there was a look of shock, of complete disbelief and, if I wasn't mistaken, genuine relief.

Because I hadn't been shanked in a shower as her sister had suggested.

I should have turned and backed out right then.

She shouldn't have been relieved to see me.

But there seemed to be no reasoning with myself right then.

I think, above all else, something inside of me was begging for some kind of connection to the outside world, a connection that didn't tie back to my prison time the way my friendship with Bobby did.

Since my family was off-limits, Autumn was really all that I had.

Even though the only reason I knew anything about her at all was through prison letters, I don't know, it felt different. She never felt tainted by it, marred with its ugly the way Bobby and I were.

Through all the letters, I had learned a lot about her preferences for movies, music, food, TV, and weather. She hated

ELI

horror, but watched *Oz* out of curiosity. She loved tomato soup, but hated tomatoes. She didn't listen to hard rock or rap, but loved indie and classic rock. She loathed summer with a passion, and thought snow was the most magical thing in the world.

Even in all those letters though, not once did she let on that she owned a sex store.

Thank fuck.

Honestly, I wasn't sure I would have been able to handle five years of that torture.

It wasn't what you would think when you thought 'sex store' either.

Was there such a thing as an *upscale sex toy store*?

If there was, this was that.

She had pristine, gleaming hardwood floors, off-white walls with glass shelving units. There wasn't a wire rack in sight. There were black display tables with chandeliers over them, giving the whole space a warm, welcoming, open vibe instead of the dark, seedy, and taboo feeling most sex stores had.

There were two doors leading to the back. One was behind the counter, saying 'employees only' which I figured for a stock room, bathroom, and maybe the break space for her. The other door was left slightly open, displaying several tables and chairs, likely the spot where she held her classes.

She had done something for herself, something she even believed in - educating the masses about enjoying sex without shame.

And she obviously had a very close relationship with her card of a sister. *Cock God*. What a trip.

She was everything I had made her up to be in my mind. And more. And then she fucking wanted me to boot?

Fuck.

I needed to walk away before I remembered that I was trying to be a good man about it. Because, the fact of the matter was, she deserved a man who didn't have to carve his heart out, who didn't need to become a hollow-chested monster so that he didn't have blackout rages anymore.

I wasn't going to let a good woman get involved in my mess.

"Yo!" Bobby yelled, followed by some banging on the floor below, making the dog next door start freaking out.

That was one thing too.

ELI

I hadn't expected Coop to remember me at all, let alone greet me like I had just left town for a week, not almost his whole life.

Dogs.

There was nothing in the world like them.

But he was her dog now. Her and her sister's.

They probably took better care of him than I ever did, and I took pretty good fucking care.

"Coming," I growled, scrubbing my hands down my face.

"What kinda lock is that?" Bobby asked as I pulled the door open, squinting a little at the harsh sun.

"Why? Did you try to pick it?"

"I was going to surprise you with breakfast," he said, holding up a bag and a tray of coffee. "That a crime?"

"If it involves picking my lock, yes," I said with a laugh. It had been a long year and a half on the inside without his ridiculous ass there to lighten shit up occasionally. "But thanks for breakfast," I added as he moved inside.

"Shit. You clean up house better than my woman."

"Pretty sure you're not supposed to say shit like that."

"Because it makes me, ah, how did she put it... oh, right. It makes me a misogynistic asshole. I heard that one when she came home from work and I asked what was for dinner."

"Yeah," I said with a chuckle. "Because she was *at work* while your lazy ass was lounging on the couch."

"Yeah, it didn't go over well. We eat out a lot," he agreed, smiling. "So, it looks like you've been busy. Nat said she saw you coming home from a walk when she was taking out the recycling. Do anything good?"

"Since I'm not supposed to be drinking, and the only place in town to drink is owned by the family I am not in touch with, not what you are thinking. I got coffee." I paused. Then, for some reason, it came out. "Then I went to see the woman who stole my dog."

"No shit! The chick who used to write you. Summer or some shit..."

"Autumn," I corrected, trying and failing to keep her face from popping up in my head.

"Yeah, Autumn. You get in?"

"Not your business, but she's not that kind of girl. And that wasn't why I went there."

ELI

"Haven't gotten your dick wet in six years, and that wasn't why you were there?" Bobby asked with an eye roll as he bit into his egg and cheese English muffin.

I decided not to get into details about how it almost went there. I knew Bobby; he would harp on it. Then I would never hear the end of it.

"It's not my main priority."

"Then your priorities are mixed up, man," he said, shaking his head as I reached for my coffee.

The raging hard-on I had been dealing with all night and part of the morning was definitely agreeing with him. But even if I did get to the point where I could consider having a woman in my life, was stable enough in my new career, could be sure that I could feel once more without it threatening to bring about my rage issues again, I knew that that woman couldn't be Autumn.

I couldn't have a woman like that, case closed.

"So what is the plan today?"

"I have to hit the gallery. They said they would give me a week to bring in some art for them to make their decision on for the next show. But I want that off my plate so I can work on the pieces for the show."

"Yeah, there's no way they aren't taking you on."

I wasn't sure if he meant because I was that good, or because I had a distantly connected wise guy to vouch for me. And while I knew Anthony Galleo had mentioned my name there when he got out a few weeks before, I wasn't going to be throwing that name around. I wanted to get shit on my own merit. Otherwise, what was the point?

"Well, here's hoping," I agreed, reaching for my food. "Because I didn't exactly have a backup plan."

Getting a straight job for an ex-felon was next to impossible. And, generally, the only places willing to take you on were the docks. Since the Grassis owned the docks, and I didn't want to have any connections to that old life, I was praying it didn't come to that.

As far as my legit businesses went, my family had obviously kept them running while I was away judging by the almost obscene amount of money in my bank account, just sitting there, not getting used, accumulating interest for six years. Eventually, I would have to find a lawyer that wasn't attached to the rest of my family, and figure

ELI

out how to sign those businesses over to them without actually having them see me doing it.

Until then, it was bringing in an income, and what I had in the bank already was more than enough to, well, sustain me for another six years even if nothing came of the art.

Hell, if I had to, I could open another new business fully on my own.

But I would prefer for the art thing to pan out.

Otherwise, it had been a waste of six years working on it on the inside.

And when you did something really well, it was only fair to wish to make a living doing it.

Portraits were how I made my money in prison, but they weren't all I was capable of. My skills stretched into many different styles from landscape to abstract to post-impressionism. I planned to, if I was going to get a wall, put up a little bit of everything.

"Hey," Bobby said, making me snap back to the present, realizing I had drifted for long enough that I had nearly finished my breakfast without having even tasted it. Call it a habit of prison. It was always better to zone out so you didn't have to think about the slop shit they fed us. "You aight?" he asked, watching me with lowered brows. "That's not a good look, bro. I've seen a lot of guys get out of the joint and have that look."

"What look?"

"That look that says you aren't adjusting. Like you thought inside was easier."

"Easier? Yeah." When someone else dictated your whole life, it was a whole new kind of simple to get through a day. "But I'm not exactly in a rush to go back, Bobby. This is all just new to me."

Being as in-and-out of the system as Bobby had been for so much of his life, starting in juvie, he had never really needed to do what I did - start over completely fresh. He always had his friends and family. He always had a slower, smoother transition to the life outside.

It didn't seem to matter that, in the grand scheme of things, it was only a small fraction of my life spent in prison. It was still a fish-out-of-water sensation to be free after so long in the same rote routine.

ELI

"I get it. It might take a while to settle in, man. I just want to make sure you ain't fixing to rob a convenience store or some shit so you can go back in. Wouldn't be the first man I knew to pull that shit."

"Don't worry about me, Bobby. I'll adjust."

To the life outside, sure.

To this hole in my chest that felt a helluva lot more empty now?

That, I wasn't so sure about.

Already that morning, my thoughts had drifted to my family more than they had in months on the inside. I guess it was easier there, since there was no chance of seeing them since I refused visitation.

But now?

Now, I could chance by one of them on the street.

I could walk over there in a weak moment.

I had a feeling it was only going to keep getting harder day after day. At least, until enough time had passed that it became as easy as it was in prison.

Someday.

"Glad to hear it. I'm gonna get going. I gotta go get Nat some flowers."

"The fuck did you do now?" I asked, shaking my head. That woman was a goddamn saint from the sound of things.

"I was trying to help! She's always bitching about the laundry piling up when I'm around the house all day. I threw it all in and now all her whites are blue from my fucking jeans, and she is going to have my balls for it; I know it."

I chuckled at that. "Man, get her some jewelry too. She puts up with a lot of shit from you."

"For real, though," he agreed, standing, and slapping my shoulder. "Well, I gotta get to it. Good luck at the gallery. I'll see you sometime tomorrow."

On that note, I showered, dressed, grabbed my canvases, and called a cab, realizing I needed to get my ass to the DMV and a dealership as soon as possible because not having a vehicle was proving problematic.

ELI

"Yo, Doggy-Daddy!" I heard as I walked out of the gallery an hour later.

And, well, there was only one person on the planet who would call me that.

I turned to find Peyton on the sidewalk in bright ass yellow skinny jeans and a long-sleeved band tee, huge sunglasses hiding most of her pretty face - the sisters looked a lot alike in the features department if you looked past the wild hair dye, the piercings, and the tattoos.

"Peyton," I greeted, giving her a nod. "Nice to see you again."

"Mhmm," she said oddly, bringing up her iced coffee and taking a long sip as she looked me over. "Alright, so. You're going to come over for dinner tonight."

"I... ah, what?"

"Dinner. The meal before the fast. Usually consisting of a meat, a starch, and a vegetable. Traditionally, anyway."

"Yeah, honey, I know what dinner is."

"Then I don't understand your confusion. You come, you eat, you..." she trailed off, shrugging, trying for casual, but I could see the way her lips were twitching.

"This wouldn't, by any chance, be your way of blindsiding your sister, would it?"

"What! Me? How could you think such an evil thing?" she asked, smiling. "Come on. She will want to see you, I promise. Plus, no offense, but you look like you need a meal or two. Where did those hot abs go?"

"Hot abs?" I asked with a smirk, knowing I did used to have them, but hadn't done as much working out in prison as I did on the outside, since on the outside, my brothers and I used to meet for a weekly workout at Shane's gym.

"What? So I stalked your Instagram. I needed to make sure you weren't the kind of guy who might kill my sister and keep her eyelids in a jar next to your bed."

"Why her eyelids?"

"See? That's how I know you're not the type. An eyelid-peeler would have tried to deny it. So, see you at six-thirty? Awesome. Okay. Byeeee!" she said, turning and disappearing before I could get my wits about me to decline the offer.

And damn if I wasn't grinning as she walked away.

ELI

Part of it was because she was just such a fucking trip.

The other part, though, there was no denying what it was. It was excitement. Anticipation.

Because, no matter how hard I had talked to myself about needing to stay away from her, the drive to see her was still there.

And I just couldn't seem to rally the determination I would need to stay away.

So... I went.

SEVEN

Autumn

"I'm not being like Mom!" I objected, offended to the core, as she knew I would be when she hurled that little ditty at me. "It's just... it would have been nice to know you were having a friend over a little more than half an hour before they show up. I'm a mess. The house is a wreck. And Coop could use a bath."

Growing up, our mother had always had this weird rule about never allowing us to bring friends over to the house unannounced. It didn't matter that the house was always immaculate - which we knew it was since we were the ones who had to clean it, followed by a white-glove inspection.

It also never mattered that she was always put together because she rose before our father to put a full face of makeup and a dress on, and carefully tame her hair. We were pretty sure that the man had never seen her without makeup on. Because we always saw her sneak out of the bedroom late at night, go into the bathroom, and come out with a fresh face.

ELI

And, well, she was a freak about getting our dogs groomed, so they were never in need of a bath.

She just had a rule that made absolutely no sense whatsoever.

In this instance, I thought my arguments were fair. I had gotten home around five-thirty after handing off the store to my night girl and guy duo, then promptly ripped off my bra through my sleeve before I was even halfway in the door since the damn thing had been poking at me under my arm since fifteen minutes after I left the apartment that morning. I had gone into the bathroom, throwing on an old Good Vibrations! Tee that I had picked up at the first sex store I had ever gone to, and a pair of flannel PJ pants. I had even swiped off my makeup, sure that no one but Peyton and Coop would be seeing me the rest of the night.

And the apartment was just due for a scrub that I had been too tired to give it. It was clean enough with just some shoes thrown about, a couple piles of books of Peyton's here and there, and a bit of an accumulation of dog hair in the corners.

But, whatever, I guess.

Peyton's friends dropped in here and there all the time. Sometimes the apartment was still smelling of floor cleaner. Other times, it looked like a bomb detonated in the living room. They wouldn't care too much.

I was making a big deal out of nothing.

Truth be told, I was just in a crummy mood.

And, yes, if you must know, it had a lot of everything to do with a man who had amazing blue eyes, inky black hair, and lips that could set a woman's panties on fire.

I hadn't been able to move from the spot leaning against that wall for an almost embarrassingly long time. My legs felt wobbly, my head a little woozy. It just seemed smart to stay in that spot until the aching need between my thighs eased enough to make clear thought possible. Then I walked myself back to my store to sit for another fifteen minutes before I started getting emoji messages from Peyton that had pictures of peaches and cucumbers. Of tongues sticking out and Spock fingers. Of a hotdog and a bagel.

Then and only then, having a small chuckle, I grabbed Coop and made my way home.

Where, well, I spent some quality time with various devices I had bought from my own store. You know, for *research purposes.*

ELI

None of it helped.

If anything, I felt even more frustrated afterward.

Then I tossed and turned, sweating through my sheets as I had vivid sex dreams about having my pants yanked down and fucked hard and dirty against a wall down a side street.

Then I dragged myself back into work after too-little sleep to discuss BDSM with a pair of new enthusiasts. I had to clean up the coffee he had brought the night before.

Then darn Coop dragged me down the side street where it all happened. Because I needed that.

The butthead.

So my snapping at Peyton had nothing to do with the house being a bit messy and me looking a wreck. Her friends wouldn't care. They were the most chill group of men and women I had ever met. They'd have to be to hang with my weirdo sister.

I just needed to get a grip.

Hell, maybe seeing some people would get my mind off things that it had no business contemplating.

"Sorry," I said, stirring the spaghetti with the slotted spoon, realizing it was a poor excuse for a meal to serve guests, but I had only been planning on feeding it to myself when I started cooking. "I'm just in a mood."

"You're in a dude-mood," she agreed, ducking into the fridge to grab the veggies she had sautéed up for lunch. "Mix these in the sauce," she instructed, and I did since it was a vast improvement in the way of making it actually seem like *dinner* and not a pity-me meal. "That is some good old-fashioned blue tubes you've got going on."

"Why do I tell you things?" I asked, shaking my head.

"'Cause you loooove me. And you know I'm just thinking of your health here. Orgasms make you live longer. It's science."

"I have orgasms."

"Yeah, yeah, yeah. Poor BOB isn't getting a break lately. Garlic bread?" she asked, reaching for what was left of the crusty bread we had bought for lazy day sandwiches.

"You're really going all out," I observed, looking for the colander.

"So?"

ELI

"So, I once saw you serve your friends Ritz crackers and vodka."

"I'm hungry!" she objected, something in her tone I couldn't quite make out, and completely didn't trust.

"Alright," I said, brows drawn together as I strained the pasta and tossed it back into the pot, mixing in the veggies and sauce as she slathered butter and garlic into slices of the bread. "Whatever. I'm going to go put Coop in my room so he doesn't hurt anyone with his enthusiasm."

I was just coming out of my bedroom when there was a knock at the door followed by Peyton's voice going all sing-song and calling out, "I'm cooooming!"

My brows drew together as I moved into the doorway of the living room. Peyton's friends had a tendency to just burst in since more than a few of them had keys in case of late-night drinking and needing a place to crash.

"Oh! Wine!" Peyton cheered, making me smile. She was a sucker for a decent - or cheap - bottle - or box - of wine. "Come on in. Hey, Autumn, Doggy-Daddy is here!" she called, obviously unaware that I had come back out.

Doggy-Daddy?

Doggy-Daddy!

Even as the implications of that settled in, she was moving out of the doorway, and there he was.

There he was.

Looking like a goddamn male model in dark wash jeans and a lightweight navy blue sweater that hugged his perfect body way too nicely. I mean, you could make out some abs there. Or maybe that was my imagination. My filthy imagination, full of sex dreams of his naked body.

"Hey sweetheart," he said, spotting me before he even took a step inside.

His smile was sweet as his eyes dipped to give me a once-over.

In all my bralessness.
In an ugly old tee.
In baggy PJ pants.
With no makeup on.
And, because I think this part bears repeating - *without a bra.*

ELI

"Your sister didn't tell you she invited me, did she?" he concluded even as my head turned to shoot *daggers* at Peyton who was just grinning at both of us.

"She failed to mention which friend she was having over."

"Of course she did," he said, giving her a raised-brow look.

"What? It totally must have slipped my mind!" she insisted, not even trying to sound convincing. "But you're here now. And we have spaghetti with mixed veggies and garlic bread. And this lovely, lovely little girl right here," she said, stroking her hands down the fancy red wine bottle. "So you might as well stay. Or she will totally let me drink all of this myself. And when I drink whole bottles of wine myself, I tend to drunk-dial exes. That is never pretty."

"Aw, honey, who the fuck would be dumb enough to give you up?"

"Save that silver tongue there, Hottie Mc Death Row," she said, digging through a drawer to find a corkscrew, seeming completely unfazed by the charm.

Meanwhile, he hadn't directed a word of that at me, and I felt lightheaded.

That was Peyton, though. She didn't get all fluttery over compliments or sweet talk. It's why nine out of ten of her relationships failed. She hated the superficial. She needed a depth of which none of the men she had ever met seemed capable of.

"And use those big, manly muscles instead," she went on, handing him the wine and corkscrew. "Oh, yeah, slide into that glass you dirty little slut you," she cooed at the wine as Eli poured it into the three glasses she supplied. "Oh, dear Lord. What *is* this? I need a lifetime supply of this," she informed him as she turned away, sipping, and leaning down to check the progress of the garlic bread.

I had been watching her, still giving her the evil eye, and I had somehow missed Eli picking up one of the other glasses and making his way across the room toward me.

One second he wasn't there. The next, there he was. Right in front of me. I got to learn right then, too, that he not only looked good, but he smelled amazing as well. It wasn't overpowering either. Whatever he had on, be it cologne or just a good deodorant, it was subtle, making you want to lean in close and get a better whiff. Maybe while you licked his neck and...

Oh, God.

ELI

Okay.

I needed to shut that down.

"I wouldn't have come if I didn't think she'd cleared it with you," he offered, holding out the wine glass toward me. My hand rose, fingers curling around the glass, but he didn't immediately release it, his fingers brushing mine.

"She's a pain in the ass like that," I agreed, voice an airy whisper.

"Would you have had me if she asked?"

God, yes!

But also, maybe not.

I was way too mixed up about the whole situation.

"I don't know," I admitted.

"That's fair," he surprised me by saying, giving me a small smile as his hand dropped. "She likely wouldn't have taken no for an answer anyway."

"You are getting to know her pretty quickly," I agreed with a small smile.

"Oh, my ears are ringing," Peyton declared, slamming down the baking sheet onto the top of the stove. "Dinner's served!" she declared, going right ahead and loading up her own plate. "So I was thinking a little slashy-slashy fucky-fucky for a movie, but Autumn here is pretty hardcore against the slashy-slashy part." She took her plate and wine over to the accent chair, balancing the plate on her thigh, holding the wine in her hand, and reaching for the remote. "So... what? Comedy? I guess we could all use a little comedy. Especially with that crummy mood Autumn has been in all day today."

I was going to kill her.

She wouldn't have to watch any slashy-slashy.

She was going to friggin experience it for herself as soon as he left.

"Sorry to hear that," Eli commented, looking at me, and his eyes were full of regret.

"It happens," I brushed it off, moving past him toward the kitchen to put food onto plates for us, mostly because I wanted something to do. I wasn't the least bit hungry anymore.

"Oh! This one looked hilarious. Buddy cop, oh wait, maybe this is the wrong audience for that."

ELI

"I have no problem with cops," Eli surprised us both by saying. At our gazes moving in his direction, he took the plate from me and shrugged. "I did something wrong. They arrested me. That's their job."

"Ah, right," Peyton said, brows low. "Except what you did was right. Any who, okay. Let's watch a remake of a classic and tear it apart instead."

Eli and I took our plates and wine toward the living room, Peyton's placement so *conveniently* meant that Eli and I would have to sit on a somewhat petite couch, ensuring that our legs and arms would brush almost constantly.

"And here we go," Peyton declared, hitting play.

And there we went.

After an awkward fifteen minutes, I began to relax. I was pretty sure the wine had a hand in that since I didn't drink often, and I had been doing nothing but pushing my food around my plate.

Peyton knocked the movie which, to be fair, was absolutely dreadful. We ate. Drinks were refilled. Then Peyton's phone started buzzing, taking her attention for a good ten minutes before she declared. "Um, I'm heading out. Doggy-Daddy, nice seeing you again. Thank you for the awesome wine."

"Peyton," I called as she moved toward the door, in such a rush to leave that she slipped into my shoes which were a whole size too big for her. I knew she heard the warning in my voice. But, as my sister, she chose to ignore it. "You kids have fun now!" she called, wiggling her brows at me as she disappeared.

"She's... subtle," Eli commented as soon as the door clicked closed.

"Yeah, no one would ever accuse Peyton of being dull," I agreed, standing, collecting the plates, and moving toward the kitchen.

I busied myself scraping plates then running water over them.

And I didn't hear him move.

But he did.

Until his front pressed into my back.

His hand slid across my belly, just a subtle pressure.

"That was a dick move last night."

I hadn't expected to discuss it. Let's face it, many - maybe most - men weren't great at communicating at all, let alone initiating conversation. Especially when that conversation was about their fuck up.

"It's fine. I... understand," I comforted him, knowing it must have been hell for him to walk away after so long a spell of celibacy.

"I don't think you do," he countered, resting his chin on my shoulder as his other hand reached out to shut off the faucet.

"I'm a good listener," I offered, wanting to extend an olive branch.

There was so long a pause that I was sure nothing was going to be said, that we were just going to keep standing there somewhat intimately as I tried my best not to think of how things could escalate.

"That night," he started suddenly, voice low, but somehow painfully tortured as well. "When I did the things that got me sent to jail a while later, that wasn't the first time I raged-out like that."

The pause was long enough for me to wonder if I should speak. "Okay."

"My brothers and I, we were raised to be different than most other kids."

"Different how?"

"Our violence was encouraged. Because my parents knew that one day it would be necessary."

Pacifist by nature - self-defense classes aside - I couldn't understand that in the least. "Why would violence be necessary?"

"For the family business," he hedged, and I was pretty sure that whatever the family business was, it was not like the military or something. It was likely something criminal. Which, well, made a lot of sense. "My Pops got his leg-up in the business world by starting loansharking back in the eighties before we were even born. He expected us to follow in his footsteps."

"So you did," I figured.

"We did. Me and Hunt, it never came natural to us. We were both I guess just... softer. Couple years before I went away, he took off, wanting to get away from it all, but seeing no way out. He didn't get to stay away though. Because you don't walk away from this shit. Not in this town. Not with such a fragile balance between the syndicates. If word got out that one of Pops' own sons ran off, it wouldn't look good for him. And while loansharking isn't the easiest

ELI

organization to run, there are absolutely men willing to step in and take Pops down if they saw enough of a weakness there."

"What happened to him?" I asked when he trailed off, wanting to keep him talking, wanting to understand.

"Shane, one of my other brothers, went up and brought him back. Then he got the only thing he could get if he truly wanted out for good."

"What's that?" I asked, though I was pretty sure I already knew thanks to all the new gang and prison type shows I had gotten into over the past few years.

"A beat-out."

Yep.

That was exactly the phrase that had been in my head.

"By your father?"

"By all of us."

The brothers.

Geez.

My back pressed into his chest slightly as I took a deep breath. "I'm sorry you had to do that."

"It was, as horrible as this sounds, just part of the job. Like all the other men I had needed to visit in the past when they didn't make a payment. But the thing is, I couldn't control it. I wasn't like my old man or my brothers. I couldn't stay connected and get the job done. I fucking... I raged-out. It was like a switch got flipped and the normal, rational, self-controlled me wasn't there anymore. Usually, when I went on a job, one of my brothers always came with me to pull me off."

Well.

That made a helluva lot of sense then, didn't it?

Sad sense, but sense.

"That was what happened the night with the woman getting beaten?"

"Exactly. Once I saw her, the switch flipped, and I wasn't even really aware of anything until a long time later when the shooting pain radiated up my hands. I have been beating people for a living since I was eighteen. Nothing ever made my hands hurt anymore. I guess that was what snapped me out of it. The man was just broken bones and blood. The woman was sobbing in a corner. And there was a small crowd."

ELI

"So you ran off."

"I figured it would blow over. The cops would take one look at the woman and agree it was one of those rare, fair eye-for-an-eye situations and put no effort at all into tracking me down."

"Except he wasn't just any man."

"Exactly," he agreed, fingers starting to trace absentminded circles over my belly. Well, to him they were absentminded. To me, they were, ah, distracting? Effective? Hot as hell? Yep, all those.

"It sounds like you and your family were close." Past tense.

"The tightest a family could get," he agreed.

"Were they mad about you going to jail?"

"No. Devastated might be a better word."

"I don't understand then..."

"When I got arrested, when I realized the ramifications of the part of me that was capable of raging out, I decided I couldn't be that person anymore."

I had a feeling I knew exactly where this was going.

"So, I cut off ties with my family. I rejected letters and visitation. I tried to shut it down, disconnect. I figured the only way for me to be a somewhat better man was to completely dissolve the man I had been before. Which gets me back to the point," he went on, making me try to scramble to remember what the point even was, where this conversation even started. "Last night, I had no business coming to see you, tainting your nice little world with my presence. And I sure as fuck had no right to put my hands on you."

But, God, it felt so right to have his hands on me.

It was taking actual concentration to keep from grinding my ass back into his crotch.

"Why?"

"Because I can't be around you and keep myself disconnected. And I can't be connected and still be sure that I won't rage-out again."

That was, well, fair.

It wasn't that typical 'you're too good for me' bullshit that guys tried to pull. It was somehow simpler, and much more honest than that. He didn't trust himself. He was *scared* about what might happen if he lost even a small bit of control. And a big part of me went out to him over that. I couldn't imagine how it felt to have something inside of you that you had never been able to control in

ELI

the past, but wanted more than anything to be able to hold control over in the present and the future. It must have been terrifying to know that you were capable of such violence.

And it must have been absolutely devastating to know that to keep that part of you tamped down, the only solution you could come up with was to stop being the man you had been all your adult life, to cut ties with the people who knew you only as that man.

Life must have been hard and so, so cold for him for so long.

My heart went out to him.

And I wanted to maybe just be a little bit of warmth he could feel comfortable around.

He deserved that, didn't he?

"Have you ever raged-out on a woman?" I asked, and felt his whole body go tense behind me.

"Of course not."

"So, I don't have to worry about that with you."

There was a pause before his arm tightened around my lower stomach. "I'd never hurt you."

I wasn't sure why I was about to say it, why I was going to agree to something that, thus far in my life, had never been something I wanted. Maybe a part of me realized it was different. It wasn't exactly casual, in the traditional sense of the word, if there was meaning behind it. Right?

"How about, when you're here, you can connect with me?" I suggested, going ahead and leaning almost fully back into him like I had been wanting to do since he moved in behind me.

"Autumn..."

"I know what I'm offering, Eli. I'm just seeing if you are interested. You want a safe place to reconnect? Why not here? Where there is no one to flip your switch, where you don't have to worry about rage or family or the man you were versus the man you are trying to become. You can just be. With me. That's it. No expectations."

Except maybe some mind-blowing orgasms.

The pause after my words made me suddenly wish I could just suck them right back in. My belly flipped uneasily as my pulse seemed to start to pound in my throat, wrists, and temples.

"I just want to be clear on what you're offering here," he said, his warm breath teasing over the skin of my neck.

ELI

Anything he wanted, that was what I was offering.

But, ah, I guess that wasn't the best thing to say to a man you hardly knew.

"Sex. A friend. Whatever you need on any given day."

There. That didn't make me sound like a giant slut because I wanted him so badly, right?

"Why?"

"Why what?"

"Why would you offer me friendship or sex?"

Okay, so there was a very distinct pre-orgasm tightening just hearing him say the word *sex*. My body was responding like I was still some blushing virgin. Weird.

"Well, we've kind of had a friendship going on and off for the last couple of years," I hedged.

I should have known he wouldn't let that slide.

"Why do you want to offer me sex, sweetheart?" he asked, his hand pressing in just in the center of my lower stomach where the pressure was already almost unbearable, like he knew that fact, and was more than willing to exploit it. Which was, well, hot. "Is it because your panties are soaked just standing here with me? Is that it?"

Good God, yes.

My head fell back against his shoulder as I took a long, steadying breath.

"I'll take that as a yes," he said, voice low. "Though, just to make sure, I should probably investigate further, don't you think?"

I felt my lips twitching at that, loving when a man could play a little, when sex wasn't always serious.

"That might be wise," I agreed, taking another deep breath, not surprised when it came out shaky.

I barely got the words out before his hand was suddenly in the hair at the base of my neck, pulling, twisting, and using it to turn me around, slamming me back against the counter as his lips crashed down on mine.

I had no idea what I had been expecting, but whatever it was, this was harder, hotter, without a shred of self-control.

His lips bruised into mine. His fingers pulled my hair until my lips parted on a whimper, giving him the space to surge inside.

ELI

My hands fisted in his shirt, my nails digging crescents into the skin beneath.

His hand released my hair, grabbing the back of my skull instead, tilting backward to give him better access, half curling me over the sink as he did so.

His lips ripped from mine, leaving them swollen and overly sensitive, to trail down my neck, his scruff scraping over my delicate skin in a way that I knew there would be beard burn there for a day or two after, and finding myself almost unreasonably pleased by that fact.

"You smell fucking amazing," he growled as his teeth scraped my neck, sending a visible shiver through my body.

I had no idea what I smelled like since I was pretty sure after my shower this morning, I hadn't remembered to put on lotion or perfume. But, hey, if my natural scent was turning him on, I was willing to give them all up permanently.

His fingers found the bottom of my tee, not even pausing before sliding under, grabbing my bare breasts in his large palms, thumbs flicking over my half-hardened nipples, dragging a ragged moan out of me.

"Fuck," he growled, yanking the shirt up and leaning down, sucking one of the hardened points into his mouth, lavishing over it with his tongue as his thumb and forefinger pinched the other one painfully.

My body, so unused to touch for so long, and having long-since forgotten the sensation of pain/pleasure through my system, trembled hard as my leg raised, wrapping around his hip, pulling his pelvis to mine, groaning shamelessly when his hard cock pressed into me through his jeans.

"Off," I growled, raking my hands down his back to grab his shirt. "Take this off."

I needed to feel his skin on mine like I needed my next breath.

He pulled backward, reaching down to pull off his sweater. I meant to reach to pull my tee off, but as his belly and chest got exposed, I couldn't do anything but watch. Each inch of exposed skin was like a treat. His skin was somewhat pale, likely thanks to years inside, but no less delicious as it hugged the subtle outlines of his abs. They weren't the same abs they had been in that poolside picture

ELI

from his Instagram, but they were abs nonetheless, and I had a sudden urge to lean forward and run my tongue between them.

Then the shirt was up and off him, showing off his strong chest, the hint of ink on his upper arms, the small scratches on the back of his neck from my fingers the night before.

My hand reached out, running over the red indentations. "Met this chick," he said, voice all gravel. "She couldn't keep her fucking hands off me," he added, smirk devilish.

"Really?" I asked, head tipped to the side, lower lip nabbed by my teeth. "Did she do this?" I asked, finger trailing down the center of his chest, moving across to circle his nipple before moving between the center of his abs, feeling my sex clench when the muscles tensed under my touch.

"Not quite," he answered, voice getting rougher still.

"Hmm. Did she do this?" I asked, hand moving down flat to cup his cock through his jeans, making a low, primal growl rip from his chest.

"You wanna play, baby?" he asked, and the promise in his wicked smile made my belly go liquid as he suddenly reached out, yanking the bottom of my shirt up and over my head, but then dragged it back down, pinning my arms at my sides. "I can play."

He turned me too fast for me to respond, pushing my entire upper body down against the counter, my sensitive nipples meeting the cold quartz with a whimper, then grinding his cock against my pussy and ass, the lightweight material of my pajama pants providing no barrier at all.

"How many times did you come last night thinking about me?" he asked, thrusting against me, then grinding against me in a circle, making his cock hit my clit perfectly. My choked whimper was not answer enough. "Tell me or this ends right now."

His cock pulled back and surged forward again, almost tripping me over the edge. "Four!" I cried out, desperate for more.

"And it still wasn't good enough, was it?" he asked, pulling back, fingers slipping just inside the waistband of my pants and panties, hooking, but not pulling down.

"No."

"Didn't think so," he agreed, snagging the material, and yanking down until I could step out of them, leaving me bare to him except for my little straight jacket of a t-shirt.

ELI

Never having been one for insecurity, shrugging off the conservative guilt I was raised in around the time I first touched a cock and had a hand touch my pussy, there wasn't even a thought to wanting to cover up. In fact, it was just the opposite. There was a strange, primal, raw urge for him to stare at me, to look at the round cheeks of my ass, to see the wet desire of my pussy. The urge was so strong that I felt myself tipping my butt up at him, inviting him to inspect what I was offering.

I wasn't surprised when he let out a low groan before his hand slapped down on my cheek, then his fingers kneaded in slightly.

His finger slid down and inward, teasing over my inner thigh, but careful not to give me any kind of relief from the torment.

"Tell me, did you think about me while I was inside?" he asked, one finger tracing the seam where my sex met my thigh, making me try to instinctively move my hips to get his touch to shift inward. But he wouldn't allow it. "Tell me," he demanded.

"Y... yes," I gasped out, my legs almost shaking from the frantic need between them.

"Doing this?" he asked, finger finally sliding up my slit and working circles around my clit, making my vision go white for a moment, sure I was going to come, certain there wasn't a force on Earth that could stop it.

Except him taking his finger away, that is.

"No," I whimpered, shoving my ass back toward him, completely shameless with the need for release.

"And maybe this too?" he suggested, and the next thing I knew I felt his hands holding my thighs apart as his tongue replaced his finger, sliding between my lips and rolling just around the outside of my clit, hinting at relief without offering any.

The tortured moan came from somewhere deep inside as my fingers spread, wanting to reach out, wanting to grab his head and hold him there, wanting contact, but being denied everything but captivity.

Just when I thought I couldn't take anymore, his lips closed around my clit, sucking it in strobes.

And I fucking shattered.

The orgasm ripped through my body with an intensity that made me struggle to keep on my own feet as he kept working me, kept intensifying it, dragging it out.

ELI

It wasn't until I felt completely wrung out that I felt the brush of his jeans against my ass before he reached down to snag the center of the back of my shirt, yanking me upward, making me arch my back, causing my breasts to press out, something he noticed because his other hand went there, squeezing one just to the point of pain before working the nipple in gentle circles.

"Bedroom," he demanded, voice a hoarse growl. Before he even finished speaking, I was shaking my head. "Why not?"

"Coop is in there," I told him, and as my brain cleared of the sex fog it had been in, I could hear him whimpering and scratching to get out.

There was a low growling noise that I took for disappointment or frustration, or both.

"I have condoms in my purse," I supplied, thinking maybe that was the hold up since everyone stored them where they tended to need to use them - near the bed. Even though I didn't have casual sex, I carried them everywhere, occasionally dropping them in the bathrooms in bars, just in case anyone needed some.

I barely finished speaking and his arm was reaching for it, undoing the main zipper, then going instinctively into the second zipper that every woman knew was tampon and condom storage. He came back with a condom that was a fall promotion, pumpkin spice flavored, and made a weird laugh/snort hybrid before I heard the slide of a zip, seeming to drown out any other thought in my head.

The desire, sated just a moment before, came surging back in a wild wave, completely taking me under again.

There was a whoosh.

Pants hitting floor.

A scrape of metal as he kicked the material to the side.

A crinkle of a wrapper.

Just when I was sure I was going to feel him surge inside, to put an end to the clawing need for fulfillment, his hands grabbed my hips and turned me.

Brilliant eyes on mine, he lifted one of my thighs, coaxing it around his hip to fold over his lower back, opening me up to him. And when he reached for the other thigh, his hard cock pressed against me as his hands sank into my ass, holding me aloft as he walked through my kitchen and into the living room, turning, and dropping down on the couch.

ELI

He had barely managed to sit before his hand was at the back of my neck, yanking me down to seal his lips over mine.

I struggled against the shirt, the urge to reach between us, grab his cock, and position it where I needed it to be so I could press down and take him in something akin to obsession.

But I couldn't get free, the material straining too hard against my shoulders.

So I dropped my hips, and ground my pussy against his cock, whimpering into his mouth as the head pressed into my clit. In response to the sound, his hand crushed almost painfully into my skull.

I knew he was lost too, likely way more lost than I was.

Six years.

It had barely been two for me, and I felt like I was losing my grip on my sanity every second that I didn't come.

I rode him, like we were fumbling teenagers too scared to go all the way, his hardness giving me just enough friction to drive me upward, to get me just right to the brink.

His lips ripped from mine as his hand sank harder into my ass, hard enough that there was a chance I would actually have bruises - a thought that made my sex clench threateningly - and lifted up.

Finally.

That was all I could think as my hips rose, as he reached between us to press his cock up against the entrance of my pussy, holding it there as a promising pressure for a long second, before surging his hips upward, and filling me to the hilt.

"Oh, my *God*," I cried out, fingers curling into my palms because they couldn't curl into him to hold on.

"Fuck," he growled back, closing his eyes, and taking a slow, deep breath.

He was seeking control. After so long a dry spell, I couldn't imagine how hard that would be to find.

And I didn't need it.

I didn't need him under control.

I needed him moving inside me, I needed just a moment or two and I would be crashing, and he could come with me.

"Eli," I called out, watching as his eyes slowly slid open, almost pained looking. "Fuck me," I demanded, moving my hips in a

ELI

circle on his lap, making a low rumbling sound move through his chest.

Whatever hold he had on his control was lost then as his hand moved to hold onto my thigh and he started thrusting upward into me - hard, fast, unrelenting.

"God, yes," I whimpered, folding forward to rest my head in his neck as my hips slammed down to meet each thrust, taking him as deep as my body would allow.

His hand left my thigh, slipping into my hair, and yanking backward. "I want to watch," he said in a harsh whisper as his other hand moved between us to start working my clit.

It was seconds.

Just seconds.

And he was making the orgasm from just a moment ago feel like child's play as another, stronger one broke through me, making my breath and cry catch in my throat for the first hard, deep pulsation, then topple out together in a gasping sob as the pleasure kept coming.

"Fuck, Autumn," he growled, surging through it even as his entire body got tight, trying to hold on until I was spent, then slamming deep, cursing out my name again as he came.

I collapsed forward into him, body trembling slightly in unexpected aftershocks, something I hadn't felt in years, something that I usually only experienced after unusually intense sex, or strong connection, or both.

"Come here," he said, when he tried for the second time to peel me off of him. This time, he yanked harder on my shirt, giving me no choice but to move. As soon as I was pressed back, he reached out, gently snagging the material of my shirt that had held me prisoner the whole time, and releasing me of it. His hand rose, finger tracing down my jaw for a moment, eyes almost reverent. "Okay, now come back here," he demanded, pulling me down toward his chest.

And, well, there was no stopping my arms from going around him, something I had wanted from the moment he put his hands on me.

His hands went out as well, one holding the back of my head gently, the other tracing sweetly up and down my spine, something that had my insides doing butterflies that I tried really hard to ignore,

ELI

knowing I had a tendency to read more into things than they needed to be read into.

"Yeah," he said a couple moments later. "I'm going to want a repeat of that."

I pulled back, smiling down at him, unable to help it. On one hand, because, yeah, I wanted a repeat of that as well - about a thousand repeats of that - but also because it meant I would get to see more of him. Though I knew that was dangerous, dangerous territory when all I had told him I needed was sex and friendship.

In a way, though, that was true.

What was a relationship, after all, but sex and friendship?

This just wouldn't have the labels.

I guess I could live with that.

"I can get behind that," I agreed, then my smile went a little wicked. "Or have you get behind me. You know, whatever you prefer."

The chuckle moved through him and somehow me at the same time as he looked up at me with those bright eyes, the tension around them seeming gone for the first time since I saw him trying to get his dog to follow a command.

"Oh, I'm gonna *prefer* a lot of things," he promised, patting my thigh. "Lift up," he demanded softly, and I did, trying to hold back my reluctance to feel him leave me. But, well, unfortunately, safe sex had its less-than-sexy sides that needed to be dealt with.

So I lifted up and he slid out of me then out from under me, moving down the hall to find the open bathroom door.

Alone, feeling a little bit too exposed, though it wasn't in a literal way, I reached for my shirt, turning it right-side-out, and slipping into it before stretching my sore leg muscles and going in search of my panties.

Eli came out a moment later, body still relaxed - a sight I liked seeing way too much for a casual sex buddy - and came toward where I was standing in the kitchen, fetching his underwear and pants, jumping into them both simultaneously.

"Sounds like Coop needs a walk," he commented as he reached for his shirt.

Me, well, I was still pants-less, but my hands thought reaching for my wine to settle my swirling thoughts was a better idea than pulling pants back on.

ELI

"Yeah, he's not usually locked up this long," I agreed.
"Wanna shrug into something warmer and walk him with me?"

And, well, I so, so did.
More than I should have.
But that wasn't going to stop me.
We took Coop for a walk.
And it was a hell of a lot like couples would do.

EIGHT

Eli

"I'm just saying," Bobby said at my breakfast table the next day, because we were, apparently, breakfast buddies now. "I know the look of a man who got his dick wet after being locked up for a long time. You got that look. And you went out last night."

"What are you the neighborhood fucking watch?" I asked, smiling because it was so ridiculous. "Watching me out of the curtains like some little old nosy neighbor?"

"I was cleaning the fucking windows, okay?" he objected, clearly caught and trying to save face.

"Yeah, sure you were. With your fucking huff of breath and your sleeve."

"You're deflecting!" he accused, though he was clearly the one guilty of such a thing.

"Yeah, I am," I agreed, leaning back in my chair, stomach full of the hash browns and breakfast burrito he had brought me. Just a

ELI

couple days out, and I was already eating better than I had six years in.

"So you did get laid! See, man, I knew it."

He knew it alright.

But to be fair, I wasn't exactly trying to hide my good mood.

Bobby was just doing some basic math.

I had been a Debbie fucking Downer for all the years he knew me inside and then the couple days I was out. Then I go out one night, come home late, and I'm suddenly in a good mood?

Yeah, two plus two equals four.

So he could know I got laid.

That was fine.

The cards I was playing close to my chest had nothing to do with the sex. Though, let's be real, that sex was fucking phenomenal. And I didn't just think that because it had been so long that I had gone without it. If you have had enough sex in life, you knew when it was just good technically because everyone involved got off and felt some good old-fashioned stress relief, and when it was more than that, when it was the kind of experience you wanted to have over and over and would never get sick of it. This was the latter kind of sex. This was the mind-blowing, obsession-inducing kind of sex.

I was sure I would never get enough of it.

Judging by the way she responded to me, she felt the same.

And Autumn, well, she owned a sex store. I bet her nightstand and closet were full of endless hours of fun.

I intended to explore that.

Often.

Enthusiastically.

Did I know there was a certain risk involved? Yeah.

I wasn't stupid.

I couldn't fuck her and not feel some kind of connection. She wasn't just some random chick at the bar. And she was, whether I liked to admit it or not, a connection to my old life. There was a thread there, small, but noticeable.

It was risky.

And I told myself I wouldn't be taking any risks.

But, well, there was no way now that I knew what it was like to be with her that I was going to give that up.

ELI

So long as the only time I was connected, opened up, was when I was with her, I figured things would be fine. I could still follow through with my plans, get my life back on track.

Hell, maybe the sex would keep me relaxed.

Relaxed, when you were dealing with rage issues, was a place you wanted to be.

"The dog thief, right?" he assumed rightly. "Tell me she's hot."

"She's hot," I agreed, but found that term wholly inaccurate. She was so, so much more than hot.

She was fucking beautiful.

I mean, I knew that going in since I had spotted her six years before outside that coffeeshop. She had a stunning, warm face, a huge, welcoming smile, and eyes that held secrets.

But last night, I got to see the whole package.

And 'hot' - while accurate - didn't do her a damn bit of justice.

She was fucking perfect.

Every goddamn subtle curve, every soft line, every dip, it was all goddamn flawless.

Add on the fact that she was confident, that she was comfortable being touched and getting touched, oh yeah, she was the whole package. Any man would have to be blind not to see that.

How the hell she was single was completely beyond me.

"So that's all you're gonna give me? No details?"

Clearly, he was offended by the prospect.

Most guys dished, no matter how much they claimed never to gossip. They did.

I had simply never been a kiss and tell kinda guy to begin with, and there was some strong urge inside to keep what Autumn and I had between the two of us.

So that was what I was going to do.

"That's all I'm going to give you. No details," I agreed.

"Man, that's cold," he said, shaking his head at me. "So what's on your agenda today?"

"I have to go back to the gallery to see how much space I have to play with so I can get to work on the pieces."

"When's the show?"

"Two days after Thanksgiving."

"That enough time?"

ELI

"I once whipped out a family portrait of three generations, including sixteen grandkids, in a weekend."

"Yeah. Inside. Where you had nothing to do but work on it. Where you had no fine piece waiting on you to make her toes curl."

That was true enough.

But Autumn worked.

And we were keeping it, ah, casual.

So that was only going to be taking a few hours out of my day.

"It should be fine."

He nodded at that, moving to stand, taking his coffee with him. "I got a nice profile, man. Just saying. I'd look good on a fucking wall."

With that, he was gone, leaving me to wonder if he was actually serious or not.

With him, it was sometimes hard to tell.

But I wasn't planning on using him anyway.

I had other ideas.

I had demons to exorcise.

And I figured that the only way to do that was to do it on paper.

--

"Eli!"

Shit.

Goddamn it all to hell.

I should have known to go to Home Depot two towns over instead of the damn small home improvement store in town. But all I needed was a drill bit so I could get some work done around the house. It seemed stupid to go out of my way for just one little thing.

But walking down the side street toward my new vehicle - a new, but not obnoxiously expensive, black pickup - and hearing my name called by a voice I most definitely recognized, yeah, it made

ELI

me see why I needed to keep my ass off the main streets in Navesink Bank.

I didn't want to do this.

This was why I had the shitty duplex in the crummy area.

This was why I only left my house when absolutely necessary, especially during the day.

This was why I should have fucking gone to goddamn Home Depot.

I didn't want to see any of them.

I didn't want to have to look them in the eye and tell them I was done with them, that they should just move on and forget me.

I didn't want to have to watch as I stuck a knife in their guts like I had needed to do countless times to my own.

But there was no avoiding it, even as I tossed the bag into the open window of my truck and turned around to face him.

My brother.

Christ, it hurt to even think that word.

I thought I was over it.

I thought I had hollowed myself out enough not to be affected by this family shit.

But, apparently, preparing yourself for the inevitable, and actually facing it up, were two completely different things.

He looked the same. A bit older maybe, like I was myself. But the same. Same inky black hair. Same eyes that I saw reflected in my mirror every morning. Same bone structure. Same height. Similar built. Same ink. And a whole fuckton of it. More than there had even been when I had gone away.

But that came with the trade, I guess.

"Hunter," I said, keeping my voice hollow, praying to fuck none of the emotion I was feeling right then could be heard in my tone.

"What the fuck?" he asked, spreading his arms out, shaking his head, the pain I couldn't express plain in his voice, in his eyes, in his very stance.

Knife, meet gut.

Christ, it hurt more than I thought it could after so long.

"What the fuck, what?" I asked, going for hollow, and succeeding judging by the way his shoulders slumped further.

ELI

"Six years, Eli? Not a fucking word? We didn't even know if you were fucking alive in there."

"Pretty sure they inform next of kin when an inmate bites it."

His brows furrowed. "What is this shit?" he asked, waving a hand at me.

"What shit?"

If there was anyone who could tell you when you were being off, it was family. If there was anyone willing to call you on it when they saw it, it was siblings.

"Did you get a psych eval in there?"

"Think I lost my mind?"

"If your dead motherfucking tone is anything to go by, bro, yeah, I think you lost your damn mind. Do you have any idea how much Ma cried over this? Try as she might to hide it, you could see it on every fucking holiday. You know how many times we sat and talked about you, worried about what could be happening to you in there? Do you have any idea what it was like to try to tell the girls that it wasn't that you didn't love them anymore; it was just that you were in a bad place in your head."

The girls.

Fuck.

Whatever was left of my heart dissipated with that comment.

"Shoulda just told them I was dead."

I reached for my door, pulling it open.

"Why the fuck would we ever do that?"

I turned back to him, looking him square in the eye, willing him to see the truth in my words.

"Because it's true."

With that, I dropped into my seat, turned the engine, and reversed right the fuck out of there, my pulse pounding in my temples, throat, wrists, fast enough that it was alarming, that it was making my head start to swim.

I wasn't going to lose it.

I wasn't going to fucking let that happen.

I needed to shut it down.

But even as I tried to, tried to shove all of it back in the box, I knew I couldn't do it.

I needed to scream.

I needed to hit something.

ELI

No.
Not hit.
No more hitting.
Not even a motherfucking pillow.
Never again, goddamnit.
I couldn't go there.
But I needed to stop the cycle.
My head was swimming.
My vision was going tunnel.
My heart was a jackhammer in my chest.
If I didn't do something soon, I was going to lose it.
And I didn't even have a target for the rage.
Could the damage go collateral?
Could I become that monster who beat on someone innocent?

Without even knowing what was happening, I slammed the truck to park down the side along the building, hopping out, and storming up, hands down at my sides opening and closing, making nearly-bloody crescents in my palms.

Losing it.

I was fucking losing it.

I wrenched the door open, seeing one person inside browsing.

I reached into my wallet, pulling out a hundred, walking up to the guy contemplating different cock rings, and waved the money in his face. "Hundred bucks to come back in an hour," I offered.

There wasn't even a hesitation before he took it, pocketed it, and almost ran for the door. I met him there, turning the sign, and locking the door.

"Eli, what the hell are you doi..." Autumn started from her position behind the desk. But when I turned, her whole body seemed to stiffen, her eyes going confused. "What's the matt..."

"I won't hurt you," I said, words barely enunciated properly my jaw was clenched so hard, sending a grinding, shooting pain up into my temple.

"Ah, okay?" she said, brows drawing together as I started toward her, grabbing a few things off the shelves as I did so.

"Not like that," I clarified.

Her eyes drifted to my hands, taking in the items I had picked up as I got closer.

"Eli, do you want..."

ELI

"I *am* going to hurt you," I clarified, watching for any sign of hesitation. Even a parting of lips would have been all I needed to know to back the fuck off. "But not like that. This is your out," I offered, slamming the packages down on the counter at her side, towering over her, letting her take in the vibration that seemed to make the air around me shake. "Take it if you want it. No questions."

"I don't want it," she said almost immediately, confidently, trusting me fully when I hadn't done one single goddamn thing to warrant that.

"Got a room without windows?" I asked as I reached into the giant bowl of condoms she kept at the register with a sign that said 'Play safe' on it.

"Stock room," she told me, voice already airy.

She wanted it.

She wasn't just obliging me because I needed it.

She *wanted* it.

It was twisted of me, wrong, unfair even, to want her to want it, to be pleased by her enthusiasm for me to hurt her.

But as soon as I walked into the store, understanding my intention, it clicked. It made sense.

It wasn't that I needed to get rid of the rage. I was pretty sure that history - even very recent history - proved that that wasn't even an option. It was going to come. It wasn't even always going to be triggered on command, or by passing by something that made me furious. The more I denied it, the better the chance for it popping up more randomly.

I never stopped to consider before that the solution wasn't to tamp it down. I didn't even see that there was another option.

To let it out.

With control.

To harness it.

Would there be pain?

Yes.

But catharsis as well.

I could release it, little by little.

I could use it, then let it the fuck go.

I could bring a small amout of pain as the rage drained from me.

ELI

Then I could bring pleasure to her, to me, to us both simultaneously, washing the rest of it all away.

Then starting fresh all over again.

"Let's go."

NINE

Autumn

He had left right after Coop's walk the night before.

And while a part of me was ready for round two, maybe an overnight so I could have round three in the morning, I still went to bed smiling.

I woke up to Peyton perched on the edge of my bed, staring at me, with two cups of coffee in hand.

"I will forgive the creep factor here since you come bearing caffeine," I told her as I moved to sit up against the headboard, reaching out to hold the too-hot Freddy cup, one she knew I particularly hated since she made me watch *Nightmare On Elm Street* as a teen.

"I would ask if you fucked, but your condom zipper in your purse was open, so I know you got down," she informed me, folding her unicorn-printed legging-clad legs under her, sitting half on her ass, watching me over the steaming cup of coffee that she was

ELI

drinking out of my Phallus-opy mug I had for a promotion once. "Was it hot? I bet it was hot."

"He trapped my arms with my tee," I admitted because, well, she was my sister, and we always talked about stuff like that. "For the whole time."

"Oh, he's fun in bed too? Ugh, so not fair! Usually, the hot guys are machine-gun fuckers. So boring."

"He's not a machine-gun fucker," I laughed. I had had a machine-gun fucker in my life too. She was right; they sucked. *Bangbangbangbangbang.* Nothing interesting, nothing unexpected, nothing fun. Just a cock slamming into a pussy. Lame. I appreciated way too many variations of sex to settle for that long-term. "It was hot. A little demanding. He likes to talk."

Her lips pursed carefully, brow raised. "Was he *good* at it? There's nothing worse than a bad dirty talker."

That was the damn truth.

"He was good."

"You lucky bitch. He's hot, sweet, funny, good with animals, and can dirty talk? Oh, wait. Was his cock small? Or all sharp angled?"

"His cock was perfect," I said with a big smile.

"I hate you," she declared, sighing dramatically. "You're welcome, by the way. I had to go and sit and listen to Ronny bitch about his boyfriend for two and a half *hours* to give you that alone time."

"Thank you," I said, meaning it, knowing that if she hadn't pushed us together, I would have woken up pissy from tossing and turning in sexual frustration again all night.

"You owe me a carton of that wine he brought over."

"Done."

"So when are you seeing him again? Since we know you're not a one-and-done girl."

"I agreed to fucking-friends," I admitted. "And we exchanged numbers. We didn't set up a date. Whenever our schedules line up, I guess."

"I didn't get a chance to tell you where I caught him walking out of."

ELI

"Where was he walking out of?" I asked, curiosity piqued. I knew I wasn't supposed to be grasping for tidbits of information about a casual sex friend, but I couldn't help myself.

"The gallery. Apparently, and I know this because I stalked their Facebook last night while Ronny went on and on about how Iggy never uses the right lube, no matter how many times he demands he use the warming one, he is getting a wall at the next show."

"That's awesome. He's really good." I only knew this because he did the one portrait of me forever ago. If he kept improving, well, I had to imagine he was pretty amazing by now.

And good for him. I loved seeing people doing what they loved in life. It was why I was thrilled when Peyton told me she was going to become a librarian even though 'libraries are in the toilet' and 'I won't have two pennies to rub together most of the time.' She loved alone time. She adored the library. And she ate up books faster than most people I knew. So what if she wasn't rolling in dough? She was happy. That was what mattered.

An artist sounded a lot more fulfilling than a loanshark enforcer.

Plus, you know, it was legal.

When he was on parole for the next year, legal was a really good thing for him.

I wouldn't go on opening night - unless, of course, he invited me - but I was going to go and check out his work. I was too curious not to.

"So, did you need to wash in bleach?"

"I'm sorry?"

"Little Miss I-Can't-Fuck-Without-Connection just fucked without connection. Do you feel all dirty or something like that?"

"It was never that I felt *dirty*," I objected immediately. "You know me better than that. I don't believe in that crap. It's just... I like sex better when I give a shit about a person."

"Ah, see. Therein is the issue here. He isn't some rando. You *do* give a shit about him as a person. I get it now. This is good, right? Like you're happy with it? Even if it doesn't go anywhere?"

"Someone very wise once told me that most relationships wouldn't go anywhere, but that doesn't mean you can't enjoy them while they last."

ELI

"I *am* brilliant, aren't I?" she asked, giving me a wink as she climbed off the bed. "Come on. Let's go for bagels. With egg and cheese. I think you will be needing extra protein for a while. And fluids."

I had a feeling she was right.

But I didn't realize I would be getting a second session quite so soon.

But then there he was in my store, paying my customer to get lost. To be fair, that customer had been hemming and hawing freaking cock rings for almost an hour. But still... a customer.

I knew immediately something was wrong.

Gone was the man I saw at the coffeeshop six years ago, and the man who had brought me coffee, who had made me see stars against a wall down a side street, who had shown up at my apartment with wine, and shared a meal, then shared some amazing orgasms.

This man was another beast entirely.

Beast.

Yes, that was apt.

I finally understood.

When he talked about rage, about it being uncontrollable, this was what he meant.

He meant it burned in his blood. It vibrated into the air around him.

It *consumed* him.

Truly, if you looked in his eyes, you barely saw the light of the man who usually lived there. They were hooded with something darker.

It was Eli, yet it wasn't at the same time.

And this Eli, he wanted to hurt me.

No, strike that.

He *needed* to hurt me.

I had learned enough from experience and from research into the matter, that for some, rough play was just about fun, just a good way to spice things up. For others, though, it was necessary. Like therapy. The dominants needed to exact control, needed to purge something. The subs needed to give over power, to trust, to relax and let go. It was catharsis for both involved.

Sex could be - and, for many, often was - like therapy.

We gave and took and exposed and released.

ELI

That was what Eli needed from me right then.

And, quite frankly, I was more than happy to give it to him.

Belly a mix of fluttering and swirling - excitement and trepidation - I led Eli behind the counter and through the door that led to the back where I had a very mini kitchen, bathroom, and a decent-sized, dark, mildly creepy storage room full of built-in metal shelving units and a few tables for laying out merchandise.

The heavy, metal-bar-enforced door slammed behind me, making me jump and turn on my heel.

And there he was, just as tense as he was a moment before, holding the items he had selected off my shelves. Items I knew exactly how to use, exactly how he would use them on me. There was no denying the thrill inside, mingled with just the slightest trace of hesitation. Not because I didn't want to explore, just because I hadn't gone that deep before. There was always a push and pull inside when trying something new. That was where the trust needed to step in.

Did I trust Eli that much? This man I hardly knew.

"Red," he said, putting a few of the items on the table beside the door, opening the biggest one with his hands.

"I'm sorry?"

"Safe words are bullshit. Green. Yellow. Red. That's all you ever need. They're self-explanatory, and you'll never forget them."

Green means *gogogo*.

Yellow means *slow down* or *this is going too far too fast*.

Red means *stop now*.

It was elementary.

And he was right, no one could ever forget them.

"Okay," I agreed, watching as he methodically moved to the next product, opening the unnecessarily thick plastic with his bare hands. That shouldn't have been sexy, but I had trouble opening those damn things with heavy duty scissors, so it somehow totally was hot.

"Take off your clothes," he demanded, the words sending a shiver through me. "Now, Autumn," he added when there was a moment of hesitation.

With an undeniable tightening in my sex, my hands went for my shirt.

Bossy Eli. I could get used to him.

ELI

A part of me felt an instinct to play, to tease, to, well, *strip* for him. But something was telling me there was no room for that in this dark back room with a pile of toys he wanted to use on me.

So I didn't tease.

I took off my clothes as he demanded.

Shirt. Pants. Bra. Panties.

And then there I was, stark freaking naked to his fully dressed.

My nipples tweaked from a mix of anticipation and the coldness in the room, making me shiver as his eyes raked over me.

"Up on that table," he demanded, ignoring me as he took a few items over to a small utility sink and started scrubbing.

Even as lost as he was in that moment, he was still managing to think straight. Maybe the focus of having tasks to complete was helping him rein it in slightly.

I looked over at the table, long, rectangular, slightly lower than hip-height because the previous owner must have been a tiny person, and cold, unforgiving stainless steel.

I was shivering at the idea of touching it even before I raised my leg and got my knee up, the rest of my body following. "Turn away," he said without looking. "Hands and knees."

I wouldn't be able to see him at all.

Why that was absolutely thrilling was beyond me.

It should have been scary.

It should have bothered me that I would never see coming whatever he planned to do to me.

Metal slammed down on metal behind me, making me jump for a moment before I felt the cuff slip around one ankle, closing tight.

"Spread your thighs all the way out."

I did.

Then the next cuff closed.

I knew what was coming.

"Shoulders to the table, hands between your legs."

Forced posture bar.

They held the legs spread wide and cuffed your hands to the center of the bar, preventing any movement whatsoever. You could pull. You could squirm. But you weren't getting free.

ELI

I lowered down, only mildly embarrassed at just how exposed the position was making me.

That being said, when it came to forced posture, this was the kindest kit. He could have chosen the arched back one that included a collar that attached down your spine to a curved, ball-topped hook that was inserted into your ass so if you tried to move, the ball pulled in a somewhat unpleasant way inside you, forcing you right back into position.

So, yeah, if he wanted me face down, ass up like any normal dom and didn't plan to put a hook in my ass, I was more than willing to get into position.

My stomach dropped slightly as I felt the cuffs slide around my wrists, as I felt my freedom taken from me.

I would be lying if I said panic didn't seize me for a moment, that self-preservation didn't rear its head. It did. My belly swirled; my air got caught in my chest.

But that was the thing.

You had to submit.

You had to trust.

While I knew he planned to hurt me, I also knew he intended to make me feel good too.

And I knew I could more than trust him with my pleasure.

I was willing to take the gamble that I could trust him with my pain.

Red means stop.

I was safe.

He said nothing, but I could feel the air as he moved away, then came back.

There wasn't a hint of what was to follow, so a whole body shiver racked through me when all I felt was the gentle whisper of leather strands over the skin of my back. Then my ass, a few of the edges sliding between, very nearly touching my pussy that was already getting wetter by the second, a fact I knew he could see very well with the position he had me in.

It traced over the backs of my thighs, my calves, the ticklish undersides of my feet.

Through this, he was silent.

Focused, was likely more accurate.

Keeping control, but also letting it go little by little.

ELI

The flogger moved back up, leather brushing my shoulders.
Whack.

Used to the softness, the sudden sting made me arch and whimper, my body instinctively trying to fold away, but the binding making it futile even to try.

Another brush.

Then a strike, right across my ass, making my hips jolt up. Then another, before I could fully register the sting of the first.

And another.

Over and over and over.

Across my ass, my upper thighs, my back, my hips.

Until there was more burning, stinging, inflamed skin, than there was not.

"Breathe," Eli commanded, making me realize he was right, I had been holding my breath, anticipating the blows.

Even as I was releasing it, though, I felt the cool liquid slide down my ass. And I knew what was coming. Because I saw that package.

The tip of the plug pressed against me, a firm pressure hinting at more, as the flogger moved gently over my skin once again, until I felt another shiver move through me, and arched my ass just a little higher.

He pushed it in, and it settled with a heavy pressure. My pussy ached with the need for fulfillment, and no matter how much the urge was there, I couldn't press my thighs together to ease the pulsating need.

His finger flicked the plug, making another surge of need course through me, wondering if he was going to work me with the plug, pull, twist, anything.

But then there was that low, rumbling noise in his chest, something akin to desire, but mixed with something else too, likely the part of him that was still raging.

There wasn't even a bit of surprise when the flogger came back, this time a little harder, a little more frantic.

Just when I was sure I wasn't going to be able to take any more, I felt the braided leather handle slide between the lips of my pussy, pressing into my clit, sending a completely unexpected orgasm shooting through my body.

This time, when he growled, it was pure desire.

ELI

There was a zip.

A swoosh.

A crinkle.

Then still on the waves of my orgasm, ass still plugged, he surged inside me.

Hard.

Burying to the hilt.

I couldn't even get used to the new sensation of getting penetrated while plugged - something akin to a pressure on the pelvic wall that which I had never experienced before - before he started fucking me.

The second thrust nearly sent me flying forward.

But his hands landed at my hips, holding me completely still, fully at his mercy, as he pistoned into me hard.

"Oh my God," I cried out as he started using my hips to push me away, then drag me back just as he thrust, forcing my body to take him deeper than I had ever taken anyone before. "Eli, I..."

One of his hands slipped between my thighs, pressing into my clit.

And that was it.

That was all it took.

I would likely never be sure if the intensity was just from the triple-zone orgasm, or the pain that was somehow pleasure as well, or thanks to being fully at someone's mercy, trusting them with you completely. All I did know was, I swear I very nearly blacked out from it. My pussy spasmed, and I could feel it in places I was sure I never had before. My vision went dark as the waves kept crashing, as he kept fucking, dragging it out before he finally found his own release.

Even after, thighs shaking, body weak and boneless, I felt only half-present, like a part of my brain was on disconnect.

Eli slid out of me.

The plug came next.

A short pause as he walked away.

Then my wrists, my ankles.

I could feel Eli drop down on the table in front of me before his hands were reaching out, pulling me toward him, resting my ass in his jean-clad lap, pulling my head under his chin, and wrapping his arms around me somehow both tightly and gently at the same time.

ELI

"I'm sorry," he murmured with his lips against my hair.

Sorry?

For the orgasm of a lifetime?

For giving me a new experience I couldn't have possibly known I would be into if he hadn't shown it to me.

I wanted to say these things, but found the act of speech just slightly out of reach.

"I'm such a fuck," he added.

The rough, tortured sound to his voice seemed to be what I needed to force the words from somewhere deep.

"No, you're not," I objected, my arms sliding around his back, holding on as well as I could with their jelly-sensation.

"If you saw your back right now, you wouldn't be saying that. I didn't even fucking realize how red you were getting."

"I might not be able to see my back, but I can feel it," I assured him. "And it's fine, Eli. I'm fine. I could have stopped you if I wanted."

"You feel fine because of the endorphins from the pain and the orgasms, sweetheart. In an hour, you're gonna fucking hate me."

"I'm not going to hate you."

"I don't do shit like this."

"Shit like what?"

"This BDSM crap."

He was pretty good at it for an amateur. But, then again, all you had to do was watch a bit of professional BDSM porn to know how to use all the toys properly.

"I don't like hurting women," he added at my silence.

"But it's not really hurting them. It's different."

"You have red marks over your back, ass, and thighs that I put there, Autumn."

"Yeah, but it wasn't--" How did you describe it? "It wasn't a bad pain." He said nothing, but his body was still tense, still - I imagined - full of self-loathing, which was unfairly placed. "It was cathartic for both of us, Eli," I assured him.

"How?" he asked, fingers sifting through my hair gently, so softly that I was sure he was worried about getting his finger caught in a tangle and hurting me even slightly more.

ELI

"You got to get rid of that anger." And it *was* gone. Every inch of him was less rigid. The air around him didn't seem to be vibrating. His speech was softer because his jaw wasn't so clenched.

"And you?"

"I got to let go."

"Of what?"

"Of... everything." It was hard to explain, especially because I didn't exactly know how it worked either. I had heard subs at conferences talking about how being tied down, having your power taken away from you, was freeing. Mostly, these women were the types who were powerful in their daily lives, who micro-managed and had iron-fisted control over every aspect of their daily routine. So giving that up to someone, having all your control taken away, it was a release like nothing else they had known before.

And while I wasn't exactly a control freak, I did have to take care of everything in my life and work. I didn't have someone else to put it off on. I was in charge of everything. So not to be in charge, even just for a couple minutes, to just have to submit and take, it was therapeutic in a way I didn't fully understand, but was thankful for.

Even just sitting there in his arms, I felt more relaxed than I had in years. Or maybe ever.

If perhaps I was a bit sore for a couple days, I somehow thought the reward was worth it. Kind of like how your legs and ass hurt so much after the gym, but getting a little more muscle tone was well worth the pain.

Flogging as anxiety relief.

Who'd have thunk it?

"Eli," I said softly into his neck when he made no response, just kept stroking my hair.

"Yeah?"

"I would have stopped it if I wanted to stop it. I'm not afraid to speak my mind about sex. I own a sex store," I reminded him. "So you feeling guilt right now for something I don't regret makes no sense."

"See if you feel that way tomorrow, and maybe I won't feel so shitty about it."

Of course he was going to be difficult.

I guess it made sense.

ELI

He went to jail for six years for doing something that was *right*, got punished even though he had been defending a helpless woman. He had guilt about that. He felt like a monster who couldn't be trusted around his own family over that.

So, of course, he was going to make himself feel shitty about this as well.

"Okay. So when I get in touch with you tomorrow and don't hate you or regret this - spoiler alert, I won't - then you will let this go? No more regret or shame or guilt?"

There was a long pause. "If you can come to me tomorrow, sore, and tired because you can't find a comfortable way to sleep, and even then can still tell me that you enjoyed it and would do it again, then, yeah, okay. I will let it go."

"So what time do you get up in the morning?" I asked immediately. "I get up pretty early because, well, Coop demands it. But I don't open the store until around ten. I can bring over coffee."

There was a humorless snort at that. "*If* you end up bringing me coffee, anytime after seven is fine by me."

"Can I bring Coop? He likes exploring - and destroying - new places."

"Yeah, you can bring Coop if you come. Actually, if your and Peyton's schedules don't link up sometimes and you don't want to leave him alone, I'm pretty much always at home."

I smiled into his neck, pressing a kiss into his pulse point.

We were going to be sharing custody of Coop, I just knew it.

And, well, I was more than okay with that.

"Sounds like a plan," I agreed as the moment seemed to be done, so I carefully unfolded from him, and slid off his lap.

"Wait," he said, hands grabbing me from behind. One of his fingers traced down a spot on my back that felt over-heated, sensitive, a spot I knew had lash marks. He pulled me back slightly, and the next thing I felt was his lips pressing near the marks.

That, well, it did all sorts of fluttery things to my belly.

When I pulled away again, I snatched my pants and panties, dragging them up carefully. There were marks on the backs of my legs, but they just gave me a slight rug burn sensation as the material moved over them. My butt? Well, that definitely was sore. Sitting was going to be interesting.

ELI

"Yeah, that's not gonna happen," Eli said, taking my bra out of my hand.

"I'm at work. I have to wear a bra."

"At a sex store? That you own? I'm pretty sure you can get away with a little nipple action, sweetheart," he said, putting the bra on the table. "Here, let me help with that," he demanded as I started bunching up my shirt to put on. "Arms up."

My arms went up, and he oh-so-carefully pulled the material down them, my head, and then over my torso, holding it outward so it didn't scrape my back.

And, okay, fine.

I totally leaned back into him slightly.

What can I say, his anger might have been molten, but his sweet was like a liquid salve, soothing it all over.

"You should probably get back to work. Someone might need to mull over the cock ring selection like it is a life or death choice again."

I chuckled at that, knowing he was right. I had to get back to work. But also a little annoyed that real life had to get in the way of what was between us.

"Alright. So text me your address when you have a minute," I agreed as we started walking through to the store.

"Will do," he agreed, but the tone in which he said it made me think I was going to have to text him first and demand it.

"Black?" I asked. "For your coffee when I see you tomorrow," I called to him as he unlocked the door.

"Yeah, I take it black. For *if* I see you tomorrow."

"When," I corrected.

He turned back to me, eyes just completely wrecked.

"If."

With that, he was gone.

And I had the strange sensation of being gutted.

He genuinely did think that badly about himself.

And that was a damn sin for someone who had shown me kindness, humor, intellect, loyalty, and generosity.

Sure, I had seen a bit of the dark side; I could understand how that level of rage was dangerous in the wrong situation. But he had been able to control it, to harness it. If maybe he joined a boxing gym or something like that, he could control it even better.

ELI

He wasn't the monster he seemed to view himself as.

And he did.

He had the same resigned unhappiness of Bruce Banner who knew there was no controlling The Hulk.

I took a deep breath, moving back through the door behind the counter, and slipping into the bathroom. I jacked up my shirt, looking over my shoulder at my reflection.

And I had to honestly say, it looked a lot worse than it felt. My skin was pale and thin and sensitive. I got burns if I used anything but ultra-sensitive soap. So it didn't surprise me that the marks were vivid red, raised, and almost bloody-looking at the ends. I knew me. I healed fast. Once I got home, took a cool, soothing shower, and maybe had my sister rub some aloe on it, the swelling would go down, as would some of the redness.

By tomorrow morning, it would look like we just had a light, gentle flogging session.

Then he would see that he was overreacting.

There was no *if* about it.

TEN

Eli

What the fuck was wrong with me?

I hadn't done enough bad shit in my life, I had to go and mark up the one little bit of good I had going for me? I had to drag her down into my darkness with me?

I meant what I said.

I had never been into the BDSM scene.

Sure, I knew about it. Who didn't?

And, okay, I had used binding and wax and plugs and hair pulling and choking and bare-handed spanking in the bedroom before. But I hadn't ever bound a woman, plugged her, flogged her, then fucked her.

I sure as fuck had never left marks on a woman before.

That was just so far and beyond what I believed was acceptable between men and women. And while I understood there were absolutely women out there who liked to be whipped bloody,

ELI

who got off by having marks on their skin, I just couldn't seem to convince myself that Autumn was one of them.

When I got home from the store, stomach swirling with an all-too-familiar disgust in myself, I hauled upstairs into my studio, working on a new piece, not knowing what I was going to make, but throwing those feelings into it.

Once I worked through the shame, getting that out of the forefront of my mind, memories of my confrontation with Hunter came about, and I abandoned one canvas for the next, a huge one, one that would likely take up a good portion of one of the walls.

They were my family

Except all the adults had their heads facing down.

And all the kids had no faces.

Even half done, it hurt to look at.

Knife, meet gut.

It was never going to end.

Not until I was off parole at least and could move, not when there was always a chance of running into them.

What the fuck was it going to feel like if I was driving down the street and saw Fee walking with the girls?

I couldn't imagine.

"Damn, that's dark."

"Jesus," I growled, whirling around to where Bobby was standing a few feet behind me.

"What?" he asked, looking innocent. "You didn't bother to lock it!"

"This might be a hard one to accept here, Bobby, but an unlocked door is not an invitation."

"What's got your panties in a bunch?" he asked, moving out into the hall as I walked toward him as well.

"I had a run-in with my brother this afternoon." I chose to leave out *then consensually beat the shit out of a girl I had feelings for.* Because, well, that one was just not somewhere I was willing to go.

"Which one?"

"Hunter, the tattoo artist."

"Ah, the one with the girls."

ELI

"Yeah," I agreed, feeling the grief well up, and forcing that shit right back down. I needed better control. The grief would turn to anger, and I couldn't slip up like that again.

"What'd he say?"

"He was angry," I told him, going into my fridge for the beer Bobby brought me that I wasn't supposed to have in the house. I really needed to get rid of the rest of it. Maybe in my fucking liver. Drown that shit down. That was why guys on parole weren't supposed to have alcohol, I supposed.

"Did you explain anything or just pull an Eli?"

"Pull an Eli?" I repeated.

"Yeah, you know what you do. You shut down or change the subject or shit like that. You never explain."

"There just isn't anything to explain. They need to let go and move on."

"They're your family, man. They're never gonna fucking let go or move on. They love you. They lost six years. They are going to do everything in their power not to lose any more."

The fuck was right.

That was the worst part.

And I didn't know how long my location would stay a secret, what lengths they might go through to get to me. Lord knew they had contacts everywhere. Hell, the only reason they knew I got arrested was because Detective Collings told them. True, he might be retired now, but he still had buddies on the force. If he pulled some strings, he might have been able to have someone bring up my DMV records that I had just needed to update the day before, realizing my license had expired and I had been driving like that. It was the little shit like that, man, that was sure to get you sent back in.

Or, maybe they would reach out to Alex or Jstorm or even Barrett Anderson to find me, hack around until they got what they needed.

If they wanted to, they could find me.

I didn't know what the fuck I would do when that happened.

Not if, when.

It was nice to get out a little early, but parole was making it impossible to be anonymous. If I got out on time served, I could have gone anywhere. I could have fallen off the face of the Earth. I could have truly started over.

ELI

"You gotta figure this shit out, man. It's gonna eat you up. You're more down out here than you were on the inside." He wasn't exactly wrong about that. "Seemed to be shaping up with the new fuck-buddy. Maybe you need to go visit her."

I couldn't.

That was the problem.

I did feel better with her.

I felt better.

Flogging her was a release, sure. But it felt even more right to hold her after, to stroke her hair, to just be near her. It was the closest to happy I had been in six goddamn years.

Because I needed the former part of that from her, I might lose the latter.

That shit, yeah, it was proving hard to accept.

It shouldn't have felt that way.

I wasn't supposed to be making any connections, let alone ones that could run deep enough to hurt someday.

Yet here I was.

Fucking moron that I was.

"Yeah, maybe," I agreed, tipping back my beer, finishing it.

"Alright, I can tell when someone wants to be alone with their fucked up thoughts," Bobby declared. That was a bit of a new one. Inside, the man would never leave me the hell alone, even if I told him to. But, I guess, on the outside, he had a house and a woman, and, well, drugs to sell. "I'll see you sometime tomorrow, man. Buck up. You're out. Out is better than in even if out sucks."

With that, he was gone.

He was right, too.

Out was better than in even if out sucked.

For example, I got to have lights on until two AM so I could keep working on my pieces.

That, at least, was an improvement.

After that, too beat to keep my eyes opened, I showered and fell into bed, not bothering to set an alarm.

I saw those lashes.

I had gotten my ass handed to me enough times growing up to know how those were going to feel given a little time.

She wasn't coming.

ELI

When I heard the slamming at seven-thirty in the morning, I rolled over to stare at the ceiling, cursing Bobby as viciously as my vocabulary would allow.

Seven?

Fucking seven?

What was wrong with him?

But, knowing Bobby, if I didn't drag my ass down there and open the door, he would climb in through a damn window or some shit.

On that note, I rolled out of bed in my black and white plaid pajama bottoms and made my way downstairs, trying to work the cricks out of my neck as I reached for the locks.

Coulda knocked me over with a gentle fucking breeze when I saw Autumn standing there, Coop's leash in one hand, and a bag and tray wobbling a bit ominously in the other.

Her eyes drifted over me, spending a little extra time on my bare chest and stomach before flying back up a bit guiltily. Once she was looking at my face again, she shook her head. "You shouldn't have said anytime after seven if you like to sleep later than that!" she accused, prompting Coop to bark along with her from his position on his ass, bouncing around though like maybe he had been given a command to sit and stay, and was trying really hard to obey even though he was excited.

"What are you doing here?" I asked, voice sleep-rough even to my own ears.

"We had an agreement. If I didn't hate you or regret what we did, I show up here, and we move on. I don't hate you or regret what we did. Oh, and Peyton would like to know if any of your brothers are single and similarly rough sex inclined."

"Peyton knows?" I asked, feeling that shame shit rear its ugly head again.

"Yeah, I asked her to help me put some aloe on. The marks were mostly gone by the time I got home. My skin is sensitive, but it recovers fast. Relax," she added, giving me an easy smile. "Peyton is into this kinda thing. She certainly doesn't think any less of you for it. But I am under threat of her donning her creepy clown mask again and scaring the shit out of me if I don't get an answer about the brothers."

I felt my lips curve up, shaking my head. "They're all taken."

ELI

"Pity. She's not going to like that. Well, anyway. I'm here. I brought coffee and food and this hellbeast who thought that my purse was a good chew toy this morning," she explained, curving her shoulder to show me the half-gnawed leather strap.

"Little shit," I said affectionately, reaching down to unclip his collar. "Go hog wild. There's nothing you can destroy in here," I told him as he bolted.

"See, now that wasn't very smart. He is going to see that as a challenge."

She moved to take a step forward, but I stepped in front of her, raising my arm to rest on the doorjamb, leaning down to catch her gaze. "Seriously, honey, what are you doing here?"

She exhaled hard at that, like something I said was pissing her off, but she was trying to control her frustration.

"Listen," she said, putting her now-free hand on my hip. "I get that you have this shitty, warped opinion of yourself right now, and it's hard for you to see through any other kind of lens. But that isn't how I see you. And short of you telling me to fuck off, I'm not going anywhere. So just buck-up and get used to it, sparky," she demanded, hand moving from my hip to tap into the center of my chest.

"Sparky?" I asked as she pushed past me to move inside.

"Yep. You're doing renovations?" she asked, looking around.

"The place was a wreck. Those cabinets were a yellow from hell," I explained, waving my hand at the fresh white coat of paint they had on them. It was a temporary fix. They actually needed to get torn out and replaced. But I wasn't sure how long I was going to be there, and it was stupid to sink a ton of money into a place you might be leaving. It just needed to be livable.

"What are you going to do with the floor?" she asked as she made herself at home, putting the food and coffee down on the pop-up table I was using until I figured out a furniture situation. "And the countertops?"

"Probably some kind of tile. On both."

"No," she said, shaking her head as she took the coffees out of the cupholder.

"No?" I asked, smiling a little at the eye roll she did, likely not thinking I would see it with her head ducked.

ELI

"You don't want tile on the counter. The grout gets dirty and looks awful. Something solid."

"Is that an offer to come with me to the home improvement store?" I asked, smiling at the way her head snapped up and her eyes brightened.

I knew that look.

And I knew it meant nothing but trouble for me.

And likely hurt for her.

Hope.

That was the purest look of hope I had seen in a long fucking time.

"Well, I can certainly do no worse than *tile*," she quipped, likely picking up on her own tells, and wanting to cover them.

"What did you bring me?" I asked, moving closer as she pulled food out of the bags.

And, unlike what Bobby brought me, this wasn't wrapped in parchment paper dripping with grease. Don't get me wrong, that shit was welcome after years of awful food in prison. But I couldn't help but wonder what kind of breakfast foods required fancy brown folded takeaway containers.

"Apple-stuffed brioche French toast with a side of breakfast potatoes annnnnd..." she said, digging through the bag for a fifth container, "fruit to share."

"Apple-stuffed brioche French toast with potatoes and you thought fruit was necessary."

"Balance," she said with a smile. "Like how I'm going to hoover all this, have a sensible salad for lunch, then have something cheesy and fatty for dinner. Balance."

"I'm pretty sure that doesn't exactly..."

"Shut it," she cut me off, small-eyeing me as she sat down to open her biggest container. "No one needs that negativity in their lives."

"You mean the truth?"

"Yeah, that shit," she agreed, giving me a smile that I swear lit up my entire sad, dark, dank fucking home.

I opened up the boxes in front of me as she opened the fruit we were to share. I'll be damned, they even had little containers of syrup nestled inside with the three fluffy pieces of apple-stuffed

ELI

toast. It smelled what a foodgasm sounded like, in case you were wondering.

And the potatoes were extra brown and perfectly seasoned.

And I was pretty sure I gained ten pounds from the one meal alone.

It was worth every last one of them too.

I sat back, hand on my stomach, reaching for my coffee.

"Where the fuck are you putting it all?" I asked as she unfolded and flattened her container. I felt like I was going to burst, and she was smaller than me and seemed to have no such issue.

"I think you forget just how much walking Coop requires in a day. If I don't eat, I will be all skin and bones," she told me as she got up and walked over to my side of the table, planning to fold my container as well.

"Yeah, wouldn't want that," I agreed, reaching up to snag her waist, pulling her down on my lap, my hand sliding up her side to rest at the side of her breast, left without a bra, as I imagined she would be for at least another day or two. "Thanks for breakfast," I told her, my hand moving up to tuck her hair behind her ear so I could see her face better.

"You're welcome," she said, ducking her gaze almost a little shyly, which wasn't a look I was used to seeing there.

"What's..." I started, only to be interrupted as Coop came barreling into the room with one of my shoes in his mouth.

"Coop!" Autumn hissed, jumping up from my lap to chase him around the living room. Which, apparently, he still saw as much of a game now as he used to as a puppy.

"Leave it," I said, shaking my head as I got up, snagging her waist again, and pulling her down with me onto the couch that I had managed to snag at Target of all fucking places. It wasn't the most comfortable thing, but it was furniture, and I had been able to bring it home that day, not wait three weeks for delivery. "It's a work boot. There is literally steel in it. Even he can't fuck those up."

"I like your couch," she said, running her hand over the charcoal-colored material. "This is one of those that they pass off as a sofa bed too, right? Like it lays down flat."

"Think it said something about that."

She turned to me, brows drawn together. "You're fixing up and furnishing, but you don't seem to care about any of it."

ELI

"I don't know how long I'm staying. Don't want to drop a ton of money into some other man's property."

"I used to say that. For years. Then I finally caved and started making the place how I like it."

"You have a nice home, Autumn," I agreed, giving her hip a squeeze.

It was homey, but not frumpy. She had nice floors, great counters, carefully selected furniture. But there were personal touches too. She had a couple collages down the hallway of her and her sister at birthday parties, concerts, on holidays, vacations. Peyton's books were lying around wherever she left them. There were blankets piled on a spare chair for movie watching.

It was comfortable.

You could settle in there.

I didn't want to settle in here.

I guess that was the difference.

"It's coming along," she agreed, smile proud. "That darn bathroom is my next project."

"I can help."

"You can?" she asked, brows drawn together.

It was right then that I realized, while we knew a lot about personal preferences, the things we enjoyed and were passionate about, there was still quite a bit she didn't know about my past.

"Loansharking aside, we all had legit businesses. My brother Mark has a construction company. I pitched in when he needed extra men on a job."

"What were your businesses?"

"Have a car rental place, a gas station, and a tutoring center - one of those chain type places."

"That is an interesting array of things."

"Pops always advised us to get into things that have an almost guaranteed chance of success. Everyone needs fuel, especially at the far side of town where my place is. It's the only game over there. Car rental is big around here. The tutoring center was a bit of a gamble, but it seems to be paying off well enough." More than. People would scoff about the passive income I had coming in from those three businesses combined, and here I was, planning to give them all up.

"Have and is."

"Sorry?" I asked, brows drawing close.

ELI

"You said have and is. Present tense. You still own those businesses?"

"Technically, yes."

"Technically?"

"I plan to sign them over to my family, but I have to work out the kinks of that. Ryan has obviously been taking care of things since I've been away. I got paid every month when I was inside."

"Why would you give all that up?"

"Because it's the past."

"And you can't have any ties to that anymore," she concluded, understanding, but if I wasn't mistaken, not exactly approving the mentality.

"Something like that, yeah."

She was quiet for a minute, seeming to mull something over. "Okay, there's no delicate way to put this," she started.

"I'm fine with indelicate, sweetheart. I just spent six years in prison. Rude was the norm."

"Okay. So you have three successful businesses that have been going strong since you went away. You are driving a brand new off-the-lot truck. So why..."

"Am I living in this dump?" I finished for her, smile big.

"Ah, well, yeah."

"I have my old apartment sitting just as I left it."

"But your family knows where that is."

"Exactly."

"You're really not going to see any of them?"

"I saw Hunter yesterday," I admitted, not knowing why I would. It was going to open up a dialog about something that I didn't want to discuss.

"Oh," she said, eyes going keen. "That makes sense then."

"I don't want it to happen again," I told her, hand going to her jaw, running my fingers along it.

"Well, I do," she said, shrugging. "Well, I mean. I don't want you getting that upset because of family stuff again," she clarified. "But I like bossy-Eli. He's kinda hot," she added, smile devilish.

My cock stirred at that, making me need to take a deep breath. "Turn for me," I demanded softly, pressing her hip to show her what I meant. She did, settling her feet on the ground between my legs, her ass on the tops of my thighs.

ELI

My hands moved out, grabbing the material of her shirt, and slowly dragging it upward. She took it from me as it got high, pulling it fully off.

She was right.

She healed fast.

The marks that had been raised like welts, and so red they were almost bloody, had flattened out, and were a much more subdued shade of red, not raw and painful-looking.

Still marks.

Still pain I had etched into her skin.

But so much better than it was.

"See?" she asked, leaning back into my chest. "Almost all better. Tomorrow, it will look like nothing happened."

I should have been focusing on her words, finding some solace in them, reassuring myself that I hadn't lost complete control.

But her shoulders were against my chest, her breasts bared, her nipples already hardening.

Any man who could focus with that before him didn't fucking deserve her there in the first place. My hands moved around and up from her hips, sliding over the skin of her stomach, before cupping the full, incredibly soft swells of her breasts. My thumbs grazed her nipples, making a shiver move through her body.

"Hey Eli?"

"Yeah, baby?" I asked, doing another swipe.

"Bossy Eli is hot," she reiterated. "But sweet Eli is pretty hot too."

I leaned over, pressing a kiss into her temple as my fingers took her nipples and rolled them, making her hips buck back into me, settling her ass fully over my already straining cock. With her strange, lightweight linen pants, there might as well not have been any barrier at all. When she shifted slightly to let my cock press against her, I could feel the scorching heat of her pussy through both our thin pants.

On a growl, I rocked my hips upward as she simultaneously worked her hips in a circle.

I swear I could feel the moan she let out in my balls.

But I needed to keep control.

ELI

After the somewhat rough first time and the too-rough second, I wanted to take my time with her. I wanted to show her that I could do softer and sweeter too.

A woman like her deserved that.

And I was going to fucking give it to her.

My hands drifted down her belly, her skin goose bumping at the contact. "Lift up," I demanded softly as my hands snagged the waistband of her pants and panties. Her hips lifted with a small grumble at losing contact with my cock. I couldn't help but hold back a smile as I pushed the material down. Once it was at her knees, she kicked it off, settling back down on me with only my thin pants as a barrier.

My hand slid between her thighs, stroking up her already wet pussy to work her clit with my thumb.

"Oh, my God," she whimpered, rocking herself against my hand. My forefinger drifted down, sliding between her lips, then sliding inside her hot, wet pussy.

Her arm rose up, slipping behind my neck, holding on as my finger fucked her - slow, soft, unhurried, driving her up as slowly as her insistent grinding would allow.

"Eli, please," she begged as my free hand went to her breast, squeezing gently, then working circles around the bud. "*Please,*" she tried again, reaching out toward the makeshift coffee table - a TV dinner stand - for her purse, fumbling for a condom, pressing it into my hand. She pulled her legs under her before leaning back against me, allowing her to lift up so I could slip the condom on.

"Here," I said, reaching for her hand before I protected us, taking it and pressing it between her thighs. "Touch your pussy for me," I demanded as I worked my cock out. She immediately complied as I stroked my cock before slipping on the condom. "Come on," I said, grabbing her waist, pulling her back and down, positioning her over my straining dick. "Take me in," I demanded softly.

She lowered down, taking me to the hilt on a soft moan.

She had barely taken me before she was rocking against me. Her hand stayed at her clit, so both of mine went to her breasts, squeezing, and teasing over her nipples as my head shifted so I could press my lips into her neck.

ELI

Her moans became desperate whimpers as my cock started thrusting upward into her, slow, almost lazy as she kept rocking, kept working her clit.

"Eli..."

"Come for me, Autumn," I demanded, feeling my own growing need for release.

"I..."

"Shh," I urged, reaching down to press my finger into hers, putting more pressure on her clit. "Just let go," I instructed her.

Then she did.

If I lived another fifty years, I was sure there would still never be a better feeling in the world than her pussy squeezing me as she came.

I came on the tail end of her orgasm, her name on my lips as I did.

She collapsed back against me, her hand reaching out for mine, squeezing, as she tried to get her breath back.

"That was it, right?" she asked a long moment later.

"That was what, sweetheart?"

"That was us moving past... everything. You can stop feeling weird about it or whatever. Right?"

I smiled as I pressed a kiss to her neck. *If only it were truly that easy.*

"Yeah, that was us moving past everything," I told her, even though I wasn't entirely convinced it was a promise I could make.

"Good," she said, giving my hand another squeeze. "Ugh, I don't want to go to work," she admitted, taking a deep breath. "I want to stay right here," she added, then almost immediately stiffened up at her words.

Like maybe she was worried they were wrong.

Like maybe she thought she shouldn't feel that way.

She probably shouldn't. Not about a man like me.

But she did.

And I was the luckiest sonofabitch in the world to have that.

So there was no way I was going to let her think that was in any way wrong.

"I wish you could stay right here too, sweetheart. But you have anal beads to sell."

ELI

She let out a surprised laugh/snort hybrid that vibrated from her and into my chest. "Oh, yes. Heaven forbid people go one day without their new anal beads," she said, lifting up, and sliding off me, going in search of her clothes.

"What are you doing after work?" I asked as I stood, pulling my pants into place.

"Ah... nothing really. I had no plans."

"How about you have your salad you planned on for lunch, but I take you out for something cheesy and fatty instead of you eating at home alone?"

You'd have thought I'd offered her a goddamn diamond ring, not just an invite to dinner. She lit the fuck up.

I so, so did not fucking deserve her.

Someday, she would see that herself.

But that day wasn't today.

Today was the day she agreed to going out with me, then gave me a kiss that made me see through time and goddamn space before she rushed off to work, leaving Coop with me for the day.

He sat down, watching the door with a whine.

"Yeah, buddy," I agreed, petting his head. "I think I am starting to feel how you feel about her leaving."

And that was going to blow the fuck up in my face eventually.

Even knowing that, though, wasn't going to stop me.

ELEVEN

Autumn

I was going on a date.
An actual, real-life date.
With Eli Mallick.
I felt like I was fifteen again, sneaking off on my first boy-girl date, butterflies in my belly all day in anticipation.
I totally drifted off a few times while a couple was explaining their sex swing needs to me since I didn't have the one they wanted in stock.
But how was I expected to focus on work when I could still feel his hands on me, his finger in me, his lips on my neck, his cock in me giving me sweet and gentle and loving?
Ugh.
Even the memory was getting me going again.
It was going to be a long, long day.
I had just gotten rid of the sex swing couple, promising to have a different model in within a week for them to see in person,

ELI

intent on sitting behind the desk and getting some ordering done, when the door chimed again.

I closed my eyes. Taking a deep breath, I turned.

Oh, thank God.

Not another adventurous couple with a thousand questions.

A group of girlfriends.

I would take a group of girlfriends over just about any other customer. It was always more laid-back, casual, even funny.

"Oh!" I said as they shuffled in, looking around, one clearly more uncomfortable than the others, a pretty blonde with green eyes that I had never seen before. But her other blonde friend? Oh, yeah, I'd seen her several times. "Fee!" I said, giving her a warm smile.

Fee was always fun when she came in, whether she was alone or with friends. She actually told me she adopted my big bowl of condoms on the counter idea and used it in the bathrooms at her work.

Her work?

Yeah, that badass chick with the best fashion sense I had ever seen owned a phone sex business.

So, of course, I thought she was awesome.

All heads turned to me in unison.

And something about the look in their eyes had me stiffening, looking between them - each just as pretty as the previous one - wondering what the heck was going on.

"I can't believe it's you," Fee said oddly, making my brows draw low.

"What? I'm always here," I said, shaking my head.

Why the hell was she looking at me so intensely? Like she had never seen me before.

"Hi," the other blonde said, giving me a sweet smile. "I'm Dusty," she supplied. "And this is Lea," she said, waving at a tall, leggy, dark-haired woman with an impossibly gorgeous face. "And that is Scotti," she added, waving at the other dark-haired woman who had incredible bone-structure and a confident air about her. "And you already know Fee."

"Hey ladies," I said, hearing the way my own voice was wavering at the oddness of this interaction that shouldn't have felt odd at all. "Are you looking for anything in partic--"

"All this time," Fee went on, brows knitted, eyes confused.

ELI

"Fee, are you feeling alright?" I asked, starting to actually get concerned.

She shook her head at that, trying to get rid of some niggling thought. "You don't know my full name, do you?"

"Ah, no," I realized, even though I had seen her on more than a few occasions.

"Fiona Mallick."

My heart froze in my chest.

Recognition hit with all the subtlety of an atomic bomb.

Oh, *God.*

Wow.

Fiona Mallick.

She was, in some way, related to Eli.

And since I only ever knew him to talk about brothers, and had just confirmed that all his brothers were taken (because Peyton was serious about the scary clown mask), then Fee must have been with one of his brothers.

"Sorry to burst in here like this," Dusty said into the silence that followed Fee's admission.

"Ah, no. It's, ah, okay."

"I bet you're wondering how we knew about you," Lea said, giving me a small smile.

"Sort of."

"The day Eli got released, everyone was out on the town looking for him, wanting to see that he was okay. Shane was on his way home to me and the kids when he stopped at a sign, and something in his peripheral caught his eye."

Oh, God.

I had a feeling I knew what caught his eye.

His brother practically fucking me against a building.

Jesus.

This was more than a little embarrassing, and totally not how I would have liked to meet his family.

"Coop," she clarified, but the way her eyes were dancing gave me the impression that she knew what I was thinking.

"We've been looking for him for six years," Scotti added. "Shelters and the vets. Nothing. Not a word." She paused there, shrugging. "Because you had him."

"But we can't figure out *why* you had him," Lea added.

ELI

The silence after demanded a response, even though they hadn't asked a direct question.

"The day Eli was arrested, I was outside the coffeeshop. He had been trying to make Coop sit for a treat when the cops showed up. They took him away. And Coop started *freaking out*. I, well, I figured he was too ugly to end up in the pound. So I took him home with me."

"You've had him this whole time?" Scotti clarified.

"Yeah. Me and my sister work opposite shifts a lot of the time, so he always has someone around."

"So he's with her now," Lea concluded.

"No, ah, he's with..." Shit. I didn't want to give anything about Eli away when he was so determined to cut off ties with his family. I already felt like I had said too much.

"He's with Eli," Lea finished for me. "Shane saw Coop that night, but he also saw you and Eli. As in, together."

Ugh.

There was literally no way out of this situation.

And I had no clue how Eli would have wanted me to maneuver it.

"We're not here to make you uncomfortable," Dusty said, holding up her hands, looking apologetic. "You just have to understand that we need to know that he's okay. Everyone has been sick for years."

I imagined that was true.

And my heart truly did go out to them.

But my loyalty needed to be with Eli.

"Look," Fee said, voice more serious than I had ever heard it before. When I did look, her eyes were full of feeling. "Hunt came home yesterday to tell me he had seen Eli. He had confronted him. You know what Eli told him to tell my girls?"

"No." But I knew it wasn't good.

"That he was dead," she said, swallowing hard. "He said it was true enough."

That hurt.

It felt like a knife in the gut.

Because I knew he did feel that way.

"Autumn," she said, voice even more grave. And when I looked up, her lip was trembling. "I've seen my husband tear up

ELI

exactly three times in our entire time together. The first time we found out we were having a baby, the day he realized Eli was going away, and last night when he told me his brother said he was as good as dead. Now, I know you don't know these Mallick men, but they are not the kind of men who cry. Not even one glistening tear. So seeing my man like that, yeah, it was the push I needed to way overstep my bounds and come in here to talk to you."

Even as she finished speaking she had to reach up and swipe a tear away, shaking her head, and blinking hard, trying to get it together.

I would have to be made of stone not to have my heart go out to her right then. My heart ached in my chest for the pain they must have been feeling, the loss their family must have endured. It wasn't just Eli who had done time; they had done time in their own way as well.

"Eli had a rough afternoon yesterday too," I admitted, the act of sitting down all day reminding me with a small sting.

"See!" Scotti said, shoving her hip into Fee's. "I told you it was an act."

"I don't think it's an act," I corrected before I thought better of it. But then all their eyes were on me and pleading for more. "Eli is terrified that any links to his old life will make him rage-out again. He doesn't want that. So he tries to disconnect. Key word there being *try*. It's not an act. He's not pretending. He is putting every ounce of energy he has to attempt to kill the man you all once knew."

"Poor Eli," Dusty said in a sad whisper, looking down at her feet. Likely, just as Fee was, struggling to keep composure.

"The part that pisses me off about this," Lea exploded suddenly, like she wasn't able to hold it in anymore, "is that he did nothing wrong! He defended a woman getting her ass handed to her. I know what it is like to have a man bully you. I know that helplessness. I know she saw him as a fucking hero when he stepped in where no one else in her life ever had. He should never have gone away for this."

That was sadly true.

"And then he wouldn't have been sitting in a cell feeling like a shitty person, feeling like he couldn't lean on us, couldn't even speak to us anymore, that he had to be someone else. Who he was

ELI

before was, ugh," Lea trailed off, turning suddenly, and taking a few steps away. Her hands rose though, pressing into her eyes.

Even just seeing these women struggling for composure was starting to make me lose mine. The sting started at the backs of my eyes, and I had to slow-blink and take deep breaths to keep from crying myself.

I didn't come from a family that loved so deeply. I mean, Peyton and I did as we grew up and grew close, but the rest of our family was just as happy without us.

What an amazing thing it must have been to be loved that deeply by so many different people.

How badly must he have seen himself to push that away?

Poor Eli. Dusty was right about that.

"Look, I get your loyalty is torn here," Scotti said, the only one who was still holding it together. "We're not asking you for his address or contact information. That's not fair," she said, giving Lea a hard look, like maybe Lea had been down with trying to force information out of me.

"Why are you here then?"

"Is he okay?" Dusty asked before anyone else could speak up.

There was no way to answer that without giving them at least a little bit of the truth. "He's... okay. He's adjusting still. It's only been a couple of days."

I could practically feel them say *It's been six years.*

"We're actually here with a request," Fee said, taking a deep breath before she launched into it. "Helen, Eli's mom, has had a really, really hard time every holiday. It seems to get worse as each year goes by."

I knew where this was going.

Because Thanksgiving was coming up.

"Fee, I..."

"You would be giving a mother her son back," she cut me off, eyes going glassy again. "I'm not sure if I can express just how huge that is. What it would mean to her."

"Fee, we just barely started..."

"But you're all we have," she rushed to stop me. "Even if you're new, you're the only link we have to him. We are begging you, Autumn - and I am not the kind of woman to beg - please, see if you can convince him to come."

ELI

God, was there any way to say no? I mean, I wouldn't push Eli; that wasn't my place. I could, however, drop hints, make suggestions, reassure him that he didn't need to kill his old self and start anew. Hell, this morning alone, I had seen sides of Eli that I didn't know existed before. Maybe, the longer he was out, the more he could shake the persona he had needed to wield in prison.

Two weeks wasn't long, though.

He had spent six years creating this mindset.

I didn't have a huge ton of hope that I could undo all that work.

"I can't make any promises..."

"We would never ask for them," Dusty assured me.

"And we aren't telling Helen or Charlie or even our men," Fee told me. "This is just between us girls. So if he doesn't show, the only one who will even know to be disappointed is us. And, please, feel free to come too! Bring your sister. We don't care. We will squeeze closer at the table. Oh and Coop. You know, whatever it might take. Trust me, if you can get him there, Helen will be kissing your feet."

Nothing like a little pressure.

The happiness of an entire damn family on your shoulders.

And here I had been excited all day over something as simple as a date with the man I had been sleeping with.

What a strange turn of events in the course of one day.

"If, and this is a huge if," I said, making sure they knew I didn't have a lot of faith in myself with this task, "I can make it happen, I need a time."

"Dinner is at four, but everyone starts filing in around noon. But I mean, whenever you can get him there," Scotti said.

"I'll try," I said, shrugging, hearing defeat in my voice.

"I know this is putting you in a bad position," Dusty said, voice soft. "We don't want to mess up your new relationship with Eli. I think having you - even if he doesn't have us or want us - is a good thing. If he lost you on top of all of us, I worry about what would go on in his mind."

"I would worry about that too," I agreed.

"So, what we're saying is," Lea cut in, "push, but don't push him away. Because at least we know he has some roots if he has you, someone to talk to, someone to give a shit about him. That's important. He needs some soft after so many years of hard."

ELI

"He really does."

"We hope we see you on Thanksgiving," Dusty said, moving back a step, obviously trying to guide the other women to leave. "But we will understand if you can't move mountains."

"Thank you, Autumn," Fee said, giving me a serious nod. Then, shaking off her heaviness, the normal Fee I was used to came shining through. "The Wand is fucking amazing, by the way," she said as she backed toward the door.

"That's why it is a bestseller," I agreed as they opened the door, and stepped outside.

With that, they were gone, and I was alone with my thoughts.

They swirled so fast that I had to sit down, cradling my head in my hands, trying to make sense of it all.

On one hand, yes. I so wanted to be the savior to their little family. I wanted to give Eli back to them. And I wanted to give *them* back to Eli. They needed one another. He might not have been able to acknowledge it himself, but it was eating him alive to stay away, especially since they were in the same town.

His interaction with Hunt, and the aftermath, showed me just how much it was hurting him. He needed to reconnect.

That being said, I didn't wear the white hat. I was nobody's hero.

And I was holding a whole family's disappointment on my shoulders if I didn't pull through.

On the other hand, I didn't want to rock the boat. Things were going in a somewhat unexpected direction with Eli. I wanted it to keep doing that. I wanted him to keep opening up to me, showing his sweeter, softer side. I wanted him to trust me.

How could I expect him to trust me when I was going behind his back?

On a groan, no less confused than I was twenty minutes before, I reached under the counter for my cell, dialing up my sister.

"This better be good. They're DP'ing her right now and it is hot as shit."

One second. That was all I needed with my sister to help lift some of the weight.

I launched into it, talking in circles, words tripping over one another to get out first.

ELI

"So don't," she said simply after listening silently for about half an hour.

"Don't what?"

"Don't go behind his back," she clarified.

"But, what..."

"Look, I know you feel bad for them. Anyone would. But your loyalty lies with Eli. And, yes, I think we all can agree he needs his family back, it is not your place to push him into that. That is his decision. And if he ever finds out you did that, you and him are over. Now, I know you're going to deny this and say I'm crazy or what the fuck ever, but I know you, Autumn. You have feelings for him."

"I barely--"

"You've been mooning over him for five years. Don't pull that 'I barely know him' shit. You know him better than that last dude I had a two-week fling with."

"Angelo No-Last-Name," I recalled. He had a last name, but he and Peyton were too busy getting it on to share that kind of information.

"Exactly. You know his last name. You know where he lives. You know he's an artist. You know what movies, books, music, and food he likes. You know he fucks you like there's no tomorrow. You know more than enough to have feelings. And, dare I say it, be already half in love with him. Don't," she said before I could even get a noise out, "even try to deny it. We both know it is true. What I am saying is, you don't fuck around and ruin that because a bunch of women showed up and went all teary-eyed on you. I know, I know, I'm a heartless monster," she went on, and I could practically hear the eye-roll she was doing. "But he matters more. His feelings need to matter more. And his choices need to be his own, not manipulated by you and some women he has made it clear he doesn't want in his life. Even if," she cut me off when I went to speak, "we both know he *does* want them in his life."

My sister, for all her crazy, for all her over-the-topness, for all her devotion to a more alternative lifestyle, was also one of the wisest people I knew. Sure, she sometimes went about imparting her wisdom in odd ways, at times referencing godawful, cheesy, campy horror movies with a negative Rotten Tomato rating. But she was almost always right.

ELI

"So what am I supposed to do? Show up and say, 'Hey, your sisters-in-law ambushed me and begged me to get you to come to Thanksgiving, so your mother doesn't cry for the umpteenth holiday in a row?' I mean... that is going to go over like a bomb."

"You come home a little early from work. Get your scrub and shave on. Do your hair and makeup. Slip into something sexy. Then you go to dinner with him. And then come home. Where you fuck his brains out. Then you bring it up. You gotta have this conversation when his guards are down. And the only time men let their guards down completely is when they are freshly fucked."

"You're not wrong," I agreed, though I didn't like the idea of sexual manipulation.

And, because she was who she was, she knew this. "You're not tricking him, Autumn. You're just getting him relaxed and a bit less likely to fly off the handle. Oh, but maybe stick a paddle in your bag in case he does fly off the handle. Okay, I have a girl to get back to who is getting plowed like nobody's business and completely unaware that her throat is going to get slit as soon as the guy comes in her. Bye!"

I snorted as I hung up the phone, realizing it was really the only card I had to play.

I didn't want to bring that kind of thing up at a restaurant. Especially if there was any chance that he might rage out again. I didn't want him in that awkward of a situation. I didn't want him to storm out, leaving me to have to deal with the bill, then finding my own way home from God-knew-where. And where did that leave him? Losing his mind in a rage with no outlet?

No.

That couldn't happen.

And the same logic went for before the date. He would likely storm off and go who-knew-where.

Peyton was right; the best time to tell him was when he was freshly fucked, completely naked, and unable to jump up and storm out before I could try to stop him.

So I did what she said.

I closed early.

I went home and spent well over an hour on getting myself together. I slipped into a black dress that was just shy of slutty and a pair of spiked heels. My back, and the cut of the dress, didn't allow

ELI

for a bra, but I picked out a special pair of panties that was black lace over my butt cheeks, but cut off at the highest point where it met a silky bow that attached to a thick satin waistband.

They were exactly made for sexual manipulation.

So I guess I was dressing for the task.

Eli had texted me an hour before I closed up, saying he would bring Coop back to my place and we could leave from there.

So I was nervously shifting my feet when there was a knock - and a scratch - at the door.

Peyton jumped up, mermaid hair all in a loose, messy bun on her head, legs in leggings covered in blood splatter and crime scene tape and a black tank top. Effortless, quirky, and still ridiculously pretty.

Some day a man would see that about her too.

"What are your intentions with my daughter?" she asked in a dead-on imitation of our father, arm stretched out to block his entrance as Coop barreled in to take her seat on the couch, resting his head on her book.

"I plan to ravish her completely," Eli said, tone deadly serious.

"Son!" Peyton declared, throwing open the door, and her arms like she was about to embrace him. She dropped her hands at the last second, moving out of the way. "She's over there looking like sex on a stick," she informed him as she walked away. "I think the 'lick' comment doesn't need to be uttered. Get your head off my book," she told Coop as she took it from under him. "Looking all innocent when we all know you're just waiting for me to glance away so you can eat it, you butthead."

"Sweetheart," Eli said, close, too close, making me realize I had been focusing on Peyton, and hadn't seen him cross the room toward me.

He looked good, too.

The Mallick men, well, they apparently cleaned up nice.

He had on black slacks and a matte black dress shirt, no tie, nice shoes, an expensive silver watch, and a matching belt buckle.

Hot.

Was there anything hotter than a man who knew how to dress?

"Hey," I said, giving him a smile.

ELI

"You look beautiful," he told me as soon as my eyes found his, making my belly do an altogether too delicious flip-flop.

"Thank you. You--"

"Look like her *ride* later. We get it," Peyton said from behind her book. "You are both sexy beasts who will be doing it soon. Coop can not stand Mommy and Daddy being all gross in front of him," she informed us, making us both smile before Eli leaned in to give me a quick kiss.

"We should get going," he agreed, reaching down to take my hand, and lead me to the door.

All I could think for the drive two towns over was *God I hope I don't screw this up. Please don't let me screw this up.*

Eli pulled up and led me into an upscale sushi restaurant I had heard amazing things about, but couldn't quite bring myself to go to since I could get decent enough rolls closer to home for a third the price.

There was a bit of awkwardness as I tried to relax, tried to be in the moment and enjoy a date I had been so looking forward to. By the time I had a glass of wine in my hand, though, things had seemed to fall into an easy rhythm, talking about the restaurant, then others, then just life and futures and hopes and all that.

And he wasn't post-prison-Eli. He was just Eli - sweet, open, joking, easy with a smile, interesting.

The guards, for those two hours, were completely gone.

And as we got in his car and drove back to my place, there was no way to stop the swirling discomfort in my stomach, the way my body was tense.

"Autumn," Eli said as we stopped outside my door so I could fish out my key, his hand at my lower back. When I looked up, his brows were drawn together. "What's the matter?"

"Nothing, I just can't find... there they are," I said, ducking my head so he couldn't see my face. I wasn't a good liar and I knew it.

"Sweetheart," he tried again just as I got the door unlocked, and pushed inside.

Peyton, having anticipated us coming home, had taken off to bed with Coop, leaving the apartment quiet except the hum of her music on.

ELI

"Autumn," he tried again, voice a little more firm thanks to my attempts to ignore him.

And, well, I couldn't keep doing that.

So, it was time for the relaxing part of the evening.

"I have something I want to show you," I told him as he closed and locked the door.

"Oh yeah?" he asked, watching me like puzzle pieces that were the last two in a giant piece, but somehow still didn't fit together.

"Mhmm," I murmured, not having to fake the heaviness in my eyelids because, well, the idea of having his hands on me was already making my panties stick to me in desire.

I reached for the side zipper, pulling it all the way down before standing straight again, then letting the material drop.

There was a quiet slam as Eli leaned back on the closed door with a groan.

My smile went wicked as he raked his eyes over me.

Once his eyes were on my face again, I turned slowly, looking over my shoulder, wanting to gauge his reaction to the panties.

"Trying to fucking kill me over here, woman," he said, shaking his head.

He pushed off the door, moving toward me, and sliding his hands up my belly to cup my breasts, pressing his hard cock into my ass.

"That was the plan," I agreed, grinding my ass against him, wondering how long it would be before he claimed that as well.

"Bedroom," he growled.

With a smile - and a shiver of anticipation - I reached for his hand, and pulled him with me to the hall, opening my bedroom door, and flicking on the light.

I still hadn't finished renovating it. But I did have the gray wood floors laid to match the dove gray walls. The bed was my old white metal bar Victorian-looking one that I wanted to replace with a charcoal gray tufted one I had sitting on an idea board for the better part of three months. Soon. I was close to getting it. The bedspread was a simple, clean white one that cost a small fortune and was a pain in the ass to keep clean, but was a favorite of mine.

ELI

Eli looked around for a second, but moved toward the side of the bed, kicking out of his shoes, then sitting off the side of it. "Come here," he demanded, holding an arm out.

And when you were naked, wet, and ready, and a hot man 'come hither'd' you, you hithered, damnit.

But if he had plans to torture me, he was mistaken. As soon as I got between his spread legs, I lowered myself down onto my knees, looking up at him with my heavy eyes as I reached to free the buttons of his shirt.

"Autumn," he said quietly as my hands slid down his stomach to snag his belt, then undo his button and zip.

Whatever he was about to say, however, disappeared as I reached in, grabbed his cock, freed it, then sucked it deep before he could even draw a breath.

He only let me work him for a couple short minutes before his hand was in the hair at the base of my neck, twisting, and yanking upward until his cock left my mouth with a soft pop.

"On the bed," he demanded, showing a bit of bossy-Eli, minus the anger, and that was just as thrilling as the angry one who plugged, flogged, and fucked me while bound. I wanted to know what this version of Eli had planned for me. I stretched out across the bed, thighs pressed together to try to calm the chaos as he moved to stand, shedding his shirt, then his pants.

There he was, naked, fucking *glorious*, with his hard cock straining, promising an end to the torment.

Just not quite yet.

He watched me as he stroked himself twice, then turned his attention to my nightstand where he pulled open the deep lower drawer where he - rightly - assumed I kept the toys.

I didn't really even know what was in there anymore, having really just used a trusty vibrator to get the job done for a long while.

The low, appreciative chuckle let me know that there was definitely more than that to play with in there.

"Perfect, he said, producing a pair of cuffs that made me suddenly really glad I hadn't replaced my headboard just yet. He waved at me, and I scooted up toward the top of the bed, raising my hands over my head, giving him a wicked smirk as he moved to straddle my waist, sliding the chain between two rails, then clamping the cold metal on each of my wrists.

ELI

He lowered down, running his tongue down my neck, my chest, circling my nipples.

But before he could go where I needed contact the most, he was off the bed and in my nightstand again, coming back with something with straps that took me a long second to recognize. A butterfly vibe. You strapped it across your thighs so you could be handless. It vibrated against your clit. And the one I brought home? Yeah, it had a small finger-type extension that slipped inside you and vibrated against your G-spot as well.

I had brought it home to test it.

Then had completely forgotten about it.

He dropped it next to my body as he moved to kneel by my legs. "Legs up," he demanded.

I pressed them together and put them straight up. He grabbed my calves and shoved them inward, pressing them into my chest as his hand moved down, rubbing my clit quickly side-to-side through my panties before his hand moved up, snagging the lacy material that was half-covering my ass, and dragging it down just slightly. His finger moved in, thrusting unexpectedly inside my pussy, making my body jump, and a moan escape me.

But before I could even get used to the sensation, his finger was gone, moving back, pressing against, then penetrating my ass.

And I knew exactly what he had planned for me, exactly what I had been wondering about just moments before.

When I rocked my hips against him, he withdrew his finger. He pulled my panties off, then reached for the butterfly, clasping it to my thighs, then pressing the little piece inside my pussy before turning it on.

His eyes closed when I let out a whimper.

"Eli, wait..." I moaned when he moved off the bed.

He didn't respond, just went into the top drawer of the nightstand, coming back with a condom and a small bottle of lube.

But he didn't use either, just watched me writhe as the vibrations pushed me upward and fast.

"You gonna tell me what you were all tense about earlier?" he asked, making my eyes go huge.

I wasn't the only one not above using sexual manipulation.

"Eli..."

ELI

"You don't get to come until you tell me," he informed me. Then, as if to prove his point, pressed between my thighs, flicking the butterfly off, making me squirm and yank against my cuffs.

"Eli, please," I whimpered, rocking my hips shamelessly, helplessly.

He watched me, eyes molten, smile evil, as he reached for the condom, slipped it on, then grabbed the lube as he pressed my knees in toward my chest again.

The cold shock made my body jolt as it slid down my pussy, my ass, dripping off of me as he kept pouring. His hand moved to work the silky liquid around my ass, thrusting a finger inside again to work me. My back arched on a moan before I lost the finger again.

But then he shifted forward and the thick head of his cock pressed against my ass instead, pushing hard, but not quite penetrating for a long minute as he watched my face for a reaction.

"Eli..." Whatever I had been about to say trailed off on a choked moan as his cock slid forward, slowly, but demanding, claiming me in one solid thrust, burying to the hilt, making me press my thighs together hard.

"Talk," he demanded, stilling inside me.

"I can't. I need you to, yes," I whimpered when he withdrew, then slammed forward again. One of his hands pressed down hard into my lower stomach, making me feel his cock scrape hard against the lower side of my pelvic wall - a sensation that almost made me come right then and there. But he seemed to sense it, pulling almost completely out of me for a long second, long enough to drag me back from the brink again.

Once he was sure it was safe, he reached between my thighs and flicked on the vibrator again, making a shudder wrack my body.

"Tell me," he demanded, voice rough, like he was losing his patience.

My hips rocked, my breathing a frantic hitching noise. "I can't think. I can't. Please, Eli. Please fuck me," I begged.

That seemed to take with it the last bit of control he was holding onto.

His hand pressed into my belly again as he started fucking my ass - hard, rough, fast. It shouldn't have been as hot as it was, but I couldn't even seem to remember to breathe as my clit, G-spot, and ass were worked all at once, driving me up, then over, then crashing down into a screaming, neighborhood-waking orgasm.

"Ohmygodohmygodohmygod," I was still crying as be buried deep, coming so hard that he half-collapsed forward, balancing his weight on a hand pressed beside my chest.

It was a long moment before he pulled out of me, reaching down to turn off the butterfly, ripping at the velcro, and tossing the whole thing to the floor.

He reached for his pants, mostly dragging them on, then walking to the door, leaving me bound as he went down the hall to the bathroom.

It was pointless to struggle, though everything within me wanted to get free, felt way too vulnerable still bound when I knew he was going to come back and demand answers.

"Please let me go," I begged as soon as he stepped inside. There was genuine desperation in my voice that made his head snap up and his brows furrow.

"Okay. One second," he said, going to the nightstand for the key. He kneeled on the bed, reaching for the cuffs, and freeing each of my hands. The metal clattered down on the floor behind my bed, forgotten, as Eli sat down and reached to touch the side of my face. "You okay?" he asked, concern dripping from his tongue. "Too much?"

And because I felt the need to, I turned, and curled into his chest, taking a few deep breaths.

"Autumn," he demanded again. "You okay?"

I managed a nod before I took another deep breath and could finally find my voice again. "That was intense," I told him, and felt his arms slide around me, holding onto me tight.

"Yeah, it was," he agreed quietly, ducking his chin so he could kiss the top of my head.

There were no further questions.

He stroked my hair, my back, seeming to brush away the stress that had been eating at me all day.

It wasn't until I was fully relaxed that I took a deep breath, pulled against his hold, and moved to sit on my knees next to him.

Even though he was as sated as I was, his eyes went a little hungry as he looked me over. "I need to talk to you about something."

ELI

"I thought so," he agreed, hand going to my knee and giving it a squeeze. "Talk to me," he encouraged, tone calm, body calm, everything calm.

I hated to ruin that.

But we had to have this conversation.

"When I was at work earlier, a group of women came in--"

"Oh, is this gonna get kinky?" he asked, eyes dancing.

I smiled slightly, but even I knew it didn't meet my eyes.

"It was all your brothers' wives."

There.

It was out.

I took a deep breath, watching as the words landed, as they moved through him. He didn't move from his relaxed position, but his entire body stiffened. "What?"

"I didn't think anything of it at first. I've seen Fee a lot of times. I had no idea she was related to you. I've never asked for her last name. She was just a customer to me, y'know?"

"What'd she say?" he asked, jaw tight, making the words come out with more of a bite than I think he intended.

"Apparently, the night you brought me coffee? When we were, ah, walking Coop... one of your brothers was driving past..."

"Which one?"

Crap. The details were getting blurry. There were so many of them. "Um, Lea's husband?"

"Shane," he supplied.

"Yeah. Well, he saw us, and I guess told everyone. And then the girls decided to come see me."

"I'm sorry they are putting you in the middle of this," he surprised me by saying, giving my knee a little squeeze.

I ducked my head, looking for the determination I needed to go through with it to the end.

"They were, ah, upset, Eli," I said, raising my gaze. "All of them."

"I know they're mad that--"

"No, they were crying," I cut him off. "Fee said she decided to put me in the middle because when Hunt came home yesterday, *he* was upset. And she had only ever seen him choked up twice before. She wanted to see if there was any way that..." I trailed off, suddenly a little queasy at having to go on.

161

ELI

His guards were back.

His eyes were blank.

"Any way that what?"

I swallowed hard. "That I could convince you to come to Thanksgiving. They said," I powered through when he went to open his mouth, "that your mother has been getting worse every holiday that passes, and they thought that this would, you know, make it all better."

Pulling the Mom-card was cruel, I knew.

But they were the facts.

And maybe he had been trying to hide from them, trying to convince himself that they were better without him, but he could only live so long with the wool over his eyes.

If I had to be the one to pull it off, and deal with the consequences of that, at least he wouldn't be blind anymore. Like that or not.

"They need to move o--"

"But they're not," I cut him off. "They're not," I repeated, voice softer. "They're not. And they're hurting. And they will never accept this, Eli. They love you. Of course they want you around."

"You don't..."

"I know," I agreed, nodding. "I know I don't understand fully. I get that. And I know that I'm just some chick that..."

"Don't," he cut me off, voice slicing through the air. "Don't finish that sentence."

My head ducked, not sure how to take that. "I told them I would mention it," I said, head lifting. "I told them I couldn't make any promises, but I said I would bring it up."

"This was why you were so tense," he concluded, watching me with a look I couldn't quite interpret.

"I didn't want to ruin dinner," I admitted.

"You thought I would get pissed," he concluded, taking his hand off my knee to rake it down the scruff on his face.

"I was really looking forward to dinner," I admitted, shrugging my shoulders, shaking my head at myself. It was silly, but true.

"We'll have to try this again on a day my sisters-in-law don't ambush you."

My head lifted, surprised, sure he was going to be resentful.

ELI

"I won't say it won't happen again. This being a thing," he said, waving a hand between us, "and them knowing that means they can use you. And I'm sorry about that. But I don't want that to fuck this up either."

This being a thing.

I wasn't sure what 'a thing' meant in his mind, but in mine, it meant something more than sex. Right? That seemed like a logical conclusion.

Or maybe that was just my heart speaking.

Peyton was right.

I wasn't just infatuated with him, with the amazing sex.

I was taking the few first tentative steps into love.

That was why I was so worked up all day, why there felt like there was something lodged in my throat when I tried to eat a very nice dinner.

I was falling for him, plain and simple.

And while it was, technically new, we had been corresponding for five years. I felt I knew him as well as I did most of my friends. It wasn't as new as it seemed. Just the physical aspect was new. The mental and emotional part had been going on for a good, long time. I suspected, for the both of us.

"I don't want anything to fuck this up either," I agreed, from, well, the bottom of my heart, damnit.

"So we aren't letting shit like this get between us."

It wasn't exactly a question, but I answered anyway. "Nope," I agreed.

"We're gonna let it drop for now, yeah?" he asked, tapping his chest again.

And, well, I pretty much flew at him.

"Yeah," I agreed.

Then we dropped it.

TWELVE

Eli

We let it drop, like I said to, for over a week.

The next morning, we had woken up to Peyton in the kitchen in full-on 1950s gear with a full skirt, a frilly waist apron, heels, her hair pulled up into some intricate up-do, and her makeup done flawlessly. She had a giant metal bowl on her hip, mixing something as the smell of sizzling bacon made my stomach grumble.

"What is this, June Cleaver?" Autumn asked, reaching up to try to pat down her hair.

"Whatever do you mean, dear?" she asked, sugar sweet. "I always get up at six AM to get ready for my day so I can get to my womanly duties."

Autumn bumped my hip as her sister turned to drop batter into a warm pan. "She's a nut. Just roll with it," she said, giving her sister a fond smile.

She was that.

A nut, quirky, a real character.

ELI

One moment, impersonating a 1950s housewife, the next, cursing like a sailor and explaining the rape-fantasy book she just read.

I took my coffee, standing back, and watching the two play off each other with the sarcastic, teasing, playful ease that only siblings could manage, poking fun without hurting feelings.

I felt it then.

A tug.

An urge.

I wasn't stupid.

I knew it for what it was.

I missed them.

See, this thing with Autumn and me, it was a mix of amazing and awful. Amazing because she was an incredible woman. I found myself thinking about her way too fucking much, missing her even though we had just started seeing each other. She was smart, accomplished, sweet, fun, and sexy as all get-out.

The shit we had going on, I had a feeling it was going somewhere.

Meaning somewhere that could possibly be permanent.

The awful part was, well, in letting her in, in letting down my guards with her, I was losing the ability to keep them in place even when I wasn't around her.

So watching her interact with her sibling was affecting me in ways I promised myself it wouldn't, that I couldn't allow.

But there it was anyway.

The next few days, Autumn went to work. When Peyton wasn't around, I took Coop back to my place so I could get my pieces done. I finished the two large ones, and moved onto some smaller pieces that ended up being softer, warmer.

I only had one medium-sized piece to work on to be ready for the show.

After work, Autumn would come to me, or I would meet her at her apartment, leaving Peyton to doggy-sit so we could go out.

It wasn't smart.

To wine and dine her.

To create memories with her.

ELI

When every day, I felt that tug again.

That urge.

That desire.

Connection.

Loyalty.

Family.

I think it was impossible when you were considering settling down with someone not to think about things like family, like foundations, like what you could bring together.

And the more that idea came to mind, the more I thought about what Autumn had told me.

About Fee crying.

And Dusty.

Scotti.

Lea.

Each time the image came up, I had to take a deep breath and try to let it go.

Then, of course, there was my mother.

I had been able to put up walls about my brothers, my father.

But my mother? Yeah, I had needed to try to completely keep her from my mind all those years. If she popped up, I knew she would ruin me, destroy all the guards I had built.

So hearing that each holiday that passed with no contact was actually weighing on her that much, that she was crying - my badass motherfucking mother who never took any shit, never let anything get to her - was *crying* every holiday? Yeah, that shit burrowed deep, took root, and started spreading outward.

Soon, it was all I could think about.

"What's the matter?" Autumn asked, pushing up off my chest, watching me with lowered brows, her silky blonde hair spilling forward and brushing her breasts.

We'd just fucked for almost an hour - rough and hard and slightly kinky, a combination that made orgasms completely wreck her. She loved soft and sweet too, but the hard and rough made her scream loud enough for the neighbors to bang on the wall.

But still, as she sat up and her body was all sex flushed still, yeah, I was almost ready for another round.

"Thinking," I admitted, reaching out to brush some of her hair behind her shoulder.

ELI

"About?"

I exhaled a deep breath.

If I had been thinking about it for a week and a half, it was about time to open a dialog about it.

"Thanksgiving."

Her lips parted and she blinked hard. That was all she gave away for a long second before she nodded. "Okay," she said, giving me a small smile. "What about Thanksgiving?"

"I'm thinking about it."

"Ah, as in thinking about it as a tradition based on the slaughter of the natives or... like considering going to your family's house for it?"

I smiled at that, running my fingers down her arm.

I would never get used to the softness of her skin, no matter how many times I put my hands on it.

"I was thinking maybe we could commemorate a terrible time in our country's history by breaking bread with my family."

I swear to Christ, she lit the fuck up.

If I wasn't sure it was a good idea before, the way her smile went proud was all the proof I needed that I was making the right decision.

"That's awesome, Eli. I'm so glad you decided to go. They're going to be so happy to see you."

"Us," I said, shaking my head.

"What?"

"They are going to be so happy to see us. I want you to come with me."

It happened almost simultaneously.

A surging joy.

Then a crushing disappointment.

"I always do Thanksgiving with..."

"Bring Peyton. She'll have a fucking blast there. She can wear one of her ridiculous 1950s get-ups."

"Really?" she asked, and there was the joy again.

"Really," I agreed.

"This is going to be so great," she declared, moving to snuggle back on my chest, planting a kiss there.

I wasn't quite as sure.

Six years.

ELI

Six years of me pushing them away.

I didn't have any idea how it was going to go, what might come up - for them, and for me.

All I knew was I had just committed to it.

Come what may.

THIRTEEN

Lea

The dining room had been expanded five years before.

When Scotti joined the family, bringing with her her four brothers. Then, in time, their women. And, of course, the litters of kids all the Mallick women had been popping out.

Charlie and Helen had decided that they didn't need their two-car garage, had it renovated, and made into a massive space that was practically like that of a venue hall. There were two long, custom-made tables almost from wall-to-wall - one for the kids, the other for the adults.

Fee was in the process of dragging three extra chairs in from the basement.

"Fee," Helen said, brows drawn low and together. "What are you doing? I put out enough chairs."

"Oh, oops," Fee said, making a grimace, pretending she just miscounted. As Helen shook her head and looked away, Fee's eyes met Lea's from across the room.

ELI

She saw a look she was worried about in Fee's eyes.

Hope.

God, there had been so much disappointed hope for them all over the years. Lea wasn't sure if any of them could handle any more of it.

And, well, Lea just didn't think there was much of a chance of him showing up, no matter how much she wished he would.

They needed him.

He was a ghost in the corners, haunting the room.

He was the redness to Helen's eyes that no matter how many times she smiled or laughed or made jokes could erase.

She had spent another holiday morning crying.

Lea had a feeling she was going to spend another holiday night doing the same again.

Her eyes went across the room to the three chairs, and her heart ached in her chest.

"What's that look for, baby?" Shane asked, coming up behind her, wrapping his arms around her center, leaning down to press a sweet kiss to her neck.

"What look?" she deflected, shrugging.

"That guarded, but sad look," he clarified, making her stomach churn. There wasn't much she could keep from him, not after so many years.

So she decided to go with most of the truth.

"Eli."

There was a pause, followed by his deep exhale, making her hair rustle as he pressed his chin into her shoulder.

"Yeah."

"Yeah," she agreed, nodding, her eyes going to the hauntingly empty chairs.

"Some day," he said, giving her a squeeze, before moving away to tear Jake and Joey apart. They were all Mallick. Five years, and all they did was wail on each other and tease one another. Usually, the Mallick way of parenting was pretty hands-off, believing the kids needed to learn to work things out themselves. The only reason he was stepping in was because they had knocked into the sidebar where the buffet was getting set up, complete with open flames for keeping food warm.

Jake and Joey, the twins.

ELI

Six-year-old Jason.
Their little one-year-old angel Sam.
Not one of them had ever met their uncle.
At this rate, maybe they never would.

She was getting accustomed to that knife in her gut sensation after so long, but it still pierced. Just not as bad as it did the time before.

She exhaled, trying to shake the mood, trying to get into the spirit, always wanting to keep holidays upbeat for the kids even if the adults were all struggling.

There was a sudden squeal from the window where Fee and Hunt's youngest girl, Mayla, six and a half years old, was standing inside the curtain, looking out. She had met her uncle, but would never remember.

"Mommy!" she shrieked, making Fee look over her shoulder.
"Yeah, honey?"
"There's a *dog* here! An *ugly* cute dog here!"

Fee's head snapped back, looking at the chairs, then up at Lea, smile triumphant.

Lea's eyes went to the chairs as a feeling she didn't even have a name for spread across her chest.

He was home.
Just like that, the ghosts were gone.

FOURTEEN

Autumn

It was a beautiful house.

If ever I had wondered about how profitable loansharking was, all my questions were answered when we all pulled up in my car - because Peyton adamantly refused to try to climb up and squeeze into the tiny backseat of the cab in Eli's truck - and parked in the winding driveway.

It had to be four-thousand square feet, easily, and every inch of it cost a fortune.

"You okay?" I asked, looking over at Eli in my driver's seat, staring at the house like it might come alive to bite his head off.

Peyton leaned up between the seats, looking at Eli's profile.

"I think this is where people are supposed to make one of those 'band-aid' comments. But I am going to appeal to your stomach. I swear I can smell the turkey from here. Plus, Coop is freaking out," she added, making me aware for the first time that he

ELI

was scratching at the window in the back. Which was weird; he was always good in the car.

"Let's go," Eli agreed, tone a bit dead, making my stomach tense.

It was good we were here.

But it wouldn't be good if he went in there all hollow, like he had been when he got out of prison.

Though, maybe they wouldn't even notice, being too overjoyed with his presence at all.

I reached for my door as Peyton fought with Coop so he didn't launch himself out without her.

She had chosen against the 1950s get-up Eli had actually seriously suggested to her. Instead, she was surprisingly subdued in a long, roomy deep teal, heavy-knit sweater that went slightly off-shoulder and came almost halfway down her thighs. She had black tights on underneath and a pair of camel-colored knee-high boots. There were three necklaces hanging down her chest in varying lengths; her hair was pulled in a side braid, and her makeup was mostly just some mascara.

She was naturally almost painfully gorgeous even if she preferred to usually go a little crazier with her makeup and clothes.

As for me, I struggled with my outfit for almost an hour, trying on one after another in front of Eli before he finally lost patience, jumped up, and went into my closet himself.

He came back with a white sweater with elastic on the waist and sleeves, tight deep brown skinny jeans, and a pair of brown flat, calf-height boots.

And, well, it was leaps and bounds better than anything I had chosen. Because he picked it out, too, I knew it was the right kind of outfit for his type of family functions. I didn't know if it was a dressy-dressy thing or a casual thing. This was something in between. Comfortable, seasonable, but put-together.

I left my hair down, did a little mascara, clasped on some studs, and called it a day.

"Breathe," Peyton said behind my shoulder as she got a hold of Coop, and Eli rounded the hood of the car.

He came up to me, reaching down to link his pinky with mine, then leading us toward the back of the house where there was a giant deck meant for entertainment, and sliding glass doors.

ELI

He didn't knock.
He didn't ring.
Hell, he didn't even pause.
I wondered if maybe he was worried he wouldn't be able to do it if he didn't just charge right in.
I squeezed his pinky as he pushed the door open, then stepped inside.
I lost his pinky, having to follow in behind him.
We stepped into a massive kitchen dominated by giant stainless steel appliances, an obscene amount of cabinets, and an island that would make Martha Stewart jealous.
The scents assaulted me all at once.
Turkey, stuffing, potatoes, broccoli, rolls.
Despite swearing I was too nauseated to eat, my stomach growled as I followed Eli as he went toward the incredibly loud sound of what had to be at least two dozen people down a hall where the walls were lined with collages I wanted to see, but was too worried to stop, following behind as he broke into the doorway, moving to the side to allow me to step in too.
"Oh, my God," Dusty managed to exhale even as her breath sucked in.
"No fucking way," one of the men said. Judging by the tallness, black hair, ice blue eyes, and perfect bone structure, one of his brothers.
All eyes turned, even kids who clearly didn't know what was going on.
But then one child stepped forward.
Well.
She wasn't a child at all, was she?
She was maybe eleven or twelve, tall, thin, black-haired, green-eyed, and almost unfairly pretty even so young.
Her lips parted as she looked at Eli.
And Eli, well, he looked *gutted*.
Eviscerated.
His insides were all sliding out.
Oh, *God.*
She must have been five or six when he went away.
From the looks of things, she was likely the only one who might remember him.

ELI

"Uncle Eli?" she asked, eyes just... devastated.

After her words left her lips, there was utter silence.

And then there was a click of heels as a woman came in from a doorway that must have led to the living room.

"Why is everyone standing around all quie..." she trailed off as she looked around.

She was gorgeous. Tall and lean, but with curves any woman would envy. She had sharp features, long black hair, and keen hazel eyes.

Eyes that landed on Eli.

And stayed.

It was a good couple of seconds of nothing before, surprisingly, it was Eli who broke the silence.

"Mom," he said, voice thick.

She almost staggered back a step before her heels clicked again as she charged across the room, stopping a foot or so in front of her long-lost son.

And then she cocked an arm back.

And slapped him across the face.

The crack was enough to make me start, my entire body stiffening, completely not understanding what was happening.

But not a second after the smack landed, the woman threw herself at her son, her entire body shaking as she sobbed silently.

His arms jerked, unsure for a second, before they raised, closing around the mother he hadn't seen in six years, and holding on tight.

I had to look away, quickly blinking the threat of tears out of my eyes. My gaze drifted over to Fee who was nestled against the chest of a man who looked just like Eli, but with a lot more tattoos. Her eyes were streaming, but she looked right at me and mouthed silently *Thank you.*

"Son," a deep male voice called, drawing my attention back to where Helen had pulled away, and was frantically swiping the tears off her face.

Eli's dad, Charlie, was a glimpse at what Eli - and all his brothers - would look like as they aged. Meaning, they would do so incredibly well. He was tall, square-shouldered, fit, with their same perfect, classically handsome bone structure, light eyes, and black hair. Except his had some streaks of gray and he had some lines by

ELI

his mouth and eyes that somehow made him not look old, but rather, distinguished.

He clamped Eli on the shoulder, then used his shoulder to pull him in for a hug. Sure, it was a manly hug, but it was a hug nonetheless.

Helen's gaze moved from the men, looking right at me, giving me a nod. "This was you," she declared.

"No," I objected immediately. "No. Actually, Fee, Lea, Dusty, and Scotti came to me and--"

"No," she objected, shaking her head, giving me a small smile. "That wasn't what I meant. Though I do think you had a part in him being here as well. But this was you. You brought him back from the dead."

The words landed with impact, making me take a step back.

Where I plowed into Peyton.

When I swirled, I found her standing there, picking stuffing off a spoon.

"What?" she asked, big-eyeing me. "It was just sitting there, looking all warm and soft and delicious."

There were a few chuckles across the room.

Eli pulled away from his father, looking at me. "This is Autumn, for those of you who didn't go behind my back to meet her," he said, sending a pointed, but not unkind, look at Fiona.

"What? Psh, you can't claim to be how I know her. She introduced me to BOB years and years ago," she declared, making me smile.

"Who is Bob?" one of the kids asked, making everyone laugh.

"And this," he said, motioning toward Peyton who wasn't the least bit uncomfortable when all eyes fell on her, "stuffing thief here is Peyton, Autumn's sister."

"Where's the ugly cute dog?" a little girl asked, coming forward.

There was no mistaking it. She looked just like her older sister. She had the same black hair, green eyes, face, and frame, though she was maybe around nine.

And whatever lightness Peyton's appearance had brought about in Eli faded as his eyes fell on the girl who would have just been about three when he went away. Just a baby still, really.

ELI

He swallowed hard, his Adam's apple poking out with the effort. "He's probably trying to find some scraps in the kitchen, Izzy," he said, giving her a smile that was clearly strained.

The girl's brows knitted a little at the familiarity, but turned to grab the hand of a girl who was maybe five or six, but blonde-haired and blue-eyed, and started dragging her toward the living room doorway. "Come on, Mayla, let's find the dog."

The silence fell again, somehow even more oppressive than before.

"Uncle Eli?" the girl who had called to him before repeated, stepping another foot forward in her black leggings and heavy white cabled sweater.

Eli took a breath that was so deep it made his chest shake before he slowly let it out.

"You're really getting good at drawing, Becca," he said, giving her a small smile.

And she launched herself at him.

He actually went back a foot, clearly surprised. I guess maybe he had expected anger, or sadness, or maybe even complete disregard from her.

There seemed to be none of that as she clung to him, her feet dangling a few inches off the ground as his arms went around her, lifting her up slightly.

He was talking in a whisper to her, clearly wanting to keep the moment private, but I swore I heard him say, "I kept them all, Beccs. Every last one."

I had to turn away again, blinking.

"Autumn," a deep voice called at my side, making me start. I looked up to see anther replica of Eli, but this one was slightly older, very serious-looking, and wearing a very expensive-looking suit. "Thank you," he said, ducking his head a little. "From all of us, thank you."

"This is Ryan," Dusty said, moving in next to him, her hand, oddly, at her throat, like she was trying to rub away something there.

Ryan leaned down, kissing her temple, whispering *Breathe* to her.

"It's nice to meet you," I said, giving him a smile because I truly did mean that. I was happy to meet them all, to get to know the people that helped shape Eli into the man he had become.

ELI

I glanced over, seeing Fee and Hunt in a circle with Eli and Becca.

"Come on," Peyton said, linking her arm through mine, giving Ryan and Dusty a smile. "Let's go mingle while your man gets reacquainted. You know," she said loudly enough for all to hear, clearly trying to lighten the mood, "it is an absolute shame to be in a room with this many good-looking men when not one of them seems single. And who are you?" she asked, stopping in front of one of aforementioned good-looking men. This one, I was pretty sure, wasn't a Mallick. His coloring was off, his hair a little darker, his eyes brown, his bone structure, while drool-worthy, was different. If anything, oddly, he looked almost like a male version of Scotti.

"Kingston, honey," he said, giving her a warm, brotherly smile. "I'm Scotti's brother. And that," he said, waving out, happy to make introductions, "is Atlas. And there's Nixon. And, finally, over there, is Rush."

"Strange names," Peyton declared as one of the guys - Atlas - moved in closer.

"Yeah?" he asked, head ducked to the side as he looked at her. "Says the chick with a name associated with a mini skirt and nosy school board."

There was a pause, Peyton's eyes going wide. They didn't know it, but I did. That look was a rare one for her. She was *impressed.*

"Was that just a *Harper Valley P.T.A.* reference?"

His smile was charmed, happy, it was clear, that she got it. "Sure was."

"You're on your own," Peyton said, turning to me, slapping her spoon down in my hand, then linking her arm through Atlas' and leading him away.

"I like her," Fee declared, stepping in beside me. "She's got balls. And don't worry; there won't be any jealous woman brawls. Atlas is the only single one of Scotti's brothers."

My head swiveled, looking for Eli, finding him in a circle with his brothers, looking completely uncomfortable, his jaw tight, his stance stiff, but not quite freaking out.

"There was a little bit of drama that went down on his release day," Scotti explained, moving in next to her brother, watching the

ELI

Mallick men. "No one could get in touch with him, and they were worried something might go down, and he would be unprepared."

I could feel my eyes rounding, my pulse starting to pound.

See, that was the weird thing.

I didn't get to see Eli being a loanshark, being a criminal, so even though I knew that was his past, I didn't exactly associate him with it. It was a bit, ah, sobering, to hear his past might have been coming back to bite him in the ass.

"Don't worry. It turned out that it was nothing, but they are likely just filling him in on all that drama," Scotti explained.

"He looks like he wants to bolt," Fiona observed.

"He's tense today," I agreed. "This was how he was when he first got out. He was rigid and guarded. Slowly, he's been letting that go. But when he woke up this morning, yeah, he was like this."

"He will adjust," Scotti said, voice hopeful.

He would.

That was true.

The biggest feat was getting him in the door.

"I honestly had no faith in you," Lea declared as she walked up, handing me a glass of red wine. "I don't mean to be offensive," she clarified. "It just seemed like such a pipe dream. But you did it," she said with a smile as she clinked her glass to mine.

"Actually, I didn't," I admitted. "I wasn't comfortable going behind his back, so that night, I told him what happened. And we didn't talk about it again."

"But you're here," Lea said, brows furrowed.

"I honestly don't know what the change was. He brought it up to me. This was all his choice. I didn't want to pressure him."

They nodded, seeming to understand, obviously not caring about the how so long as he was there.

"Is Becca okay?" Scotti asked.

Fee shrugged a shoulder. "She's too stubborn to admit it even if she was upset. She's with Helen in the kitchen getting the gravy ready."

"She looked broken up," Kingston observed.

"She was six when he went away," Fee agreed. "She asked me where Uncle Eli was every single time the family got together for over a year."

ELI

"I almost wish my guys had a recollection of him," Scotti started, then winced. "Is that bad to say?"

"No," I said, shaking my head. "I understand that. I'm sure he wishes he knew who, well," I paused, but there was no delicate way to phrase it, "any of the kids are."

"Poor Eli," Fee repeated the mantra of the day, exhaling hard. "This must be kind of disorienting after so long."

I was pretty sure that was a huge understatement.

"I can't believe Helen slapped him," Dusty said as she moved in, seeming a bit more relaxed than she had a moment before.

"Really?" Lea asked with a smirk. "She whacked Shane across the shoulders last Easter because he went to reach for the food before she finished serving. Broke the wooden spoon," she added with a smirk.

"So," Fee said, looking over at me. "What has Eli been doing? I mean, aside from you," she said with a smirk.

"And on that note, I'm out," Kingston declared, walking over toward a woman who was sitting on the floor playing with one of the kids.

"Um, mostly he's been working on his pieces for the show."

"Pieces? Show?" Lea asked, brows together.

Crap.

That really should have been his information to hand out.

He was so proud of himself for getting on his feet with his art.

And, judging by the few small non-gallery pieces he let me see, he had every right to feel amazing about himself. Even from the wonderful sketch he had done of me, he had come so far.

"Oh, ah, Eli has a wall at the gallery in a couple days."

"What?" they all asked in unison, eyes wide.

"You mean he finally did it?" Dusty asked. "He's been passionate about art all his life, but just never pursued it."

"He, ah, pursued it in prison. It was his, um, hustle while he was inside. He used his commissary money to buy art supplies, then did pieces for the other prisoners. For a profit. One of the guys liked him enough to drop his name at the gallery. When he got out, he went and showed them some pieces, and they wanted him on the spot. So, yeah, he's been working on his pieces for that since he's been out. And doing some renovations on his place."

ELI

"That's one thing about these Mallick men," Lea said with an appreciative smile, "they all know how to swing a hammer. It's obnoxiously hot."

Okay.

That was so true.

I mean I was always progressive about gender roles, and often dated men softer, sweeter, more clueless about plumbing than me. But I was sure there was something primal about seeing a man who could fix things. Like maybe we saw them as better protectors and providers or something.

I had totally jumped Eli one night after watching him lay flooring at his place. All those muscles clenching. The hint of sweat. The big strong hands. Oh, yeah. It was effective.

"Autumn," Eli's voice called, making me jump and turn on my low heel. "Come here for a sec," he asked, holding an arm out.

"Aw, he wants you to meet his brothers," Fee declared, smile going warm. "Go on. We'll discuss aphrodisiacs later."

I moved away from a group I was somewhat comfortable with and across the room to one I didn't know, aside from Ryan thanking me.

But then Eli's arm went around me, pulling me in close. I think, just as much for his comfort as mine, and all felt better in the world.

"You met Ryan," he said nodding his head toward him. "This is Hunt, Fee's husband. And that is Shane, Lea's. And finally, Mark, Scotti's husband."

"It's nice to meet all of you. I'd say I've heard a lot, but that would be a lie," I admitted, and I could feel Eli silently chuckle as he gave me a squeeze.

"So you're the one who stole Coop," the big one - Shane - accused, smirk toying with his lips. "Know how many animals shelters I've trolled these past six years?"

"No one put up any fliers!" I accused, big-eyeing them.

"No one had any pictures," Shane said with a shrug. "Though Hunt did draw some shit up, but I dunno. Guess they never crossed your path."

"He's had a good life eating shoes and destroying copies of *Die Muthafucka*," Eli supplied, giving me a knowing smile. He had totally hunkered down, went searching, and tracked down a signed

ELI

copy of the book for Peyton that he planned to give her for Christmas.

Because he was thinking that far ahead.

About her, so therefore about me.

My heart squeezed every time I thought about that.

And maybe I wondered what he was going to get me.

"And I got updates."

Oh, shit.

I felt myself stiffen, not knowing why he would bring that up. Things were going smoothly. That was a huge bump in the road.

"Updates on what?" Mark asked.

"Coop. How he was doing."

There was a strained silence as that sank in. "You took her letters while you were inside?" Ryan asked, jaw tight.

"The first one because I had no fucking idea who she was," he admitted, obviously just wanting to clear the air. "She told me she had Coop and that he was okay. Then there were other letters after that."

You could feel it vibrating off the men around us, an uncomfortable throbbing anger they were all desperately trying to keep under control. Because they had him back, and they didn't want to push him away.

But he had refused their letters for six years, while receiving those of a woman he didn't know from Eve.

There was a sinking in my belly at that, at the clear hurt in Mark's eyes, in the clenched fists of Shane's hands.

"Autumn!" a voice called, making me start. I looked over my shoulder to find Helen standing in the doorway. "Want to come in the kitchen and help out?"

"By that she means she is going to give you the third degree," Eli supplied. "But don't worry. The fact that you own a sex store really works in your favor. Plus, she has the wine refills. You'll be fine," he assured me, kissing my temple, then pulling his arm from around me so I could follow Helen to where she disappeared into the kitchen.

My stomach knotted as I looked around for my sister, thinking a buffer would be ideal. I found her in a corner having what seemed to be a good-natured, but heated argument with Atlas.

ELI

Sensing my eyes, she looked over, but gave my desperate look a shrug. She wasn't going to save me.

With that, I left the room, taking a deep breath, reminding myself that wine refills would certainly help soften the social discomfort.

"No, I'm just saying, you guys all need to get a Wand," I walked into Fee declaring to them all, brandishing a slotted spoon, half-turned away from the stove.

"Fee," Helen said, smile wicked. "Those first went into production in the sixties. I've had one since before you were even born."

"Oh, shit!" Lea said, smiling huge. "Your mother-in-law just schooled you in sex toys. How embarrassing for you."

"Says the woman who didn't even *own* a *vibrator* before I took her to go pick one out. I mean how did you survive for so long without your own personal Buzz Nightgear?"

I had been taking a sip of my wine, and almost got reminded how unpleasant it was for it to come out of your nose I snorted so loud.

"I was in a spell of celibacy!" Lea insisted, rolling her eyes.

"With a hair chastity belt to boot," Fee agreed, smiling. "Grew that shit out like Rapunzel."

"Oh my God, Fee," Dusty whisper-hissed at her, eyes big. "Autumn doesn't know you're joking."

"I'm not joking," Fee clarified. "She thought if she gave up shaving, it would keep her from falling into bed with the wrong type of man. A for effort though, right, Lea?" she asked, giving Lea a fake-angry look because Lea was giving her one first.

"I would tell you they're not always like this," Scotti said, moving in beside me, already refilling my wine glass. "But they're always like this. On Easter, Fee used the term 'invagination' at the dinner table."

"It was the dessert table and the kids were in the other room trading egg goodies. Geez!"

Helen looked over at me as I smiled between them, liking the ease with which they discussed things, enjoying the openness, it reminding me of my sister and me. "Welcome to the family, Autumn," she told me. "Better to jump on the bandwagon now, or

ELI

they will get you drunk and make you admit things like they did with Dusty."

"You make us sound like monsters," Fee objected. "We got her drunk *on her birthday* where she *just so happened* to admit to doing some midnight jackhammering during her shut-in days."

"Oh, my God," Dusty whimpered, closing her eyes, her cheeks heating, but she was smiling.

Feeling for her, knowing some people - no matter how open with sex they were with their partners - just couldn't discuss it in mixed company, I decided to jump in. "You know what one is worth a try?" I asked, watching as their eyes went to me. "The butterfly. Hands-free," I added. "It straps on. Especially if you get the one with the G-spo..." I trailed off as a pretty little toddler came swaying in.

Fee gave me a smile. "Know your audience," she advised. "Three and under, you can pretty much get away with saying anything you want. Three and a half and up, they start repeating stuff and asking questions."

"Like when Mayla blared out over Sunday dinner that a man at mommy's work must have been really bad because he got a spanking."

I laughed at that.

"She's leaving out the part that the man in question is this super alpha asshole coach at Becca's school who is a secret submissive."

"I think I know exactly who you're talking about," I chimed in, smiling. "He comes into the shop with a coach shirt on, always being a complete asshole unless I bark at him to take his attitude somewhere else. Then he's like an obedient little puppy."

"Alright, I hear the alcohol is in here," Peyton's voice declared. "What?" she asked, looking at the bemused faces of all the women. "What were we talking about?" she finished as she took my wine out of my hands.

"Submissive men," Lea supplied.

"Who like getting spanked," Fee finished.

"Who *doesn't* like getting spanked?" she asked, casual as could be, not a worry in the world. You had to respect that about her. She genuinely did not give a fuck.

"She makes a good point," Fee agreed, turning back to the stove to stir whatever was in the pot.

ELI

"Scotti, your brother is yummy, but his taste in movies is absolutely abysmal. So, obviously, we're over. I apologize in advance for his broken heart."

"You know," Scotti said, watching Peyton with a look I didn't quite understand, "I totally believe that that is possible."

"So, Autumn owns a sex store and steals dogs," Helen declared, smirking. "What do you do, Peyton?"

"I scare little old ladies from behind the desk at the library. And read a lot of twisted horror porn," she admitted openly, clearly charming Helen who - as I was starting to see - was nothing like your usual mom. I guessed when you raised five loansharking sons while married to their loansharking father, that kind of went with the territory.

"Well, you guys seem like you will fit right in," Helen declared, holding out two bowls. "Now get to filling so we can eat."

With that, we did.

I had never seen so much food in my life. Endless platters left that kitchen to fill the chafing dishes that ran along the sideboards from one end of the room to another. There was turkey, stuffing, mashed potatoes, sweet potato fries, green bean casserole, broccoli, corn, balsamic glazed carrots, peppers, onions, and zucchini, cranberry sauce that was clearly made from scratch, and three different kinds of rolls.

They were going to have to wheelbarrow me out of the damn house.

"Coop!" Charlie snapped, getting the dog's attention from where he was whining at the kids' table. To everyone's - especially my - surprise, Coop jumped up, ran over, and laid down at the man's side, silent for the entire meal before Charlie patted his head and declared, "Alright, go ahead." And he nearly toppled two kids to dive under the table and clean up the mess the kids had made of the floor.

Over dinner, conversation had been kept light - mostly thanks to Fee, Mark, Peyton, and Rush, with everyone else simply piling onto their conversation starters, keeping everything upbeat and easy, something that had Eli relaxing in his seat beside me.

Once he finished eating, his hand went under the table to give my knee a reassuring squeeze.

ELI

"Alright," Kingston said after a couple minutes of after-dinner talk. "We got the clean-up," he declared, sending his brothers and sister a hard look that had them all moving to stand.

"King, that's not..." Helen started.

"Have some family time, Helen," he demanded, voice soft, eyes wise, as he started collecting plates.

With that, the Mallick clan, sans the Rivers clan and their women, got up and moved to the living room which was decidedly smaller than the enormous dining room, but still a good two times the size of the average living space with a long gray sectional, a few accent chairs, and a collage of pictures lining one whole wall.

Squished, I took a page out of Lea's book and sat up on the arm of the couch beside Eli as the kids came barreling in and out, making conversation a bit more of a concept than an actuality.

I had never seen thirteen children all in one space before. And while Becca was more on her way to adult than child, her playing mom to the littler ones was creating just as much noise as the four, five, and six-year-olds.

It wasn't until a good fifteen minutes later, much of the cleaning clatter in the kitchen dying down, that a three-year-old came walking in, calm, quiet, looking around.

She, well, looked like a Mallick with her short black hair and light blue eyes. But as she got closer, you could actually see an odd hint of brown flecks in his eyes as well. If I had to bet, I would put money on her being Mark and Scotti's. There was just something in those eyes that looked like the Rivers brothers (and sister).

Any conversation that had been going on halted immediately as she locked eyes on Eli, then confidently made her way over, like it was the most normal thing in the world.

She climbed up in the small space between Eli and Helen who was seated next to him, then went right ahead and sat down on his leg, watching him with those unique eyes.

"I'm Eli," she said with a firm nod, like it was the most normal thing in the world.

Eli.

Likely short for Elizabeth.

My heart seized in my chest, every inch of me going tight.

This was what I was sure he was dreading.

ELI

The adults were one thing, adults who had him for thirty some-odd years.

The kids, these kids who had no idea who he was, that was what he was dreading.

The questions.

The lack of recognition.

"Hey Eli," Eli said, voice thick, giving her a smile that was clear was pained.

And then the adorable, innocent little thing did it.

He gutted him.

"Who are you?"

I felt a knife to my own gut, could see the same pain on everyone else's faces. I couldn't even imagine how he was feeling.

My gaze found his, his eyes glassy. He half-turned away, more toward his mother, his hand raising, pressing into his eyes, struggling to keep it together.

"Little Eli," Becca's confident voice called, old enough to be able to sense when the adults needed a minute, good enough to be willing to step in and give them it. "Come here."

Little Eli hopped off her uncle's lap and ran over to her. "I'm not *little*," she declared, voice firm as she led her out of the room.

"It's okay," Helen said, her arms going around Eli. His forehead fell forward into her shoulder, his body shaking as he sucked in a breath. "I know," she said, kissing the side of his head. "I know."

I had to look away, reaching up to swipe tears off my cheeks.

When I looked up, everyone else was similarly affected, the women turned into their men's shoulders, men who were barely keeping it together themselves.

Hell, even Peyton as she stepped in and saw the scene - having been helping with the clean-up - looked taken aback. If there was one thing I knew for sure about Peyton, it was that she was a hard nut to crack. I didn't remember the last time I had seen her cry. It might have actually been when we were kids. She quipped when I was getting the, as she called it, 'waterworks,' that she had sold her tear ducts on the black market to finance the upkeep of her amazing hair.

So seeing her eyes go wide then glisten slightly was another knife to the gut.

ELI

Sensing my inspection, her gaze found mine and her eyes went *horrified*.

Oh, fuck no, she mouthed before turning on her heel and disappearing.

When I looked back, Eli's breathing looked even, and his mother was whispering something between the two of them into his ear as she stroked his hair slightly.

Whatever it was she was saying seemed to help him bring his composure back.

A moment later, he took a deep breath and pulled away.

Her hands cradled his face.

"Now fuck your parole. Go get a drink. It looks like Autumn needs a refill too," she added, making me start and immediately jump up.

I knew a mom-command when I heard one.

And even though she wasn't actually my mother, I felt compelled to do exactly what she said.

"Yeah, I'm empty," I said with a smile I hoped met my eyes as Eli's head turned in my direction.

He gave me a smile that must have matched my own, and, yeah, it totally didn't reach. "Can't have that," he agreed, standing, and moving toward me, putting an arm around my hips and leading me out of the room.

But not toward the kitchen where the booze was. No, he led me out toward the front of the house, setting my glass away, grabbing some random jacket off a hook, and pulling me outside with him. He didn't stop pulling until he was leaning up against the back of my car, reaching to pull my front to face his, then draping the jacket across my back, using the sides to pull me against his body.

His arms went around my center, his face in my neck.

There wasn't even a hint of hesitation before my arms went around him, holding on as tight as he was holding me.

"This is even harder than I expected," he admitted, voice rough, raw - a half-healed wound ripped open.

Having no words, no comfort other than my presence, my listening ear, I just squeezed him tighter, and let him drain it out.

"She has my fucking *name*, and she doesn't know who I am."

Oh, God.

ELI

I needed to keep it under control. I was supposed to be the one comforting him; I couldn't bring on the tears again.

"She will know you, Eli. She's so little. Most of her childhood memories will have you in them."

"And Becca?" he asked, voice barely more than a choked whisper. "And Izzy? They're closer to teens than kids. Izzy wouldn't even come close to me."

That was, unfortunately, true.

Most of the kids had kept a bit of a wide birth around me, Eli, and Peyton, all of us being strangers to them.

"Becca remembered you," I tried.

He swallowed hard, pressing his face into my neck. "She told me she thought I didn't love her anymore, Autumn." Oh, hell. Okay. There was no way to stop a few tears. "Since I never responded to any of her letters. I did that. I ripped away the comfort that she should have had in knowing that her whole family loved and supported and appreciated her. I made a part of her, maybe only a small part, but a part of her perfect little self think that there was even a chance that she was unlovable. I fucking did that."

"You did what you thought was best," I tried, hearing the thickness in my voice, trying to breathe through it, get control over myself.

"And I fucked everything up," he growled, voice getting an edge that had me stiffening.

Angry.

At himself, sure.

But still angry.

And because I knew him, I knew that the last thing he would want was to lose it at his first family gathering in six years, a gathering he had convinced himself would never happen.

My hands slid down his tense arms to curl around the fists he had curled behind my back. "Hey," I said, pulling back slightly so I could look at him. "Don't do this."

"Do what? Say the truth?" he asked, a mix of broken and pissed, a combination that would not be good in another minute or two. "All I have done since I walked down that street that night was fucking wrong. I have fucked everything up with every choice I have made."

"You don't believe that--"

ELI

"I haven't--"

"No," I cut him off. "I'm talking," I clarified, pleased when he looked taken aback for a second, the new emotion wiping a bit of the anger away. "You don't believe that what you did that night was wrong. In fact, not a single person in the world - including the asshole you beat up - thinks what you did was wrong. You did the right thing for the right reasons and got the wrong judgment in court."

"I beat a man half to death, Autumn. The judgment wasn't wrong. I did do that."

He wasn't wrong, and I was having a hard time coming up with a rebuttal, but I wanted to keep him talking. His body was relaxing with every word.

"You're talking about it like you walked up to some random innocent and beat him. You stopped a bully from possibly killing a woman he was supposed to honor and cherish. He should have gone away for that. In lieu of that, you should have been up on charges that were thrown away given the situation. It was a miscarriage of justice from the second that battered woman was allowed to be taken away by the very people who allowed her abuser to keep hurting her. You did the right thing in trying to protect her."

"You don't have to raise your voice, sweetheart," he said, making me realize that I had almost been yelling. I wasn't the best with strong emotions, and they had a tendency to burst out of me in almost manic explosions of feeling. "I'm listening," he added.

"I can't imagine what it felt like when you realized you were going to lose six years of your life, Eli. I, I just... I can't fathom that. But because I can't even wrap my head around it, I know - not *think* - know that whatever decision you needed to make to be able to survive those six years was the right decision. There are consequences to every choice we make, good and bad, you just have to deal with them as they come. You're here now, Eli. You can make amends. You can spend the next forty years showing Becca just how perfect she is, how lovable. You can meet all those kids and show them how awesome their Uncle Eli is. You can mend bonds with your brothers, sisters-in-law, and parents. You have that chance. But you aren't going to accomplish that by being out here bitching about a choice that didn't go the way you planned."

There.

ELI

That about covered it.

I felt like I was shaking, knowing some of the things were a bit aggressive, worried it would drive a wedge, but knowing down to my marrow that he needed to hear it regardless.

When I finished though, he didn't seem mad or upset.

Instead, he was watching me like I had sprouted another head and it started singing in Swahili.

He looked at me like I confused him.

Then, slowly, his lips twitched, then tugged upward into a smile. "I've had my ass handed to me a lot in my life," he started oddly. "My mom used to whoop it when I stepped out of line. My brothers did it just to fuck with me. It came with the job as I aged up. But I've never had my ass handed to me *verbally* before. That's quite a hook you got there, sweetheart."

"Well," I said, feeling oddly confused and proud at the same time, "you were losing your shit. You needed your ass kicked a little."

"Guess I did," he agreed, smiling fully. "Thank you."

"Hey, if ever you need an ass-kicking, you know where to find me," I said, trying to keep things light, especially because there was something deep in his eyes that I couldn't place, and therefore felt worried about.

"Good to know. You can verbally whoop mine," he agreed, eyes going molten, "and I can physically whoop yours from time to time."

This was *not* a good time - or place - to be getting completely turned on, but it was totally happening anyway.

"Don't tease me," I said, leaning into his chest.

"Not teasing," he said, hand sliding out from under the jacket to go to the back of my neck, sliding into my hair, and pulling to make my head angle up. The pain seemed to spread from my scalp and shoot right between my legs. "We're going back to my place tonight so we don't have to worry about traumatizing your sister."

"Right," I said with a grin, "because she's such a shrinking violet."

"Might have to stop at your store for some goodies though," he added, eyes full of promise, making an almost intolerable pressure press into my lower stomach.

ELI

"You!" Peyton's voice called, making me jolt backward a step, the jacket started to fall, making me reach for it to pull it back up as she walked up, pointing at Eli.

"Me?" Eli asked, leaning back against the car, smirking at her.

"Yes, *you!*" she hissed.

"What'd I do?"

"You made me *feel* things, you monster," she declared, crossing her arms, small-eyeing him.

To that, he threw his head back and laughed a little. "Can't be having that, can we?"

"No," she agreed, shaking her head in exasperation, "we absolutely can not."

Eli reached out, dragging a very stiff Peyton in for a hug. "Don't fucking change, Peyton."

"Why would I?" she asked, trying to pull off unaffected, but I knew my sister, and she was totally having a moment. "There's no improving on this," she added, even as her hands went up and gave him a quick, tentative hug back. "Okay, you big sap. Let me go," she added a moment later, pulling away. "What? You're not getting enough affection from this one?" she asked, waving a hand at me. "She's like a clinging vine for chrissakes."

I totally had to force affection on her from time to time. Mostly because I felt like she needed it, no matter how much she denied it.

With that, though, she turned on her heel and started toward the house.

"Also, we're having dessert. And it looks like you guys will need to cut my fat ass out of the wall and take me out with a crane."

"Some day," Eli said, shaking his head at her, "some guy is going to come around and throw an entire Home Depot department full of wrenches in her works."

"Won't that be awesome to watch?" I agreed, moving in when he held out an arm for me to step into.

"Thank you," he told me a second later, pressing a kiss into my temple.

"For her? I don't think you've woken up to her standing in a corner with a knife yet. You might not be thanking me then."

He chuckled at that, giving me a squeeze.

ELI

"Yeah, for her. For you. For this. For taking that hollow shell I was when I got out, and steadily filling me back up."

Oh, my poor heart.

I couldn't take any more of the up and down.

But thank God we were ending the conversation on such an up.

I filled him up.

That might have been the best compliment I had ever received.

"You're very welcome," I said, meaning it. "I really love your family."

"They'll be happy to adopt you. It seems like Ma just keeps building a longer table."

"Well, that's good. Because I don't think Peyton will ever give them up. She follows her stomach. She swears the only time she's ever been in love was with the absolutely perfect cheesy lasagne we got once at a restaurant that went out of business a week after she had it."

"We better go help her eat the dessert so she doesn't bitch the whole way home about how much we let her eat."

She would totally do that, too.

We walked into the dining room, making our choices.

Eli stopped on the way back to the table, going by habit toward his mother, but stopping, and moving to sit down next to Little Eli instead.

"That's a nice truck," he said as I stood watching, my breath caught in my chest.

"It has a backseat," Little Eli declared, holding up the bright blue pickup.

"I see that. I have a truck just like that. With a backseat."

"Yeah?"

"Yeah," he agreed as Mark walked over to sit down on Little Eli's other side. "Maybe one day your daddy can bring you over, and we can take a ride in it."

"To the beach?" she asked, perking up immediately.

"Anywhere you want," Eli agreed, giving her a smile. "And my name is Eli, by the way."

"That's my name!" Little Eli declared.

"You stole it from me," Eli agreed.

ELI

Little Eli looked at her father. "Did you?"

"Sure did," Mark agreed. "I thought Eli was pretty cool, so I thought you'd like to have the name of someone cool."

"He has a truck!" Little Eli declared, adorably oblivious to how big the moment was.

"I have a truck too," Mark insisted.

"He has a *red* truck."

Eli and I laughed at that, knowing his truck was not, in fact, red, and that hopefully Little Eli didn't have her heart set on that.

"I owe you," a deep, smooth male voice said as he moved to stand beside me, watching Eli *zoom zoom* with Little Eli's truck, plowing right through the kid's slice of cheesecake, an action that the little girl found hilarious.

Charlie Mallick.

There was something intimidating in him, something that spoke of his past, something in the way he carried himself. But I had seen him throw a little girl up in the air until his arms must have felt like Jell-O. Being a grandparent had obviously softened him.

"No, you don't," I objected, shaking my head. "Believe me, I wanted this too. He needed this so badly."

Oh, crap.

I was getting all misty-eyed again.

What was wrong with me?

"There isn't a doubt in my mind, hon, that we never would have seen him at our table again if not for you. He told his brother that he was dead just a couple weeks ago. You brought him back to life. I owe you. From what I hear, you have your life on track. You don't have need for anything I could usually offer. But I can offer you this," he said, waving his hand out toward the room as a whole.

Oh, Jesus, with the waterworks.

Peyton was never going to let me live all this crying down.

But, the fact of the matter was, family was nice.

I had always had Peyton, and she meant the world to me, but I never really had a chance to experience a fun, loving, supportive family. Just getting a couple hours in one made me want more.

And Charlie was offering it to me.

It was one thing when it was just acceptance, just the fact that you had to have a place at your table for your child's spouse. It was a complete other to welcome them with open arms.

ELI

Sensing my tears even though my head was ducked, Charlie's arm went around my lower back, pulling me close enough to kiss my temple. "Welcome to the family, Autumn."

Eli chose that exact moment to look over.

And his eyes went heavy with feeling, seeming to understand exactly what was happening.

"Bitch, get it together," Peyton declared as she moved into the spot Charlie vacated. "Or drown it in chocolate cake. You're embarrassing the family," she declared in a dead-on mobster impression, hand motions and all.

But I was still being a sap.

"I think this is our new family, Peyton."

She thought on that, looking around, then gave me a nod.

"Fine, then you're just being a sap. Ovary-up, woman! Oh, is that an apple danish?" she asked, making a bee-line for the pile.

"I think she was serious about the crane thing," Eli told me, walking right up, and pulling me to him.

"She doesn't do much by half," I agreed.

"Pops just welcomed you to the family, didn't he?"

I felt like this was shaky ground.

What if Eli wasn't at that place yet, and his father was overstepping?

"Ah, kinda," I admitted, because it was true.

His arms folded around my back, pulling my hips to his.

"Honey, wait till you see Christmas."

And, well, I maybe sorta kinda totally lit the heck up.

I was part of the family.

Maybe, possibly, someday, I might actually be a Mallick myself.

FIFTEEN

Eli

We left it there.

It wasn't something we discussed or planned on, but something that had just happened.

After Helen stuffed a plate for Peyton to take home, and she spent the five-minute car ride back to their place complaining about how we could let her eat so much, we took Coop for a short walk which wasn't even necessary since the kids had run him ragged, and we both got ready for bed.

And we didn't talk about it.

Autumn had needed to go back on our plans to get kinky at my place, to pass out almost immediately because, apparently, sex toys were a hot commodity when put on Black Friday sales, and she was even soliciting Peyton to help her out. I had offered, but she had a kind and roundabout way of - essentially - telling me I would be in the way. Because Peyton had worked for her here and there, she knew how to use the system and where all the items were while I

ELI

would likely just keep asking questions which would only slow them down.

I understood that.

So when I got up, them so long gone that the coffee machine had already bleeped off, I took Coop with me back to my place so I could put the finishing touches on the pieces for the show.

One day.

Before, it had seemed like a monumental thing, like a life-or-death situation, like it was my only chance in life.

That day, as I put a splash of color here or a small detail there, it suddenly didn't seem quite as life-altering.

If it went well, great.

If it flopped, well, I'd survive.

Maybe, subconsciously, I had been putting so much pressure on myself to earn the approval of others when all I really had needed all along was the approval of those who loved me.

I won't say it was easy walking in there, facing them down, knowing that while there was more relief and love than anything else, that there was also resentment and anger as well. They wouldn't tell me that. In fact, I suspected all of it would likely not come out for a good, long time.

By then, I hoped I would be better prepared for it.

Because that entire day just showed me that whatever pain I felt in prison with cutting them off paled completely in comparison to having to go there and deal with the consequences of my actions.

My parents.

My brothers.

My sisters-in-law.

But most especially, the kids.

Becca who was hurt most by it.

The ten others who I didn't even know, hadn't ever met, had to *ask* whose were whose.

That shit gutted me in a way I wasn't aware of before.

But I was going to make an effort. I was going to get together with them all, family by family, and I was going to get to know them, let them get to know me.

My mother had been right.

I had plenty of time.

Most of them were six and under.

ELI

Almost all their memories would include me.

As for Becca, well, I had some work to do.

But she was willing to work at it with me.

We would get there someday too.

I hadn't given them my address because, with everything else going on, it simply hadn't come up. But I had made sure I had given my mother my cell. As such, I had thirty-two texts from her, Pops, Ryan, Mark, Shane, Fee, Lea, Dusty, Scotti and - because she apparently had her own cell - Becca.

I could tell as I fetched my phone by the squeezing sensation in my chest that this was the right thing. I had forgotten over the course of six long years what it was like to feel it, the love, the loyalty, the sense of belonging.

It wouldn't be easy, I knew.

There was still work to be done.

On myself.

If I couldn't shut them out, if I couldn't shut myself down completely, well, then I needed to find a way to keep control, even when the anger came.

I wouldn't be going back into the *family business*.

I was sure no one was even thinking that was a remote possibility.

But even without that, there would be triggers.

Pretending there weren't would only set me up for failure.

Autumn had been right one night after a session that had left marks on her back and butt again, when she said I had her now. I did. And having a safe, consensual, mutually enjoyable outlet like that was helping more than I could express.

She had also suggested boxing.

Which, well, was a great idea.

I was a little pissed at myself for not thinking of it sooner.

I needed that hitting sensation.

That was why using a flogger, a paddle, my bare palm, on Autumn helped.

That violence was necessary to purge the rage.

So hitting a bag - or another person - at a boxing gym was the perfect way to keep myself under control.

I was going to look into it as soon as my show was over.

198

ELI

"Yo yo bro," Bobby called, letting himself in as I was becoming accustomed to. "You barely been around, man," he said, coming around the bend to the kitchen, coffees in hand.

"Been with Autumn. And yesterday, I went to Thanksgiving."

He paused in handing me my cup. "Like with your family?" he asked, voice hesitant.

"Yeah, with my family."

"Man!" he said, grinning huge, like it in any way affected him. "That's good fucking news. See? I knew you needed to dip your wick. A woman has a way of putting shit in perspective. Fuck the stupid and stubborn right out of you."

Eloquent he was not.

Wise, well, he often was.

"So, me and Nat are excited for your show, man. She went shopping and got me, what she called 'appropriate attire.' Apparently, nothing I own would work."

"Remind me to buy Nat something nice for Christmas, man."

"Don't deserve her."

"Nope," I agreed, but gave him a smile. "I don't deserve Autumn either. But here we both are."

"Two assholes who lucked the fuck out," he agreed, tapping his cup to mine.

"You can say that again."

"Don't look at me."

That was how Autumn greeted me at her apartment later that night, coming in at almost ten which meant that she had spent sixteen hours on her feet at that store.

"Um..."

"Don't look at me either," Peyton demanded as she came in, closing, and locking the door.

And, well, of course I looked at them.

The day took a toll on them.

ELI

Autumn was pale with purple bruises under her eyes. Her mascara was swiped in an arch on her eyelids. But otherwise, she looked like herself. In need of food, a shower, and bed, but herself.

"I said don't!" Peyton shrieked as my eyes went over to her.

And Peyton, well, she was fresh-faced.

As in, without a single trace of makeup.

And she was actually dressed in plain bluejeans that I didn't think she would be caught dead in, and a simple black long-sleeve tee. Sure, she had her multi-colored hair and her nose ring. But that was it. She was without any of her usual embellishments.

She looked about five years younger.

And almost painfully sweet and innocent.

I think I finally understood why she worked so hard on her makeup and style. She didn't want anyone to see her and think 'sweet and innocent' or anything even akin to it. And, to be fair, it would be a pretty big shock to them if they saw that and then she opened her mouth and proved it wrong.

I mean, she absolutely *was* sweet, but only to her select few people. She certainly didn't want that getting out to the masses.

"My turkey coma made me sleep through my three AM alarm that would have made this," she said, waving a hand at her face, "disappear. Ugh, I need a shower. And a good kill," she declared, moving across the room, snatching a book off the coffee table, and disappearing down the hall.

I looked over at Autumn, leaning against the counter, dead on her feet. "Come on, I'll give you a foot rub, and you can get some sleep."

"That was practically porn," she said, attempting a tired smile, and following me into the bedroom.

So I rubbed her feet and she went to sleep.

And we didn't talk about them.

My family.

Which was why, the following day, I hadn't been prepared.

"I can totally wear a corset dress and leather boots, right?" Peyton called from the hall as Autumn fiddled with her outfit.

The show was in an hour.

I had gone over early in the morning to get everything all set up and get the plans from the coordinator. Then I had met Autumn for a late lunch when she closed the shop early.

ELI

I stopped by my place to snag some clothes, then made my way to the girls' apartment to, well, wait - and in Autumn's case, watch - for them to get ready.

"Oh my God!" Autumn hissed, eyes huge in her reflection. "No, you absolutely can not wear a corset--"

The door burst open, and Peyton walked in in a simple, rather elegant, cocktail dress. Her hair was down, but curled. Her makeup was minimalist. The only thing she had on that screamed 'Peyton' was her black shoes that had rainbow-colored unicorn horns for heels.

"Ha, look at that face," Peyton said with a smile as she moved to sit near me at the edge of the bed. "I know how to dress for things, *Mom*," she said, rolling her eyes. "I like that dress."

I fucking *loved* that dress.

In fact, I loved it so much, that when she came out in it, I had to peel up the skirt, and fuck her against the wall until she screamed my name.

It was a cobalt blue with a slightly lighter blue lace over it. Where the bust scalloped on the lower level, the lace went to her neckline. Sleeveless, and just short enough to show off some leg and keep it classy, it set off her eyes, her skin, her hair, and was fucking perfect.

I'd have been proud to have her on my arm wearing a potato sack - or the hideously oversized tees she sometimes wore to bed - but having her on my arm at my first show looking like she did? Yeah, I was fucking puffed up in the chest.

"Alright," Autumn said, taking a deep breath as she took one last look at herself and turned. "I'm ready."

I moved to stand. "One last thing," I said, as I moved toward her.

"Did I forget to zip?" she asked, trying to look down her back.

Which was perfect, because I could reach for the jewelry box without her seeing. When she turned back around, her gaze fell on the hard-to-describe, but the closest I could get was robins-egg-blue, box with a simple satin white bow tied around it.

"No," she said, shaking her head. "Whatever that is, it's too much."

ELI

"Is she always this bad about receiving gifts?" I asked, looking over at Peyton who made no attempt to hide the fact that she was watching the interaction.

"She once shrieked and *threw* a birthday present I gave her."

"Because you filled it with fake spiders, you jackass," Autumn objected. "That *moved.*"

"Well, you wouldn't buy it if they were just all still," Peyton said, rolling her eyes. "Open your present. You don't turn down a present from a man who rubs your feet and gives you good orgasms."

Oh, Peyton.

"I still say that this is unnecessary, and that you don't need to buy me things," she said, giving me a firm look as she reached for the box.

"Noted. But that won't stop me," I agreed as she untied the white ribbon. It didn't exactly escape me either that her fingers stroked over it after she carefully laid it on her dresser. Autumn worked hard and made enough money to pay bills and have some leftover, but I was pretty sure she didn't have enough money lying around to buy designer jewelry.

It was superficial, sure, but it was a small little experience I was happy to give to her.

"Oh," her air whooshed out as she pulled open the box, then the little robins-egg-blue satchel to pull out the diamond earrings. "Eli..."

"Well, I mean there are no cool blood splatters on them," Peyton said, moving to stand. "But I guess they're nice," she said, giving me a wink. "I'm assuming you're going to thank him from an upward-facing position, and I don't need that trauma in my life," she declared, walking out toward the living room. "I'll wait in the car."

"Thank you," Autumn said, voice a little thick after we were alone again.

"Literally the least I could do," I said, reaching for the box so she could turn and put them on. Once she was done, she twined her arms around my neck, and kissed me until she swayed on her feet.

The whole goddamn drive to the gallery involved a pretty severe case of blue balls, even though I had just had her less than an hour before.

"Ooh, fancy," Peyton declared to the server who came to us with champagne as soon as we arrived.

ELI

We had about twenty minutes to hang around, talking with the other artist who had a wall that evening, an older woman who did social commentary pieces that had Peyton engaged in lively conversation with her until the doors finally opened, and people came in.

Those people?

My entire family, sans kids, and the Rivers men as well.

My gaze went to Autumn, finding her eyes huge and her lips parted. "Oh my God. I totally forgot. I kind of slipped and said you had a show today. I'm so sorry. I should have--"

"Sweetheart, it's fine," I said, putting an arm around her waist, and pulling her in. "I was just surprised. It's fine."

And it was.

As soon as I saw their faces, my heart did an expanding thing in my chest.

I wanted them there.

I hadn't even known it until I saw them.

There was also a small part of me that was immediately nervous, a sensation that I wasn't all that familiar with. Not because I thought they would think my work was shit - they had always praised it in the past, but because several of the pieces revolved around my darkness, around the hollowness, around their absence.

In fact, the painting their eyes went to immediately was the large one with all their heads ducked and the faceless children.

And every last one of them looked taken aback, then sad.

"I think it will help them understand," Autumn said, reading me. "They can see that you hadn't been able to actually shut them out like you thought you did. They were always there, always haunting you. I think that is good for them to see."

"Oh, my, this is a good turnout," the coordinator said, looking around at my family as they milled around, looking at walls.

As if on cue, the door opened again, and in walked some other familiar faces.

See, you didn't work in the underbelly of Navesink Bank without making some friends - and acquaintances - that existed down there as well.

For me, that meant Breaker, Shooter, Paine, Sawyer, and the Grassi family.

And, somehow, they all knew about the show.

ELI

"Eli," Antony Grassi, the patriarch of a dock-owning local mob family said, coming up, taking my hand. "One of my men, Anthony Galleo, told me to keep an eye for your show, that I might want a piece for myself. I can see his taste is as impeccable as usual. Glad to see you are back on your feet," he added, clamping a hand behind my shoulder before moving away.

"Ah, isn't that the guy who owns Famigilia?" Autumn asked as she watched him join his sons in greeting the other artist. Manners, that *family* always had them in spades.

"Yeah," I agreed, enjoying watching her mind race, something that was clear in her eyes.

"But he said one of his guys... oh," she said, turning to look at him again, then back at me. "Are they like... *the mafia*?" she whispered in excitement.

"I sense a *Sopranos* marathon in my future, huh?" I asked, then laughed when she looked guilty as charged.

"This is really something," Hunt said, coming up after all the friends had greeted and congratulated me. Coming from him, someone whose artistic skills had always surpassed mine, even though now, I was comfortable saying we were pretty neck-and-neck, though our canvas was different, it truly meant a lot. "Fee wants to hire you to do a portrait of the girls. I'd be offended," he said, giving me a smirk, "but you're clearly better at portraits than I am."

By the end of the night, most pictures on each wall had sold stickers in the corners, though they would continue to stay up for a few more days.

"I've done four shows here," the other artist, Magda, announced after everyone had filed out and we - Magda, me, Autumn, and Peyton - were handed one final round of champagne, "and I have never sold more than one painting on the opening night. You have many cultured friends," she praised, beaming, this night a clearcut success for the both of us. "I will share a gallery with you anytime," she added, clinking my glass, draining hers, then making her way out the door.

"Eli," my mother called, she and Pops being the only two who didn't have babysitters to go save from their, as Fee called them, demon spawn, and had only walked out a moment before.

"Yeah, Ma?" I called back, brows drawn together.

ELI

"Tomorrow is Sunday dinner. And in case you forgot, attendance is mandatory. That goes for you girls too," she added, giving Autumn and Peyton a very firm Helen Mallick don't-fuck-with-me look.

"Mama Dukes, you have food, I'm there," Peyton declared. "I mean that literally. You order a little too much extra Chinese, you can call me over like a dog to clean up the leftovers."

Ma smiled at that, it being clear she was a fan of Peyton's particular brand of absurdity.

"We'll be there, Ma," I agreed, giving Autumn a little squeeze.

The *we* thing was still new, but somehow completely comfortable at the same time. I guess that was maybe how you knew it was right.

"Let me know if we can bring anything," Autumn added.

My mother took a second, looking at us, clearly still a little emotional at having me - and us - around, but then gave us a smile, and was gone.

"Mandatory, huh?" Autumn asked, moving around to press her chest to mine, her arms behind my shoulders.

"She's serious about that too. She will hunt us down. There is no excuse good enough not to show. It looks like people are going to have to go without their cock rings and butt plugs on Sundays from now on."

And so they would.

We never missed a Sunday from that day forward.

After all, I had a lot of catching up to do.

EPILOGUE

Autumn - 1 month

We were having two Christmases.

Of course, we had to go to Charlie and Helen's for the absolutely massive event that Christmas was for them. I had been shown pictures. Gifts flooded the living room; people were everywhere; there was a huge feast after gifts.

It was a big deal.

Luckily, it didn't start until the afternoon since everyone needed to do the Santa thing at home with the kids first.

It worked out too because Peyton and I had our little morning tradition of a huge home-cooked breakfast that we made while belting out horribly off-key carols. Then we ate while watching *The Christmas Story*. After that, we opened gifts while watching *Christmas Vacation*. Normally, the afternoon would include some heavy eggnog usage and more movie watching before we popped in a pre-made lasagne we made earlier in the month and froze, and pigging out.

ELI

We were happy to give up the latter part of the day, deciding homemade dinner by Helen was leaps and bounds better than reheated lasagne.

But we weren't giving up on our morning traditions.

"I'm coming," I whispered at Peyton who was waiting in my doorway wearing a pair of red and green striped leggings and a red long sleeved tee with a picture of Santa that begged the question *Where my hoes at?*

I slid out of bed away from Eli who had given me an early Christmas present - actually, three.

It was barely six. Eli wouldn't be up for at least another hour. It gave us time to get things rolling food-wise, and get the presents under the tree.

I grabbed a sweatshirt Peyton had bought me with one red and one green bulb on it, saying simply underneath *Balls.*

"Flick on the tree," I demanded as we passed it - our pride and joy. We had a tradition since we moved in together that we bought each other a bulb for each year. Every single one on there was dated and had some special meaning. This year, one of my gifts to Eli was his first ornament too.

I had totally teared up when I wrapped it.

Because I was becoming a big old sap lately.

"Okay, I'm on the French toa... wait," Peyton said, stopping mid-stride, then turning back to the colored tree, some of the strands blinking lazily, but most of them solid. "Santa came!" she whisper-shrieked, mouth wide, eyes dancing.

I doubled back, seeing the pile of, well, badly-wrapped presents in bright red and white paper, that only a man - or child made all of thumbs - could have wrapped.

"He must have snuck out while I was sleeping and put them out," I said, smiling at the pile, anticipation a happy, swirling thing in my belly.

"Oh!" Peyton gasped from where she had squatted down in front of them. "*Half* of these have my name on them! We officially share him now. He's half mine. You get the half that includes nudity. I don't like him that way. But the other half is all mine, damnit. One big poly family."

I laughed at that as she got back up and headed into the kitchen.

ELI

Some day, she was going to get a man of her own.

Until then, I was happy to share the non-nude parts of Eli with her. He already loved her as much as any of his sisters-in-law. And while she would never, ever admit it, she needed a man like him in her life. Someone safe, stable, loving, considerate. After our shitty, judgmental father and then her string of shitty partners, I was pretty sure she didn't even know what one of them was like.

He was good for her.

And he was great for me.

Oh, the heart squeeze.

I was getting really used to that.

I was no longer stepping into it; I was drowning in it.

Love.

And I never, ever wanted to surface.

"Alright, I'm hoping one of you guys got me a pair of noise-canceling headphones for next Christmas," Eli greeted us about forty minutes later, just as the potatoes, French toast, eggs, and bacon were finishing.

"Not our fault we weren't blessed with the note-carrying gene," Peyton insisted. "What we lack in skill, we make up for in enthusiasm."

"Sure about that?" he asked, giving her a hair tug as he passed her to grab the coffee. "This looks amazing."

"Can I open my presents?" Peyton asked, slamming down the last platter on the island. "Come on, you can't keep me in suspense like this!"

Eli shot me a look, eyes dancing, lips tipped up.

"One," we said in unison, making us both laugh because it was such a *parent* moment.

We hadn't exactly discussed that, it still being a somewhat new relationship. But judging by his family, and his determination to win the love of his nieces and nephews, he was going to want some kids of his own.

And we weren't getting any younger.

But those were thoughts for another day.

"No way!" Peyton shrieked, having, of course, chosen the book-sized package. She was holding up a copy of *Die Muthafucka*. "And it's signed!" she added, eyes huge. "How... I looked for months!"

ELI

"Santa must be really well connected," Eli hedged. I actually didn't even know how he pulled that one off.

After that, we all sat to eat in front of the TV, though Peyton was mostly re-reading her book since it had been discontinued in ebook, and she hadn't been able to track down a copy.

We opened the rest of our gifts after, Eli positively beaming at his ornament as he put it on the tree, having heard - and loved - our tradition when we put up the tree on December 1st.

"I'm just saying," Peyton said as we all went off to dress, "it would be much easier for me to eat today if I could just wear these pajamas!"

An hour later, we were dragging huge black bags full of gifts into the house, arriving twenty minutes earlier than the scheduled time along with all the other men to arrange all the gifts into sections to make unwrapping easier.

The full Santa experience, I realized as I stepped back into the kitchen since there was almost no floorspace in the living room once everyone was done.

"Totally, I can come be a taste-tester anytime," Peyton yelled back at Helen as she moved toward me with mashed potatoes on her spoon. At my raised brow, she shrugged. "What? I told her it needed more garlic. Geez. Holy shit," she said as she looked at the room. "And I bet there isn't one box full of fake, crawling spiders. What a waste."

Eli - 2 months

ELI

"You're overreacting," Autumn said, keeping her voice calm as I paced the living room.

"How the fuck am I overreacting about this?" I asked, turning to give her my full attention.

We hadn't had anything even resembling a fight yet, but I was seeing red over this, and she was calm as could be. Like there was anything even remotely normal about this situation.

"It's been going on for years and--"

"Years?" I cut her off, feeling my blood start to boil. "How the fuck have you put up with this for years?"

"If you would let me *speak*," she said in that ultra calm voice still. I wasn't sure if she was just always so calm in heated moments, or this was in response to my getting angry, worried I might lose it.

That was always a possibility, though I had started the boxing. Between that and the sex, yeah, my ass was staying practically zen-like most of the time.

This was as angry as I had been in months.

And neither of them were even worried about it.

No, they had been just... accepting it?

Fuck no.

Not on my watch.

"I'm listening," I said through a clenched jaw.

"She doesn't mind, Eli. Believe me, I've had a round or two with her about this."

"Why are you even leaving it up to her, though? Why aren't, I don't know, the cops involved?"

"Ease up there, Hottie Mc Death Row," Peyton said, coming out of the bathroom in a robe.

"Peyton, the fucking asshole was standing outside the window watching you take a bath," I objected.

I had been walking Coop, and just so happened around that side of the building. And I knew Peyton was in the tub because she had it running when I left and was murmuring something about 'sizzle you hot bitches' at, I imagined, her bath bombs.

Luckily, Coop had barked and spooked the guy before I could break out of the dazed shock I had been in momentarily.

I might have killed the guy, making Peyton's nickname for me come true.

ELI

"I know. He tends to do that. If I were paranoid about it, I would shut the curtains."

"You shouldn't fucking have to because he shouldn't be looking in them. Peeping Toms are committing crimes, Peyton. And, fine, maybe you don't mind--" Though I sure as shit did. "But what about the other women in this building who may be spied on, who might not even know they are being watched?"

"The only other apartments on our level are men and a little old lady. I doubt he's peeping there."

"Jesus Christ. There's no talking to you about this, huh?"

"It's not--" Autumn started.

"A big deal," I finished for her. "I get it."

"Where are you going?"

"To the gym," I answered, not feeling the need to tell her I was making a stop at Ryan's office first.

"What's this?" Autumn asked a couple of weeks later when it was official.

"The deed to this apartment building."

"*What!*"

So, she wasn't happy about it. To be perfectly honest, I expected that, and it didn't matter. Since I had no proof that Randy was a Peeping Tom - and it could take weeks to get some - and Peyton likely wouldn't testify, and the owner didn't give a shit if the super was a creep so long as the rent checks came on time, I was left with little other option.

"I get you're pissed," I said, rocking back on my heels. "But it was the only way to get Randy out of here. He's packing as we speak."

"You can't just... just buy everything to fix problems," she objected. "I mean, what, if I struggle to cover the rent at the store, are you going to buy that too?"

"Stop," Peyton said, smirking, "you're giving him ideas now."

"You can't own my apartment building."

My.

See, that was another part of the surprise that day.

"That's the thing. I was wondering if you would think about moving in with me in my old apartment."

She had been there several times with me, helping me get my new shit in there, you know, the stuff I was keeping from the duplex,

211

ELI

which was very little. She even spent the night a few times. She loved the decor there, the building itself, the common rooms, the land around it. I actually caught her lovingly stroking the countertops while she sipped her coffee.

There was a heavy silence following that.

I knew what I was asking.

I knew that the dynamic with Autumn and Peyton and me was important to them, to me as well. I loved having Peyton around. But we couldn't all be roomies forever. Some day, she was going to find herself a man too, and then there would be a rush for everyone to figure out living situations.

"I'm not saying full-time," I qualified. "You can keep your room here, and we can spend as much time here as you want. Oh, and the rent here is dropping. That asshole was gouging all of you to fund a gambling habit."

"Okay, wait," Autumn said, shaking her head. "One thing at a time. You bought this building."

"Yes."

"How?"

"I sold the tutoring place to a friend of my father's which gave me enough. It's a smart business move - income properties. That's why Shane has one."

"Ah, okay," she said, eyes a little unfocused like she wasn't getting it. "So... this was your solution to the thing that we told you wasn't a problem?"

"Look, sweetheart, if you're moving in with me - and, yes, I know that is still an if - but if you do, Peyton will be here alone most of the time. I know he's seemed relatively harmless up until now, but do you want to take that chance? I don't."

"Aw, Autumn, he *loves* me. He wants to protect my quote-unquote *honor*."

"Something like that," I agreed. "And since we're taking Coop, you're getting a dog of your own."

"I get my own apartment *and* a puppy? Dude, you're moving in with him. It's not even a choice. Buh-bye. I will pack your shit while you finish your little snit."

"It's not a snit!" Autumn called after her as she disappeared into Autumn's room.

ELI

"It's totally a snit," I objected, moving to sit beside her on the couch. "You're pissed at me. You can admit it."

"You can't just go behind my back and do things, Eli," she said, exhaling hard.

"I did try to talk about it with you."

"And you didn't get your way, so you pretended to let it go, and plotted behind my back."

Alright.

Put that way, it did sound shitty.

"No more buying buildings that I live in - or work in," she was quick to clarify, "without speaking to me first."

"That's fair," I agreed, resting my arm across the back of the couch.

She barely even hesitated before she curled in.

"I like that you want to look out for Peyton when we move out."

"When?"

"Yes, when."

Eli - 1.5 years

Sometimes you did it backward.

Sometimes it wasn't the rock, the ring, the wedding, the baby.

ELI

I had given Autumn a rock six months after we started dating.

But before we could get to the ring part, there was a missed period, a trip to the drug store, and a stick that went blue.

And it didn't matter what order the world expected us to do it in, we were fucking thrilled.

I had been away for so long, had resigned myself to a future that had no softness in it. So I hadn't planned on kids.

But after spending so much time with my nieces and nephews, I realized the pull was still there.

So learning that was what we were working toward, yeah, I was a happy man.

We painted a nursery. We went to doctor visits. We bought clothes and diapers and blankets.

Then it happened.

Autumn got sick.

Not the kind of sick that meant she had to maybe take it easy, be on bedrest.

No.

It was the kind of sick that had us calling the doctor at night because she was way beyond morning sickness and suddenly couldn't stop vomiting and was too dizzy to walk on her own. It was the kind of sick that had him telling us to get to the emergency room immediately, that he would meet us there.

When a doctor tells you that he would meet you at the emergency room in twenty minutes when it was three o'clock in the morning, you knew it wasn't good.

Her blood pressure was one-ninety over one-fifteen.

A hypertensive emergency.

They had hours to get it down before she risked organ failure, seizures, stroke, or the death of her and the baby.

I'd had a somewhat crazy life. I had seen things and done things that would scare most people half to death.

But I could say with one-hundred percent certainty that nothing was anywhere near as terrifying as that night beside that hospital bed with her.

Until, of course, the night of the delivery.

C-section, because it was the only option.

They had to get him out.

For both their sakes.

ELI

Even though it was four weeks early still.

We can't wait anymore, the doctor had told us when her blood pressure refused to get and stay low, no matter the medication they tried. *We are taking an unnecessary risk. We have the best neonatal unit in the state here. The baby will be fine.*

So, with little choice, Autumn was wheeled down and prepped.

I was scrubbed and dressed.

I stayed up by her head, holding her hand, every inch of me more tense than I had ever been before.

"I love you," I told her as her eyes went a little glassy."

"I love you too," she said back with a smile as we heard a faint, then louder cry.

The smile on her face was something that was burned in my memory.

Especially because three minutes later, she started seizing.

And I was sure.

I was so fucking sure.

This was it.

This was the ultimate 'fuck you' from the universe to me.

I knew I had never deserved her, had never done anything to earn the right to call her mine.

So I got her for too short a time.

And she was going to be taken from me.

"What do you mean they won't let you in?" Peyton shrieked, slamming her fists into my chest until my arms went around her, squeezing too tight for her to keep pounding.

Then it happened.

Peyton broke.

Fucking shattered.

And I was right goddamn there with her.

"What's the update?" my mother asked, barreling down the hall in her four-inch boots, looking like hell on heels, ready to take on the world.

"We haven't gotten one," Peyton said, scrubbing her cheeks.

"Oh, fuck that," Ma said, turning on her heel, and stomping back to the nurse's station, looking every bit the mama bear she was.

It was barely two minutes until her doctor came out, looking tired, looking strained.

ELI

I was sure it was the talk.

The "we did everything we could" announcement I had been dreading for forty minutes.

"She's stopped seizing," he said instead and my fucking legs gave out. I slammed back against the wall on an exhale of breath I had been holding for so long it hurt. "Her blood pressure is stabling out. But this is still serious. Now that the baby is out, her body should slowly start to regulate itself. But it can take months for her blood pressure to go back to normal. Right now, we're not as worried about that as we are keeping her stable through the night. If we can manage that, she will be out of the woods."

"And the baby?" my mother asked, making me feel like the biggest shit in the world for forgetting to ask. But he had been crying. No one had been rushing to his side.

"The baby is fine. He's under the Bili lights right now because he was just a little jaundiced which is perfectly common in premature babies. It's more precaution than anything. But he's been through a lot the past few weeks; we just want to be overly careful."

"When can I see them?" I asked, trying to focus on continuing to breathe.

"You can see your son through the window up in the NICU right now. In a couple of hours, we will take him off the lights so you can hold him, but for now, we want to keep him there. You," he said, looking at me, "can see Autumn at any point."

"And me," Peyton insisted, eyes red-rimmed, makeup everywhere, a complete and utter mess, but her voice held more conviction than a general leading his men into battle.

"And you," he agreed immediately, but gave us a firm look. "But only you."

"Why don't you go see your son?" Peyton suggested. "I will go sit with Autumn until you get back, then we'll switch."

That was exactly what we did.

For the entire night.

Autumn drifted awake several hours later, having been drained from the stress, the blood loss and transfusion, the seizure, and the accompanying seizure migraine.

"The baby..."

Those words were out of her mouth before she even fully focused on me.

ELI

"He's fine," I said immediately, giving her hand a squeeze. "They have him under the blue lights just to make sure he stays fine, but all the tests have come back great so far. He's a little small, but he will be a huge, hulking Mallick in no time."

"My head hurts," she admitted. She didn't even need to say it; you could see the pain behind her eyes.

"Yeah, they said they would give you a dose of pain meds once you were conscious. I'll call..."

"I'm okay," she said, oddly.

"Sweetheart, you have a splitting..."

"No," she said, shaking her head. "You're watching me like I might drop dead. I'm okay."

"You weren't," I said, hearing the heaviness in my own voice.

"But I am now."

"See this?" I asked, showing her the front of my shirt that was smeared black.

"Yeah?"

"Peyton losing her shit."

"She cried?"

"She bawled," I corrected.

"And I *missed it*?" she said, looking ridiculously disappointed at the idea. "Almost dying, that's what it takes for her."

"Yeah, well, we aren't going to take that risk again just so you can see her with her mascara running."

"Ugh, *fine*," she grumbled, but she was smiling softly. "When can I see him?"

"Tomorrow. They said we could come up and hold him and feed him if you're up to it."

"I'll be up to it."

And she was.

We got to hold our son, feed him, and, finally, name him.

Celen.

"It's a mash-up of Charlie and Helen," she informed me as she looked up at me, her finger in our son's tiny hand, her eyes a little glassy.

"How long have you been sitting on that?"

"Since I knew it was a boy," she admitted, giving me a sweet smile.

Nothing.

ELI

Not a goddamn thing in the world to deserve her.
Or him.
Yet there they were.

Autumn - 5 years

I couldn't have any more.
With the Mallick clan, they all seemed to have litters.
I had wanted to carry on that tradition as well.
But it had taken six months to get my blood pressure down to normal without medication.
Then we had forgotten all about things like other babies because we had been so wrapped up in the one we had. One that had eyes just a shade darker than Eli's, a mix of both of ours, and hair that was just shy of black.
Eli had been right.
Once he got out of the hospital, he grew like a weed, kicking dirt in every preemie chart the doctors tried to measure him by.
At three, he was tall, wide-shouldered, and dense.
He had a strange mix of the roughness all the Mallick boys possessed, always getting into trouble, always getting hurt, and a softness that his father possessed more than his brothers did, a quietly reflective side even at his young age.
It wasn't until Celen celebrated his third birthday that we went to the doctor to talk about the possibility of another.
And it had been a very firm *no*.
I guess I had suspected as much.

ELI

I wasn't stupid. Once I felt well enough to listen, I had Peyton read me the online pages about pre-eclampsia. I understood that the risk factors increased with each child. And it was ill-advised even when you had mild complications.

Mine were severe.

So I think a part of me had known.

Yet I felt a really strong sense of guilt as we walked out of the office.

Then I felt shitty for feeling shitty because we had Celen.

"Thank God he said it."

"What?" I asked, confused, sure I misheard him.

"Thank God *he* said it."

"I don't understand," I said, turning to lean against the car.

"Look," Eli exhaled, putting his hands on my hips. "I know you got to be blissfully unconscious through it, but seeing you seizing, not getting updated for forty-minutes, that was the worst time in my life. And I'm counting the six years I spent inside. I'd take six more over watching that happen again. I'd give up six years of freedom to never have to think I was about to lose you again."

My heart squeezed in my chest at that, in the conviction with which he said it.

"But all your brothers..."

"Have exactly how many kids they are supposed to have," he cut me off. "And, sweetheart, so do we."

"But you love all the kids..."

"Yes, I do. Of course I do. But loving them doesn't mean I need to have five of my own. Autumn, I never saw myself here. I never thought I would get my family back, have the love of a good woman, have any children at all. It seemed so out of the realm of possibilities for me. I am fucking thrilled with what we have. I don't need one goddamn thing more."

It was like a weight had been lifted.

Would it have been nice to have more?

Yes.

But I loved our little family.

I loved the undivided attention we could give Celen.

And he had seventeen cousins to play with. He would never feel alone or lonely.

I didn't need one goddamn thing more either.

ELI

Eli - 10 years

"I can't fucking do it again. I swear to shit, they're trying to kill me."

That was Hunt, sitting off the side of his couch, scrubbing his hands down his face.

Mayla was seventeen.

As the rules went, she was finally allowed to date.

So she had her first one later that night.

"We agreed to these rules," Fee reminded him, watching him with a smirk, clearly enjoying his paternal dilemma.

"Yeah, when they were all in elementary school still. When I was sure this day would never come."

"They're almost all grown up," Fee went on, purposely adding salt in an obviously open wound, clearly enjoying herself.

"Don't say that. They're little girls."

"Becca is twenty-two, living in her own apartment, likely dating..."

"Don't. Babe, you're just making it worse."

"I know. I'm evil, aren't I? And Izzy..."

"Stop."

"Izzy and her guy are going on a year now."

"You're being ridiculous," Shane said, snorting.

"Um, bro," Hunt said, looking up, shooting him a look, "Sam is gonna be a teen soon. This is you in a couple years."

"Nah, man. Sam isn't dating until I'm dead. We made a deal."

"Yeah? When was that?"

"When she was eight. But it still holds."

ELI

I laughed at that, leaning back, enjoying the struggle of a father of girls. I knew because I had been a guy that dating was different for us. I understood Hunter's freak-out, his wish for more time for the girls to just be girls.

Statistically speaking, Autumn had reasoned with me when I had brought it up earlier, *girls start 'dating' much later now than most times in history. Historically, Becca would have at least three kids by now, Izzy two, and Mayla would be freshly married.*

When put in that perspective, I was pretty fucking glad these girls lived in the time that they did.

Even if it meant having to listen to Hunt bitch about it being too soon for an hour while Autumn was in the other room having a *talk* with Mayla.

Not the sex talk, of course.

Fee was progressive. The girls got small sex talks every year as new information became appropriate.

This was a different talk.

Autumn called it a "pre-date talk" that was, apparently, about pressure, consent, safety, and her right to go as fast - or slow - as she wanted. She had given similar ones to both Becca and Izzy the day before their first dates. It was also one of the most in-demand classes she had, next to couples tantra, and the *talk* talk.

"You told her to carry her knife too, right?" Hunt asked as they walked out. "Right in the thigh, Mayla," he told her.

"And twist," Shane chimed in.

"Punch to the groin for good measure," Mark added.

"You still have the mace I got you for your birthday too, right?" Ryan asked.

"God," Mayla said, looking around at all her uncles. "You guys are so weird."

We all shared a smile as she walked off, shaking her head at all of us.

"Did I ever thank you for giving me a son?" I asked as Autumn dropped down on my lap.

"Every time I have to have this talk with anyone," she agreed, smiling.

"Well, thank you for my son," I told her again.

"Speaking of, we should go pick him up. Knowing Bobby, he is letting them play with sparklers unsupervised."

ELI

Bobby was still around.

He eventually did get locked up again, doing a year for possession, getting out early on good behavior as he always did.

When he got out, he had practically needed to crawl over broken glass to get Nat back.

I gave him the super job at the apartment building when the old super got married and needed to move on with his life. They got married. Then they had three boys that, well, were so rough and tumble that they put Mallick boys to shame.

She really wasn't exaggerating in her worry about sparklers.

"I wish Peyton still lived there to keep an eye on things."

Autumn - 11 years

"Why would you get rid of Cock God?" Peyton asked, wrapping her arms around the massive human-sized phallus statue that had been just inside the door of the store since about two months after I first opened it. "He's done nothing but stand here and inspire everyone to pick out a nicely shaped dildo."

"I'm not getting rid of him. I'm just trying to redo the store a little. I haven't done anything different in too long."

"But why must Cock God move? He is the store mascot! The store is *Phallus*-opy. He's the phallus. The glorious, giant phallus."

"I just think that maybe he's a bit 'in your face' there."

"This is a *sex* store, Autumn. Cocks in the face are kinda part of the whole shebang. I mean, except for the girls who dig girls. But we can just get like a giant pussy to put on this side!" she exclaimed, waving a hand out to the other side of the door.

ELI

"I am not putting a giant vagina up next to the door, Peyton."

Now there was a sentence I never could have anticipated saying before. Even owning a sex store, that was a bit, ah, unusual.

"Eh, yeah. I mean even if the girls who dig girls don't like the men attached to the dicks, they like the dick shape too. Cock God stays, I vote. I mean, where else are you going to put a Santa hat at Christmas if not on his lovely, curved, shapely head?"

"I love you, but you're ridiculous," I declared with a laugh as I sorted through a box of various types of handcuffs.

"If you get rid of him, I'm taking him home with me."

I chuckled at that, looking up, finding her serious. "I don't think your man will want a giant cock in your house."

"Oh, please. If he can get used to my penis flower pillows, he can get used to Cock God."

"You're supposed to be here helping me plan, not making demands on one small statue..."

"She didn't mean it," she said, putting her hands on the head of the cock. "You are perfectly adequate. Though we all know it *is* partly the size of the boat, no matter how the saying goes. Alright, fine," she said, reluctantly getting serious. "Show me the swatches."

Eleven years, and she never lost an ounce of her crazy.

Love had come to her, like I had predicted, but it hadn't softened her, it hadn't rounded out her rough edges, it hadn't calmed her crazy.

In fact, it was the oddest thing.

It gave her comfort to be herself, without having to *prove* anything. More and more often, you could catch her without her war paint - makeup - and completely comfortable with it. She stayed in more. She just became a more laid-back version of her usual self.

It was a sight to see.

I was so happy to see her happy.

And raising her own little one.

Just like me, just one.

But more by choice than happenstance.

A little girl just a bit younger than Celen.

I hoped she would grow up to be every bit as confident, imaginative, and fearless as her mother.

Just like I hoped Celen grew up to be as kind, determined, loyal, generous, and strong as his father.

ELI

He was already on his way there.

Sometimes, when I walked in the room to say something to one of them, and I caught them sitting working on homework, or building a model ship, or just lounging together watching TV, it simply hits me.

The whole of what my life had become.

The crazy, amazing twist of fate that led me to that coffeeshop on that day to watch that man and his dog. To witness his life take a turn in the worst possible direction, leaving me to take in Coop, and feel compelled to update him on his well-being.

The pen pal friendship.

His release.

Our budding relationship.

His connection with Peyton, and mine with the Mallick and Rivers Clan.

Then, finally, Celen.

I went from such a small, though fulfilling life, to such a huge, amazing, beautiful, wonderful one so full of unique personalities, so much loyalty, so much love that it was almost painful to receive it all at once.

And in some moments, when my mind was on other things, when I wasn't prepared for it, it hit me.

With actual impact.

I would often go back a step.

My eyes would glass over.

And I would have a moment of complete and utter appreciation for this man, this amazing, wonderful, beautiful man who once upon a time didn't believe in himself, who had needed me to show him how perfect he was.

Then he spent every single day after proving to me just how worth it that all was.

"Incoming," Peyton said, turning away from the window where she was holding swatches up to the light.

There was an odd look in her eyes that I didn't quite understand until the door burst open, and in all three of them walked.

Eli.

Celen.

And some godawful, hideous mutt.

ELI

See, Coop had given us fourteen loyal years before old age took him from us, peaceful in his sleep, no illness, no pain, just a release from his duty to us.

I had sobbed for weeks.

Peyton had joined me.

Celen as well.

Even Eli got choked up over the loss of the amazing, pain in the ass creature who had, essentially, brought us all together.

Afterward, we simply never could bring ourselves even to try to replace that void.

Apparently, fate had other plans for us.

"Seriously, though," Peyton said, looking at the dog. "Where do you find these freaks of nature?"

To be fair, he was ugly.

He was all legs with a skinny center, pointed ears, and a tail that could clear tabletops. What made him so unfortunate looking was the fact that the only places he had hair was on his head, ears, the center of his back, and his tail. The rest of him was skin.

He looked like he was out of some sci-fi nightmare.

Some kind of genetically engineered dog.

I looked up to find Eli grinning at me.

"Let's see what kind of adventure he can take us on..."

XX

DON'T FORGET!

<u>Dear Reader,</u>
Thank you for taking time out of your life to read this book. If you loved this book, I would really appreciate it if you could hop onto Goodreads or Amazon and tell me your favorite parts. You can also spread the word by recommending the book to friends or sending digital copies that can be received via kindle or kindle app on any device.

ALSO BY JESSICA GADZIALA

The Henchmen MC
Reign
Cash
Wolf
Repo
Duke
Renny
Lazarus
Pagan
Cyrus

The Savages
Monster
Killer
Savior

Stars Landing
What The Heart Needs
What The Heart Wants
What The Heart Finds

ELI
What The Heart Knows
The Stars Landing Deviant

Mallick Brothers
Shane
Ryan
Mark

--

DEBT
For A Good Time, Call...
Vigilante
The Sex Surrogate
Dr. Chase Hudson
Dissent
Into The Green
Dark Mysteries
367 Days
14 Weeks
Stuffed: A Thanksgiving Romance
Dark Secrets
Dark Horse
Unwrapped
Peace, Love, & Macarons

ABOUT THE AUTHOR

Jessica Gadziala is a full-time writer, parrot enthusiast, and coffee drinker from New Jersey. She enjoys short rides to the book store, sad songs, and cold weather.

She is very active on Goodreads, Facebook, as well as her personal groups on those sites. Join in. She's friendly.

STALK HER!

Connect with Jessica:

Facebook: https://www.facebook.com/JessicaGadziala/
Facebook Group: https://www.facebook.com/groups/314540025563403/

Goodreads: https://www.goodreads.com/author/show/13800950.Jessica_Gadziala
Goodreads Group: https://www.goodreads.com/group/show/177944-jessica-gadziala-books-and-bullsh

Twitter: @JessicaGadziala

JessicaGadziala.com

<3/ Jessica

<<<◇>>>

Made in United States
Orlando, FL
07 July 2023